WHITE PLAINS

FICTIONS

WHITE PLAINS

Pieces & Witherlings
by Gordon Lish

LITTLE ISLAND PRESS

Lodgemore Lane,
Stroud, GL5 3EQ

Published in the United Kingdom by
Little Island Press, Stroud

First Published 2017
This paperback edition 2018

ISBN 978-0-9957052-6-5

Series design by t.r.u
typographic research unit

Typeset in Bembo MT
Printed and bound in Great Britain

CONTENTS

WHITE PLAINS

The nonreferentiality
of the hurt body,
or the referential
instability of the hurt body ...

ELAINE SCARRY

Outside
it was raw and windy.
The trees were broken
and shorn of leaves.
The ground, too, was broken and stiff.
There was a faint fusty odor everywhere.
And cold.
All was cold.
Still, some solitary bird
was flinging out its frail song.

JOY WILLIAMS

Ariel was glad he had written his poems.
They were of a remembered time
or of something seen that he liked.

WALLACE STEVENS

THE 12 SIGNS OF OLD AGE

WAYNE HOGAN

FOREWORD

What do you say we make room for a quality of writing (the written) less susceptible to the giddiness and caprice of a fountain-pen owner subject to his tipping over the ink bottle, bumping into the walls, unthinkingly loosening the lightbulbs ornamenting the grand fixtures of his (well, mental) habitat, and thereafter (oh, there's more?) scrupling that he shall operate in the bestrewn yet squintedly mappable dark, all bullying and whim and lawless egoism subdued for as long as he, his own best unavoidable sickened victim, might bear it? So what say you that we try such a romp? – and do it altogether as soon as we can (ach, momentarily, almost now!) – quick, quickened, aquick before the ink bottle runs dry and the fellow's last glimpse of the world flies deathward with it, or, if you prefer it, with it deathward?

What say you to lending some instants to a scheme of the kind?

Is he (I, Gordon!) soliciting an unearned dispensation? You had better bet he is!

Will we be at all likely to conclude at all fairly how such an exception to local practice would strike the temperament of the uncommon reader out on the avenue in search of a venue promising a bit more in the fashion of a gracious welcome and all the ensuant accusatory effects flowing from the famous convenience of history (hurry, hurry, O accomplices, there! now! the criminalities, they hastily hasten onward! – or isn't it rearward we've been sentenced to say?) made present to the page historiographically?

Jesus! – errorfully, errantly, awry, askew, begogged. Whew!

Well, let's see.

We open a door, then, do we not, to a not unfamiliar tableau, a foursome of the human all-in-all, all of them at table in what can only be the family dining room. The householder himself, we find him arranged in his armed chair, his mistress, herself, is seated opposite, in a chair detectably less comfy, the children, a girl almost a teenager, let us not yet stumble into disagreeing, the boy years enough her junior, are revealed, the pair of them, at stations to either side of their, mmm, progenitors, neither of these subordinates discoverable at rest in a grade of furniture worth the noting – but no, no, you mustn't make allowances for the importunate – for however it's turned, the narrative template is never not aglint with a fury of lowlights now caught in the blazing torsion of time's (auctorial) glare. Such words, such words! – the muddled mania of metaphors mixed – not to mention the municipal litter of alliterative reflexes reading themselves on and on and onward, all too maddeningly on the loose. Alas, what is culture but the revenge of the spoken, what is language but its vehicle for conceiving inconceivable trickeries? Properly rebarbative, the ruthless scourge released, by gum, isn't the all-in-all action forever taken under the banner of the deranged perfectionism of getting the fuck even?

Nothing crueler.

The blackmail of rehearsed (not a jot less unrehearsed) speech.

A caustic testament bound to its terms exacting its cost of whatever trials to afflict (sure, sure, who – *whom* – in Christ does the Yid think he's scaring?) its thoroughly accidental beneficiaries. Friend (oh, sure, sure), how elsewise the means of the wordwise to be featured at all defeatingly, save in the speech of speakage and, not unslyly, the faked stammerings of unutterably uttered defeat? It is not that I hate – it is, rather, that I fear – but, dammit, I do hate fearing, so, mustn't it be stated, I hate plenty plenteously that I, your author, am a plenitude of hatreds, an unremitting, unrepentant hatefulness, with neither days enough, nor zing enough, to reserve what's left of me for some small show of decency, some snap of the humane, some hint of the least glance at the impecunity of, ooooh, fellow-feeling. And yet I refer to you (I 'reference' you – my God!) – take care you not trip into the blandishment of a certain form's formalities, though what's not form but the deformed in a moodier rankle of mood? – as friend, as friends, nay, as very accomplices all! – not in any entreaty for you to forgive me my spite, but solely for us, for you and me, in twain, as twain, all alit all right, then as a flock, to do what we may to keep the habituated keptness going.

False, false, false! – that's what the shoedog (ladies' shoe salesman in Fiedler's 'Nobody Ever Died from It') shrieks, in defense of himself, in judgment of the jurors, since what else is he, or we, to do? Feign? You jest with me, feign! It's what I, here at this inaugurating of 'things' aheadward am utzed, jussively, to place, impulsively, before you. Listen, I ask no more than that you conspire with me for not that terribly much in order that I might, over the course of this one last fraudulence, sense myself coming, thereby, into a fiction of an extension of existence.

It's my scam, you see.

Not art, no – not that, positively not!

Not suggesting anything so rash as that, never! – just saying pay attention to what I have insofar as, hey, that's *all* I have. In a word, this.

The rest is fancy, folly, further defraudings – plus, not implausibly, a bit of money in the bank. Not for me, pray no, but for my grandchildren, may they, as we Jews are said to say, live and be well. For them, mayhaps. Whereas what is it that you – as a friend, as friends, as, you know, as my unimprovable accomplices, then – might get out of it for yourselves? (Here, stiffen yon kishkes for the come-ance of the swindler's shvindle, yon ancient bait & switch.) Ah, to wit – come to me, come to me, then, come on, come *on*, all you need do is for you to nip with me along with me to just behind yon skimpiest of curtains – and so be portfolio'd to snatch the nakedest of forbidden looks.

What?

What?

That's not a sufficiency for you?

Then, pal o' mine, do us both a favor and piss off!

INVOCATION

O egg custard!

One will say no more.

Save this:

If you happen to have around the house a recipe for egg custard anywhere on a par with what Aunt Dora and Aunt Esther and Tante Lily and Tante Ida spooned from a bowl into a saucer and then placed that saucer onto a table where I had a chair pulled well up to it with a napkin tucked in under my chin, be nice, be merciful, exhibit your gratitude for all the glorious times which I, Gordon, will be going out of my way to, yes, like an infinite food, deposit in front of you in the course of the forthcoming delights. Waste not a thrice in making every effort for you or for any of your assigns to make fast to every family cache of receipts in search of a formula for that wonderful stuff and, if anything promising is found, let the finder seek to achieve touch with any of my children or with any of my grandchildren or with the distinguished David Winters himself (not to worry, he will, not impossibly, understand), or, further, with the equally angelic Andrew Latimer, the foundational fundament of the happy liberating of these pieces and witherlings under the auspices of the Little Island imprimatur, whichever, let the good news be spread Lish-ward before I, your petitioner, yon fresser, do plotz into the sod laid open for him in Farmingdale, where else, New York.

Please, Lord, give all who hear this not hesitate to shake a leg.

Lord, it's egg custard I'm talking about, albeit any semblance of nishy, real or dreamed, as your erstwhile servant Barry Hannah, famous arthur, was wont to say, will not be refused, rebuked, or marked return to sender.

This, Lord, is my prayer.

I only said 'invocation' because I thought it better to play it safe. So that's it and that's it – yessir, yessir! – offered to You in lieu of all other couchments, fruiticles, oodlings and koots.

All thanks to whomever and, of course, to Him.

I'm absolutely convinced I had the word 'compline' in the original version of this – but, you know, at the moment, what with my being pretty egg-custardless and all, I honestly don't think it would be fair for Anybody to hold me responsible for my slipping into blankitude at a moment (shit, the moments!) like this.

Aw-main.

Oh yeah – I hope You're noticing I didn't forget to capitalize the A.

He said, 'You know what I think of when I think of us?'

She said, 'Tell me.'

He said, 'The chair.'

She said, 'Us in the chair.'

'You with your leg up,' he said.

'My left leg,' she said.

He said, 'Right. I mean, your left leg – right.'

She said, 'I'll think about this tonight.'

'The chair?' he said. 'Our time in the chair?'

'No,' she said. 'The way you said it,' she said.

He said, 'How I said it was how it came to me to say.'

She said, 'Nothing just comes. It's all rehearsed.'

He said, 'You think that's the way we are?'

'It's not what I think,' she said. She said, 'It's what is. Or was,' she said.

'Take it back,' he said.

'Look,' she said, 'I have to get off,' she said.

He said, 'Sorry. I wanted to talk.'

'More past tense,' she said.

He said, 'You listen too closely.'

She said, 'Wasn't that the thrill?'

'Of course,' he said. 'It had its charms. Everything known,' he said.

She said, 'So it seemed.'

'Not just talk,' he said. 'Everything else,' he said. 'Nothing not given.'

'Hang up,' she said.

'Exactly,' he said.

* * *

'Hi,' he said.

She said, 'Okay, have it your way.'

'That's funny,' he said. He said, 'You know what?'

'Tell me what,' she said.

He said, 'You're still funny.'

'Nothing funny about this,' she said.

'Don't you mean *that*?' he said.

'I mean you're calling too often,' she said.

He said, 'Can't seem to help it. You want me to help it?' he said.

'Make an effort,' she said.

He said, 'You think I'm not making an effort?'

'Make more of one,' she said.

'Yeah,' he said. 'You're right,' he said. 'But I close my eyes and I see the chair,' he said.

'Cut it out,' she said. 'Who has to close them?' she said. She said, 'It's not right where it was? You're impossible,' she said.

He said, 'Yeah.' He said, 'Nothing's changed.' He said, 'Everything's right where it was.'

She said, 'Get off the phone, please.'

He said, 'Make me.'

She said, 'I'm hanging up.'

'Who's stopping you?' he said.

'Oh, for God's sake,' she said.

'All right,' he said. 'I think I hear her anyway.'

'Give her my best,' she said. 'Look,' she said, 'if you're so dying to talk about the chair, talk to her about it,' she said.

'Hang up,' he said.

She said, 'Consider it done.'

'I'm waiting,' he said.

'Enough,' she said. 'Don't call,' she said.

He said, 'I'll think about it.' He said, 'I'm thinking about it.' He said, 'Did I say it's right in this room?'

'You said you hear her,' she said. 'For everybody's sake, hang up,' she said. She said, 'Please, I'm getting off.'

'Fine,' he said. 'Get off,' he said.

* * *

He said, 'How nice of you to call.'

She said, 'This a bad time?'

'It's a safe time,' he said. 'Been thinking?' he said.

'Never not,' she said.

'Fine and dandy,' he said.

'That's nice,' she said.

He said, 'Nice.' He said, 'It's nice when it's nice.'

She said, 'Are we remembering it as it was?' She said, 'That's not possible, is it?' She said, 'But it was nice, very nice,' she said.

'Couldn't have been nicer,' he said.

'The chair,' she said.

'Right,' he said.

'That's all I wanted to say,' she said. 'But call me,' she said. 'When it's safe,' she said.

He said, 'Of course.'

'Yes,' she said. 'Of course,' she said.

* * *

'I remember things,' she said.

'The chair?' he said.

'You said she had it recovered, didn't you?' she said.

'Reupholstered,' he said.

She said, 'Mmm.' She said, 'Nothing stays the same.'

'That's deep,' he said.

'There's no reason to be mean,' she said.

'Right you are,' he said. 'You know what?' he said. He said, 'You're right.' He said, 'But not everything does,' he said.

She said, 'What?'

He said, 'Change.'

'Oh, God,' she said.

'Yeah, sure,' he said.

She said, 'Tell me what you remember.'

'You tell me first,' he said.

'This is awful,' she said.

He said, 'You're telling me.'

She said, 'Uh-oh. Hanging up.'

* * *

'Are we thinking?' she said.

'Let's think,' he said.

'Let's fuck,' she said.

He said, 'Christ. Christ,' he said.

'My thought is this,' she said. 'My thought is it's impossible to think,' she said. She said, 'My thought is it's better if we quit calling.'

'Okay,' he said.

'Okay,' she said.

* * *

'You want to hear my thought?' he said.

'We agreed,' she said.

'Nothing doesn't change,' he said.

She said, 'Which of us said that?'

'Too deep for it to have been me,' he said.

'Is she there?' she said.

'Out,' he said.

She said, 'At the upholsterer's or at the reupholsterer's?'

He said, 'How would you like it if I said at chemo?'

'Say it,' she said. 'Go ahead and say it,' she said. She said, 'You think everyone doesn't die?'

'I think we'll die,' he said.

'Who's not already dying?' she said. She said, 'When are we not dying?' she said.

'We were alive,' he said.

'We were,' she said. 'It felt like we were really alive,' she said.

He said, 'Say as if,' he said.

'As if,' she said.

* * *

He said, 'Are we making this up?'

She said, 'What other course is there?'

He said, 'Then we're lucky for that.'

She said, 'Lucky how?'

'That we can,' he said.

'That one wants to,' she said.

He said, 'There's no out-talking you.'

She said, 'Oh, yes there is.'

'I think I hear her,' he said.

'She's not dead?' she said.
'Is he?' he said.

* * *

He said, 'You remember what it was covered with?'
She said, 'How couldn't I?'
He said, 'Then tell me how was it?'
'This a test?' she said.
He said, 'What isn't?'
'Pity the pedestrians on the Rialto,' she said.
He said, 'You don't remember, do you?'
She said, 'Am I the expert in what I remember?' She
said, 'I have done all I can do to remember how to spell
it anymore.' She said, 'You think I haven't forgotten
your name sometimes?'
He said, 'But then you remember it.'
She said, 'I sometimes remember your phone
number faster than I do your name.' She said, 'It was
rose-colored or something.' She said, 'Velvet maybe.'
He said, 'Likelier velveteen.'
'Lovely,' she said.
'Lovely,' he said.
She said, 'The word, I mean.'
'The word,' he said. 'To be sure,' he said.
'Velveteen,' she said.

* * *

'It wasn't that,' he said.
'What? What,' she said, 'are you talking about?' she
said.

He said, 'What it was covered with,' he said.

'In,' she said.

'Okay, in,' he said.

'You know what I'm wondering?' she said.

'Tell me what you're wondering,' he said.

She said, 'Tell me why it was I who provided the sheet.'

'The bedsheet?' he said.

'Yes,' she said. 'I'd like to know how come it was always me who did. It was your place,' she said. 'How come was it that it was always I?' she said. She said, 'What was the strategy with that?' she said.

'What a word,' he said.

'Strategy?' she said.

He said, 'Jesus, that's the worst word I ever heard come out of your mouth.'

She said, 'Did it never occur to you the chance I was taking?' She said, 'What were you thinking when it was all me all of the time who was taking the biggest risk?'

'Bigger,' he said. 'Better to have said bigger,' he said.

'Good God,' she said.

'Exactly,' he said. He said, 'I'm tired.' He said, 'I think I'm tired,' he said. He said, 'I'm sorry – I'm going to go take a nap.'

'Then go,' she said.

He said, 'Yeah, I think I must.'

She said, 'Fine. He's due any second now anyway.'

'I'll phone,' he said.

She said, 'Yes, of course. You do that,' she said.

* * *

He said, 'Why this tack to harden yourself?'
'It's working,' she said. 'I'm harder,' she said.
'Think what you're doing,' he said.
She said, 'Think? Who thinks?' she said.
'Oh, Jesus – please,' he said.
She said, 'That was the car. Goodbye,' she said.

* * *

She said, 'He read me something this morning.'
He said, 'The latest from Hallmark?'
She said, 'A bit from one of the journals he gets.'
'I'm all ears,' he said.
'He's no lout, you know,' she said.
'I'm all apologies,' he said.
'This is childish,' she said.
'I said I'm sorry,' he said.
She said, 'Try to put your back into it,' she said.
He said, 'I'm listening. Go ahead,' he said.
She said, 'That no matter the woman ...'
He said, 'Oh, this is going to be deeply deep,' he said.
She said, 'There's a man who's weary of her.'
'That's it?' he said.
'That's not enough?' she said.
'Pretty profound,' he said.
She said, 'There's a point there.' She said, 'Don't you
think there's a point there?'
He said, 'It applies all around,' he said. 'Try this,' he
said. 'Try no matter the person,' he said.
She said, 'We'll speak another time.'
He said, 'Talk now.'

'Not in the mood,' she said.

He said, 'Oh, begging the lady's pardon, a mood, is it, then?'

She said, 'I'm saying goodbye.'

He said, 'So say it.'

'Goodbye,' she said.

* * *

'Hi,' he said.

She said, 'I think he's in the house,' she said.

He said, 'It happens I know for a fact she is.'

'Then let's not either of us risk it,' she said.

He said, 'Are you forgetting what we risked?'

She said, 'I'm not comfortable,' she said. 'This is unintelligent,' she said. 'We're asking for trouble,' she said.

'Fine,' he said. 'Let's let comfort be our aim.'

She said, 'Call when you're thinking straight.'

He said, 'All right, I will.'

'Then do it,' she said.

* * *

'I miss you,' he said.

'Oh,' she said, 'so much missing, so much missing, so much missing.'

He said, 'Don't worry, there's plenty more where that came from.'

She said, 'Who'd ever imagine?'

He said, 'That we die, that we're dying, that we're every minute less alive.' He said, 'It's not slipped your mind, has it?'

31

'Not for a fucking instant,' she said.

'Let's talk about the chair,' he said.

She said, 'How about the floor, how about the bed?'

He said, 'I shouldn't have called.'

'On the contrary,' she said.

'Then hello,' he said. He said, 'I believe I said I miss you.'

She said, 'Aren't we at our best on the phone?'

'Good for you,' he said. 'Getting more callous by the day.'

'Look,' she said, 'this isn't a very good time,' she said.

He said, 'Oh, yeah – time,' he said.

'Just say goodbye,' she said.

'Perfect,' he said. 'Perfectamundo,' he said. 'Goodbye,' he said.

She said, 'Another time.'

'Oh, positively,' he said. He said, 'There'll come a time,' he said.

'Next time,' she said.

* * *

'It just so happens he reads Agamben,' she said.

He said, 'What's that?'

'Never mind,' she said.

He said, 'No, I'm interested,' he said. 'This is the kind of thing that really interests me,' he said.

'What does she read?' she said.

He said, 'Don't know.' He said, 'She's secretive about it. Hides her books,' he said. 'Burns them,' he said.

'Donates them to the starving,' he said. 'Thinks reading's capitalism's last stand.'

'This is beneath us,' she said.

He said, 'Speak for yourself,' he said.

She said, 'She doesn't really have cancer,' she said. 'Does she?' she said.

'Thinks she does,' he said.

'Thinks what?' she said.

'Cancer,' he said. 'All varieties,' he said. 'Just another one,' he said, 'of, you know,' he said, 'of one of capitalism's last stands,' he said.

She said, 'Was the chair beneath us?'

He said, 'The floor, the bed.'

'The bedsheet on the floor,' she said. 'The bedsheet on top of the bedsheet on top of the bed,' she said. 'My bedsheet,' she said.

'True enough,' he said. He said, 'Yours.' He said, 'Never one of mine,' he said.

'Mine to wash,' she said.

'True enough again,' he said. 'Yours to take home and wash,' he said. He said, 'Any more exposition called for?'

'We had something,' she said.

He said, 'Don't we still?'

'Yes – death,' she said.

He said, 'But until death?'

She said, 'Is that a question?'

He said, 'An invitation. A solicitation. A dare.'

'Rhymes with chair,' she said.

'Hell,' he said. 'Does Agamben somewhere get to that?'

She said, 'You'd do well to do as well.'

He said, 'Very nice. Anything else?' he said.

'I'm thinking,' she said.

'Ah, rehearsing, is it?' he said.

She said, 'Want to drop all this?'

He said, 'All what?'

'Oh, please,' she said. 'Can't you grow up?' she said.

He said, 'You know how old I am?'

She said, 'It's hopeless.' She said, 'You're hopeless.'

'That's not how you felt on the chair,' he said.

'You want to know what I felt on the chair?' she said.

He said, 'Make it good and hard and tough and mean and as callous as you can. Show me your stuff,' he said. 'Do unto me as you did unto me on the chair,' he said.

She said, 'Since you asked.'

He said, 'Oh, go ahead. Didn't I ask?'

She said, 'Next time.' She said, 'He's coming.'

'Always another time,' he said.

'That's right,' she said. 'We live with other people,' she said.

'We die with them,' he said.

'We die alone,' she said.

* * *

She said, 'Didn't you say she redid the chair?'

He said, 'We talked about it.' He said, 'You can't have forgotten we talked about it,' he said. He said, 'The chair, the carpeting, the plumbing, the viaduct, the forests in the Sudan.' He said, 'Years ago. She recovered everything,' he said.

She said, 'With what?'

He said, 'Don't know.' He said, 'A sort of leather-like thing. But maybe not,' he said. He said, 'I'll take a look and report back to you the next time I get back to the bedroom,' he said.

'Skip it,' she said. 'Lost interest,' she said, 'the instant I asked,' she said.

'What?' he said. He said, 'What was it you asked?'

'Could we fuck on it?' she said.

He said, 'Would we or could we?'

'I don't want to talk about it,' she said.

'Where couldn't we fuck?' he said.

'I'm getting off the line,' she said. 'Don't you hear something on the line?' she said.

He said, 'No.'

She said, 'Your hearing's going.'

He said, 'It's yours that is.'

She said, 'Let's not take a chance.' She said, 'Hang up.' She said, 'If you won't, I will.'

'Oh, but of course,' he said. 'No end to the theories of the Agamben guy. Hey,' he said, 'you ever hear of Alexander Graham Bell?' he said.

She said, 'I'm having a test tomorrow.'

'Aren't we all?' he said.

She said, 'Did you hear what I said?'

He said, 'What did you say?' He said, 'Didn't you say you're hanging up?'

* * *

He said, 'What's the verdict?'

She said, 'It didn't come in yet.'

He said, 'It'll be okay.'

'Probably,' she said.

'No question about it,' he said. 'Take it easy,' he said. 'Did you tell him?' he said.

She said, 'Tell him what?'

'I guess you started to,' he said, 'and he was, you know, reading,' he said.

'Thanks for checking in,' she said.

'No trouble at all,' he said.

She said, 'It's not unlikely you think there's a prize involved.'

He said, 'Isn't there always?'

'Shit,' she said, 'that's so Jewish of you.'

'A fella's got to keep trucking,' he said.

She said, 'You're not even living in this century,' she said.

He said, 'Yeah, but I'll die in it, won't I?'

She said, 'Call me Thursday. Chances are I'll have heard by Thursday.' She said, 'I want you to be the first to hear.'

'Me too,' he said. He said, 'The same'd go for me,' he said. 'Isn't it crazy?' he said. He said, 'After all these years,' he said.

'After all the years,' she said.

* * *

He said, 'So?'

'All clear,' she said.

'Thank God,' he said.

'Yeah,' she said. 'Until it's otherwise,' she said.

'Not to dwell on it,' he said.

'Right,' she said. She said, 'But we dwell.'

He said, 'What is that?' He said, 'Is that Agamben again?'

'Just common sense,' she said.

'Alas,' he said.

'Alas, your ass,' she said.

'I'm thinking yours,' he said.

'I'm old,' she said.

He said, 'We're always old. It's ours to live,' he said.

She said, 'I can't.'

'You won't,' he said.

'The chair,' she said.

He said, 'Picture it.' He said, 'Can you picture it?' He said, 'We'd lay a sheet over it.'

'Drape it over it,' she said.

He said, 'Drape,' he said. He said, 'You'd bring it and we'd drape it.' He said, 'Together,' he said. He said, 'Are you seeing it?'

'I don't know,' she said.

'See it,' he said.

She said, 'All I'm really seeing is the telephone. All I'm really seeing is what I looked like when the call came in. All I'm really seeing is his peeking into the back of the car when I'd forget to get the sheet out of it.'

He said, 'But that never happened, did it?'

She said, 'No, it never happened. But I was so afraid,'
she said. 'I could never remember,' she said. 'I was
always thinking all that night did I actually get it out of
the car and get it into the washing machine.'

He said, 'That's what you were thinking?'

She said, 'I was thinking had I or hadn't I?' She said,
'And then I'd get up in the middle of the night to make
sure I'd run a load and gotten it into the dryer or at least
stuck the sheet at the bottom out of the way under the
other stuff.'

'Whereas me,' he said, 'whereas I,' he said, 'I was all
that night thinking Jesus, your leg, your ankle, your
foot – my hand, this hand.' He said, 'My right hand,
your left leg – knee, calf, ankle, foot.'

'I was terrified,' she said.

'Don't be terrified,' he said.

'What if the report had come out different?' she said.

'Ah, yes, that,' he said. 'It's always that.'

She said, 'He's back. I hear him. He's back.'

'I'll call,' he said.

She said, 'Yes – call.'

* * *

'You okay?' he said.

'Yes, I'm fine,' she said.

He said, 'I'm sorry. I'm suddenly stumped,' he said,
'for what to say.'

She said, 'Look at it this way – you just,' she said,
'managed to say something,' she said.

'Okay,' he said. 'It's just that I all of a sudden don't feel …'

'Not another word,' she said. 'We'll get together soon.'

He said, 'You mean that?'

'On the phone,' she said.

'Yes, got you,' he said. 'On the phone,' he said.

* * *

'You know what I used to think?' she said.

He said, 'What did you used to think?'

'A woman's work,' she said.

'You mean the sheet,' he said. 'Well, I'll tell you what I,' he said, 'used to think.'

'Watch it,' she said. 'I'm not ready for any more guff,' she said. 'Not from you,' she said. 'But go ahead and tell me what,' she said.

'Fine,' he said. 'I'm going to tell you,' he said. 'How tired my arm was,' he said. He said, 'In the midst of all that, how tired.'

'That's sweet,' she said. 'It's sort of endearing,' she said. 'It's a remembrance I'll take to bed with me tonight,' she said.

'Listen,' he said, 'I don't think I'm so certain you even know what guff means. You know what I mean?' he said.

'I know what pain means,' she said.

He said, 'I'll bet you do.'

She said, 'Don't kid yourself, buddy-boy. I know what I know.'

He said, 'You know what you think you know.'

She said, 'I'm not for an instant suggesting you hurt me.' She said, 'You do understand that, don't you? But there was pain,' she said.

'Really?' he said. 'As in pain, you mean? As in ow, you mean?'

'Believe it,' she said.

'I don't,' he said. 'You're confusing me with him,' he said. He said, 'It's been so long now, you don't know which is which.'

'Oh, I know,' she said. 'Don't be so quick to flatter yourself. You dealt out your share,' she said. She said, 'Body pain. Not hurt, buddy-boy. Not just hurt, buddy-boy,' she said. 'But pain, darling. Not,' she said, 'just a weary arm, but how about cramps in my leg?' she said.

'This is childish,' he said.

'Beneath us,' she said.

He said, 'We had the chair beneath us.'

She said, 'We had the carpet, the bed.'

He said, 'The floor sometimes. It was lovely on the floor.'

'Sometimes,' she said.

'All the time,' he said.

'Now,' she said, 'now there's no time,' she said.

'There's time,' he said. He said, 'We could arrange it,' he said.

'I'm old,' she said. 'I'm fed up with everything,' she said. She said, 'I'm fed up with myself,' she said.

He said, 'Outgrow it,' he said.

'Heart's not in it,' she said.

'Try another part,' he said.

'I heard something,' she said.

'You heard me pleading,' he said.

'Ringing off,' she said.

He said, 'How Brit of you – wow.'

'Goodbye,' she said.

'Goodbye,' he said.

* * *

'Naugahyde,' she said.

'Hunh?' he said.

She said, 'Years ago you said it was naugahyde.'

'I don't understand you,' he said.

She said, 'You said it, you said it.'

'Said what?' he said.

'Said,' she said, 'that she had had it recovered in nau-gahyde. Or with naugahyde. Reupholstered in it. You said it, you said it,' she said, 'you did. Years ago, for God's sake.' She said, 'Of all the things, Jesus.'

'I couldn't have,' he said. 'What's naugahyde?' he said. He said, 'I don't even know what naugahyde is,' he said.

'You heard me,' she said.

He said, 'Heard what?'

She said, 'You let her, you let her.'

'Let her what?' he said.

'Skip it,' she said.

He said, 'What are we talking about?'

'It doesn't matter,' she said.

'She's downstairs,' he said.

She said, 'That's right.' She said, 'Of course she is.'

'Women,' he said.

'It's an old saying,' she said.

'I'm not following you,' he said.

'For every man,' she said, but did not say the rest.

* * *

Afterwards, for no few times afterwards, he would seek to remember, and she would seek to remember – each succeeding a little differently from the other – remembering when they would be given to slide all as one down off the lip of the chair, oh so shiningly slidingly, together, together, each mindful to reach back a little to drag the bedsheet down along with them down onto the floor with them, her foot, her ankle, her knee, her leg, none of it not ever for an instant not still gripped in his hand, the ecstasy of it, of their rolling over and over in this unforgettable zeal of theirs, smashing into the whole household together, smashing into everything everywhere together, forever rolling over and over in the whole wide world together, rolling the two of them together in the rolling feeling of love.

JELLY APPLE

Sure, you've been through some tough times, don't I
know it! – and, hey, I'd be the last one to say you've not
weathered the lot of them in grand good style, believe
me, believe me – not that I'd want for you for an
instant to think that I myself (Gordon, Gordon!) have
not, from period to period (time to time), had it pretty
rough too, you know? Let's get one thing straight
– my hat, it's off to you, the way you've gone ahead
and – pretty stylishly, if you don't mind my saying so,
taken the bitter with the smooth, unless – I don't this
minute right now know if it's 'with the sweet' a person
is supposed to say. I mean, they're always changing
these things. A fella turns around and the next thing he
knows, they went ahead and took away one word and
put a different one in its place – 'smooth' one minute,
'sweet' the next – you know what I mean? I mean like
take 'jelly apple', okay? A fella goes to bed and the next
thing he knows he gets up in the morning and the first
thing he has to deal with, even before he's had time to
blink, the newspapers are all telling him, 'Forget it, bub
– yeah, it was jelly apple last night but it's candy apple
now and you just better get yourself adjusted to it or,
like, get out of town, okay?' I mean, you know what
I'm saying? It's the way of the world – a fella gets used
to something, a fella gets himself good and comfortable with something and – *whamo*, Bob's your uncle! –
the bastardos take it away. Come on, I don't have to tell
you. It's tough, it's rough – it's pretty goddamn lousy

for the whole human race, what with every whip-stitch waking up and finding out the bastardos have gone ahead and changed everything around the minute you turned your back and went ahead to get yourself a decent night's rest.

It's not right. Am I or am I not right on the beam here – not morphing it from jelly apple to candy apple, for the best example I can this minute think of, and nobody even tips you off about it until you lay out for the price of a newspaper or turn the radio on or maybe fire up the television or one of them crazy new species of gadget it takes a postgraduate education just for you to get the hang of how a citizen is supposed to get the battery for it in.

Batteries! I mean, fuck it, they're sometimes these things which a fella can't even with two regular fingers in good working order pick up for him to get one of them into something futuristical, they're so itty-bitty and everything and all. You need a specialist, if you're maybe lucky enough to be on speaking terms with a ten-year-old, plus got for yourself a bank account in a bank which didn't already swipe every dime of your lifetime savings out of it and turn your name over to the axis powers for them to dope out brand-new types of crimes against humanity and the inhumanly maimed.

Okay, granted, granted, I'm sitting here horsing around a little bit. Guilty, I'm pleading guilty – so sue me. Because, buster, I'm leveling with you, I'm taking you into my fucken confidence as a person I can go ahead and open my heart to – so, okay, I'm like straining, if that's, please God, if that's still the word today for me to attempt to convey to you the impression that I'm a pretty good guy, that I'm, you know, imbued, if you follow me, with what they call the common touch and that you can go ahead and drop your guard and put down your defenses and place a certain amount of trust in me as an individual who is dedicated to giving you the straight scoop about this and that as to the news of his kishkes – because, I'm telling you, there's no two ways about it, if I don't get to get some items off my chest, I'll like, you know, pop a gut or something.

So, okay, I'm taking it I can let down my hair with you and not have to pay for it in the morning. I mean me as my actual self and not me as some ventriloquistic type who's sitting here selling you a bill of goods as to his ordinariness. I mean, I went to college for a little bit and I know about the guy in the poem who's leaning out of the window in his shirtsleeves, I think it is. Maybe it's guys. I suppose I don't know exactly, but I don't think exactly's got anything to do with the point. What I can promise you is this: I'm a guy like that, I feel like I'm a guy like that, or guys like that, all of us ladies and gentlemen who have the feeling something's come along and knocked us on the head and it, let's face it, it hurts, it really hurts all over all of a sudden and there's nobody who's interested and we're probably a little dizzy from it all and it's not going to get better and the sun is going down and the air is all steamy and sticky and suffocating and colorless and all we can do is lean on a windowsill all day and get soot on our arms and our hands and our shirtsleeves and, okay, on the floor of our heart and, you know, not be able for us to do anything else but look out the window and get dirty and stare.

You listening to me?

Because I feel as if that's me in a nutshell.

Now, I mean – I mean now that something's happened.

Anyway, that's me in a nutshell.

It's not impossible it's just as much you yourself as well.

Anyway, right or wrong, that's how I heard it when I heard it in college and sat in that fucken classroom and heard that poem being read on a record which the teacher had by the poet himself. I'm going to tell you something – dollars to doughnuts, the poet, the man, he couldn't have said what he said – that little thing, just the little bit which I remember, words, hardly any of them at all, but it's got to be how the man felt all the way down to his last word. It was the truth. You with me on what I'm saying? It was the real deal. I'm swearing it to you – I'd fight for that guy – I'd smack anybody right in the mouth for that guy – if anybody so much as whispered to me their opinion the guy was a bullshitter or was a bullshit artist and was just a guy who was in love with the words he had and the mood he was in and with faking everyone out with a pose he in the instant – *in the instant* – figured he could get away with.

Well, you and me – nah, forget it – you and I – we're no poets, you know, at least probably far from it, speaking for myself, but here comes the word about the soot which was once this one particular time all over everything here in my household – and which nothing, which not anything, has ever since gotten even anywhere close to getting rid of since.

That's twice – for good measure.

A double's worth of sinces – since it's the right trick to get it said right. As far as I'm concerned, this thing I'm going to talk with you about, it can't have too many nor too much of anything. So be it with desolation, which they had better not try to vaporize on me, come tomorrow and dishonor, come the morning and indifference, come the rest of my life and newly cherished poses, come the scruple of candor undercut by skeptics, come death and what I leave behind, some tepid gesturing at the awful triumph of the woman who, despite appearances, is the principal (just wait) playmaker – no, let's say mastermind – in this piece, not a shade, not a line, not an inch other than she was in a still life from whose frame it was drawn.

Not that I'm not going to prove the least tardy in readying myself to bow deeply (take a deep bow) for the imminent burst of applause when you've been all so copiously put in the know and have, resultantly, been rigged to hail the hell out of me for my rushing right in there, hurling the heft of my infamously pugnacious nature right in there into the midst of the melee, or the fray, say, or, what there is of the shock of the action. Hey, you're at liberty – nay, encouraged – to get a fix on me as a seasoned scrapper, a little fellow forever – or, better to acknowledge – à la a mini-spring once upon a time pretty tightly (truth?) violently wound, later to be discovered, concomitant with the on-coming discoverable awaiting you on-comingly ahead, revealed (theoretically) loose, revealed (implicitly loosened), reckoned (innuendo'ishly) to be good and decommissioned, played the piss out, he himself, at the first hint of the catastrophic, having got himself all exercised to hunker himself down and kick the ghastly luck a sharp one in the nuts, take charge, buckle down, spread calm, minimize, minimize, get control of the uncontrollable, laugh off the curse, plow on through, chin up, shoulders squared, fill out the suit of 'head of household' when I had, in fact, all I could do to hang on to my blankie, suck a corner of it obeisantly, and wondering if I would not do better by my dropping to my knees, break with tradition, see what an almighty might have in the way for a miracle for the deserving, or just fall all to pieces, sobbingly ahead of the game, make it with the help of Chinese medicine, of Indian medicine, maybe less lucklessly still, make it revivified by the magic of the astringent applied by an ingenious perfection of (eureka!) medicinelessness, make it, please God, to the distinguished ribbon marking the end of the marathon – and then, to, thereafter, collapse into the sanctuary of an afterlife whose border-crossing is to be audibly recognized by the abrupt muting of the principal bystander's repertoire of hysterics. Whereas as for our child, as for our son, as for the stripling made motherless by no commonplace means, he, it's certain, will, when it's warranted, devise far righter, far truer, run of figurations.

I repair to the days of tykehood, when tyke-like, one took into hand a double-scooped cone. Oh, you wanted it, not implausibly with sprinkles on it, and set off strolling, your free hand in the hand of the mother, the father, the uncle, the aunt, in the hand of the available chaperonic grown-up willing to treat you to a visit to the playland, in the course of which, thereupon, still treatingly wise, to a doubly scooped divertisement of something mountainously diverting, the other hand of which steward would have grasped in it the napkin held in good sense for coping with the torrent of meltage to ensue all too ensuingly.

A napkin?

Nay!

Likelier, ever more sensibly, many napkins, a grabful of napkins, a proper proportion of them dipped in waterfountain water for the downfall unignorably due.

O the fucken entropic!

The drogue congenitally hung from every (not-quite-yet-cragsome) contour of yon infant's cuddlesomeness.

Figurations.

Well, what the fucken else are you fucken expecting else from me? Is my fucken mind on words or are words – figurations – are they not chickenshit placeholders for what the fucken mind could never begin to bid you to translate into craven locutions in any language far and wide?

My apologies.

Losing tone here, not retaining purchase on stance

here, falling all to pieces with the coward's frolic among the phraseological here.

You know.

Shit-faced.

Beshitted.

Mountainous composition commencing to succumb to the science of things in the (now both) hands of the eager but, what else, inexperienced initiate. Look at the kid. Just look. Madly, deliriously licking his head off to keep the drippage from outflanking his frantic tactics to interrupt (O the ick of it, O the fucken ick!) the cascade of good times dropping from his grasp and settling in the dust all around his Buster Browns – nay, sawdust, in the sawdust – graphing the carnival's limits.

O the impotence of the conical biscuit, no match for the chemistry, or for the weatherman's sortilege, nor for the physics of it plain and simple, the evil ensemble of it afflicting all the rim's arcs of it all fucken all at once, lapping over the edge in some unassimilable onrush of reality, speeding earthward, too far gone to tarry a tick within recourse (resort?) to rescue, going, going, gone, unsalvageable, the forecast cast in favor of teasing a merciful remission from the merciless despotism of gravity – O the all-at-onceness of it! – the dissolving, the dissolution, of the unimagined delight!

Oh man!

And then, likeliest, it would be your ma who would snatch out the tissue she forever had tucked well away out of the way of superhuman sight and fucken rub it at you, shove it at you, swab you all over your fucken shame (ugh, ugh, quit it, please, Ma, I'm clean, I'm telling you, I'm clean, I'm clean!), as if you were not made of the same unendurable, fragile stuff she was.

Oh, we all of us are well aware you had it tremendously wretchedly awful back in your own execrable epoch or three, but if it's your conviction you can sit there and match me torment for torment of the type of torment I just sat here and proffered my heart out to you about, this for your personal benefit, sort of semi-illustration-wise, listen to me, what do you say you try this one on for size? – e.g. a kid comes up to you and the kid stands there and he says to you I bet you can't catch your shadow and, crikey, right up to that very point in the cultivation of your greenage, had you ever even given the slightest consideration as to what a shadow was?

Or is?

So am I right or am I right?

You bet I'm right.

I mean, *really* – don't you dare sit there convinced to the gills you can tell me what the question is – if it's whether to be or not to be, for an upmarket for-instance – or if it's (the question, that is) better spelt, more practicably spelt: what the shit, what the fucken shit?

What's it going to be – contumacy or contumely? – if you're anywhere near fathoming the repertory of the various jigs and jags individualizing the hardware laid out for us in our circling, circumloquaciously, ever closer to sneaking a teensy squint at the grisly array of thumb-screws and head-vices and claw-hammers intrepidly prepared to substitute themselves in the civilian enterprise to keep us at a safe distance from the grotesquerie of actualities fastened to actualities in a fusion of the flourishing disrepair visible in the slugfest between the believable and the unbelievable.

Ah, dickens and tarnation, the question's not looking so all-fire unanswerable – so long as you've got language and people and the impasse of making yourself passably understood. Oh, to be sure, it's all's a person can do – yeah, I said all's, you got it? – either stand there transfixed and take it like a mensch and do the best you can to blow off the thought of the thoughtitude of one's confusitation of going for the whole crazy split or, or, or! – go for throwing, instead, for the likelier, for the solitary, extinguishable pin.

My Christ, the substitutions, supplantings, mishmash of analogues and analogues and the dodges and tropisms galore, isn't it all a Christian can do to bear protesting the grace of an instant's absolution to be quarried from the organization of the organizing of the agonies to be counted up for the occasion of inventorying the resources bundled for our maintenance of (not to mention, entertainment in) the God-made world?

As was the fucken case with the wife and me when we had us …

Hold on a minute. Can you hold on for a sec? Because I'm changing the register here – I'm switching it to a whole different deal – if that's the way for a thing like this to be said – the tone, the tenor, the – oh, you know, isn't it the pressuring of the text for all it's superficially worth – for, anyway – or anyway for – a cursory flirt with straight-talk and the real?

I mean, inasmuch as you and me, you and I, weren't we talking tough times?

Okay, so here we go, the shambolic approached for the best of the symbolic in it – the never-to-be-spoken-of-case-with-me-and-the-missus, okay? – for it was when we had us a flock of nurses all flocked all around on all of the walls around here, every last one of these ladies and gentlemen keening holy fucken hell for how it was that their backs were killing them, for how they were kvetching holy hell was on account of how their backs couldn't take it anymore, for how their having to howl their hearts out for how their backs (mercy, mercy, yon aching back!) were fixing to exterminate them from their having to lean on over and then on farther and farther on over to fucken tend to her when there was neither nerve nor muscle anywhere in all her person which was willing to do the job the gods had designed it to be capable of.

That's right.

You heard me right – *nada nada nada*, as the man said.

By the time the nurses had all wandered in and took over whatever could be taken over.

Nada.

Except her eyes.

And, I don't know, I fucken don't remember, maybe them granting an exemption as well, the gods of us being, after all, the fucken gods, to her eyelids as well.

Which blessment – nay, blessmentation – delivers us unto the matter of the medium locally famous for its role under the aegis of the letterboard but which we – that's this time I the husband and you the interpellator – we're going to leave untouched, untinkered with, ever so gladly unattended where it's come to insist upon a moment's lie-down for itself.

You see it?

Never before seen a letterboard, have you?

Look, for crissake, yonder!

There on the floor laid out right in yon fucken foreground for you – but back between me and the last dependable trouper from among the squadron of forever-on-the-fritz suction machines (no fewer than six of them, one sucking ardently after the other, for the afflicted to get through the fucken night with – until the agency comes – or maybe doesn't get the frantic message to – with six overnight overhauled more).

Here's hoping you're not inviting the notion I'm sitting here discounting what the flock of them were up against. Their labors, let me tell you from first-hand witness, they, the labors, they were hard on them, on the ladies and gentlemen. It was terrible to see two at a time of them teamed up to lean over and over and on and on down over for them to turn her.

Tend to her needs.

Which were without number.

Which were numberlessly greater than what yon newborn would need.

Well, which of us has not seen for himself – presto, change-oh! – a hospital bed?

So, fine – so go ahead and phone all around the universe to find a service willing to fetch to the premises such an appliance of you-crank-it variety – and, lo and behold, it comes, if sans the shoehorn to shoehorn it in.

Took four big men to get it up the freight elevator and then get it back out of it and then shimmy it in through the side door and then fit it on through the kitchen and then thereafterwards shove it along the front hall and then heave it along the back hall and then – at last, good grief, jam it all of the way into the chuggyjammed sickroom where the afflicted lay the night and the day every night and every day not a jot other than how the afflicted had lain all foregoing nights, all foregoing days – unless, until, for the love of the fucken gods, all hands were at the ready, every hand in the fucken house, came to the marital bed and leant in – down, down, down – to get her turned.

Whereas now the afflicted might be raised up.

Whereas now my beloved might be lifted aloft.

But no, she wouldn't be moved to it.

No!

No concession granted, no easement entertained, the answer is no, goddamn it to hell, no this for that, no trade-off, no deal!

Oh, did you ever see a lassie go this way and that way and this way and that way, did you ever see a lassie ...?

Need further remark be made?

No matter how inert the deathbound inhabitant in there.

No matter how exhausted the deathbound ether in there.

No!

The afflicted's position is posted via the letterboard.

N O

Listen to me.

Did you see it?

See her eyes see yours? – thereafter first here, then after that, then there?

N O

But who can really remember?

Isn't it enough to have marveled, to recall the marveling as you stood there nonplussed?

The obstinance.

Stubbornness.

Contempt for the importunings of the next event.

Did you ever see a lassie, a lassie, a lassie …

The afflicted would not be budged, would not be rearranged, would not consent to reason – not even when the news had come to breathe its malignancy all of the way down into her face.

My wife.

Refusing the unparsable grammar of non-being.

Oh, to devour the jelly apple and then to remain, impervious, among the horrors of the midway, sticky-free.

Please – who doesn't have it rough?

You ready yet? – for not the worst of us shall be cheated of the chance to stage a quality performance.

Refusal, of course.

Revenge wreaked upon the irreversible.

Of course.

But the genius of it, just think! – nothing stated but N O, nothing keeping the exchange between you and yourself conceding to forgive the living their freedom from torment incommensurate with your own.

Yessir, that's my baby now!

UP THE WHITE ROAD

The secret I had in mind, which I have never not had in mind from as far back as I have any trace of memory, I can, if you will allow the use of simulation, please, I can just about sit here and get the tips of my fingers on and tease it, tease it, work it out of its, draw it out of its, tempt it to come into my hands enough for me to say it was, in a word, wrongness – that the secret I felt I had to keep secret in myself was a feeling of deep-felt wrongness, of unmendable wrongness, the bottomless kind, chthonic, which isn't pronounced like it looks, but which I have no choice but to anyway use if we can have any honest hope of us, of me, getting to the character of the secret, the sense of it, the, say I said, the sensorium of it, of this feeling I had in my kishkes if we're going as far back as I have any hope of remembering, or of retrieving, or of getting, so to speak, my hands on it, like as unto maybe possibly grasping it, or getting a pretty good grip on it, of my having any hope of succeeding to grab it and bring it anywhere up into the light of day with us – wrongness, a feeling of unriddable wrongness, chthonically lodged in, or stuck for good down there upon the bottommost surface of the bottommost level of my kishkes – because, we have to come to grips with it, we have to, so to speak, face it, if you and me are going to get anywhere with each other – because there's first and foremost the element of nature, which in your case I am totally ignorant of, over my head about, out of my depth, the best expression is, which we can possibly, if we team up, unravel together, get it unpacked, as they say, shine a proper light on in all its fullness of difference, but first of all, first and foremost, the floor is mine, the book is mine, Latimer, given name Andrew, has so declared it, ordained it, made it the case we're here to deal with – this chthonic thing I have, up to this crazy instant, secret as all get-out, the sense I'm wrong, wrong, wrong, but not wrong about something – heaven knows I haven't the least interest in me being right about anything – it's not a question-and-answer thing, it's not you ask me a question and I give you an answer and it's either the right answer or the wrong answer, but deeper than that sort of thing, far other than that sort of thing, outside the realm of anything like I know this and I don't know that, anything, everything well apart from that sort of thing, like learning, like knowledge, like a person's getting around in the world what with trips and so forth, or with sitting herself or sitting himself down with a geography book, or with a book which deals with the topic of geography, and studying it real hard, really going ahead and applying herself, or applying himself, and then, facing the phalanx of questioners, or interrogators, or investigators, best of all, inquisitors, facing them and the various and sundry tests they're going to set you, the tests which they are honorbound to sit there and set you, facing that phalanx of them, the inquisitors, or the inquisitive profession, and then you having to go ahead and field their interminable queries, or inquiries, all of them devised for you on what we call an individuated basis, no, no, no, that's not the thing, that's not what I'm talking about, that's not what I mean, not at all, wrongness and rightness, or rightness versus wrongness on a rivalrous basis, on the basis, on an axis of this way you got it and that way no but instead on a basis of different from that, not on a basis where you're judged, or scored, or graded in terms of your placement somewhere, heaven knows where, along, so to speak, you know, along the continuum of an axis of that type, no, no, no – it's nothing like that, it's not anything like that – it's, you know, it's totally chthonic instead, it's totally congenital, if you are really making an honest effort to know what I mean – *congenital*, that's the word I've been wandering all over the pages in search of – just look at them *now*, if you will, because that's what I mean, for your information, when I broach the matter of the whereabouts of the lodgement of the secret in me, it's the whereabouts of the feeling which is never not attacking the status of the kishkes in me – it's chthonically congenital, or, since it's six of one and half a dozen of the other, let's say I'm saying it vice versa, as per: congenitively chthonic – man oh man, the chthonicism of the kishken feeling of wrong.

Which is to say the secret one.

Until now.

Right up until we've spent these nice quiet minutes together – you and me, or vice versa, me and you – confessor and confessorand, which is a word which I just this minute made up, in case you're the type of individual who goes for the facts and who turns around like as to say he or she is saying fuck it and leaving the rest of it alone.

The piffle.

The unfounded. The whole opinionated rigamarole.

And feature this, me figuring you still have a few more minutes to hang around where we've settled in for some peace and quiet – confessor and confessorand – engaged in a heart-to-heart examination of my nature as an American citizen who, as an American citizen, has, if I don't mind me saying so, to coin another apt as-they-come expression, who has, you know, been around the block.

Well, to Worcester, for one.

Also, to a foreign country, for two.

Like when I was a teen.

You can see me at it – no shit – to this day there's a pic of me there on this foreign street there – that's it, just me on a foreign street there, a bonafide American citizen, just getting on an aircraft and going when I'm not even more than a middle-aged teen yet, me being, as they say, abroad.

I like that.

You like that?

It's got some zing of an historical ping in it – an American citizen abroad.

You know – ping.

You can hear it if you're sitting there listening to hear it. But forget it if you're not. It's not an issue. I'm making an issue of it. There's nothing intended issue-wise here. It's just like a lackadaisical interplay between individuals who just happen to fall in with each other on the road of life, just two-teaming everybody else with each other, shooting the shit like lackadaisically, which I don't even know if I'm spelling it correctly, but does it matter?

Ask yourself. Inquisitate yourself – *does* it, does it actually?

But fine, I'm going to go ahead and take another even chancier chance with you, which is me coming clean apropos as to the Brokaw kid – inasmuch as must be eminently clear by now, I have, throwing caution to the wind, sat myself down here for me to break with my traditional habitual silence and, if a touch rashly, touch (you see, you see? – me doubling it, doubling *down*, as the featured speakers of the New American Lingo do speak) upon myself, my age-old secret and, if you will, what this portends for the nation of which I am a constituent part, if not a part of the constituted electorate at hand. Hence, the Brokaw kid, where does the matter stand? By the by, before we endeavor to ferret out adumbration on a side-topic such as that, or say I said an ancillary one such as that, there's a little formality we had better get straight between us right here at the start.

Another adumbration, as it were, adumbrated, as it were, strictly between us, as it were, which is to say not between you and I but between you and me. Are we clear? Enough, preponderantly, said? Unless it's preponderantly which is to be said since preponderantly looks, as

a word, to the future, which we are, of course, getting to
– there! – you catch the tide of it *there*? – word by word.
In any case, this is called, or is subsumed, as they say,
under the title 'Up the White Road'. Well, we're getting
to it, as we, so to speak, speak. It's all about temporality,
not to mention politics, which is why I am already exer-
cising every inch of caution in me, which is never to lapse
in my policy to cheat to the safe side, to conceive, then
review, and thereafter not to actuate all utterances until
they have been inspected for their loyalty to policy, for
fidelity to probity, never venturing, never letting any
of them venture into speculation, no matter how much
I hate the person, or fear the person, despite me being
protected by the laws of the United States of America.
You see this might have been devised as the commence-
ment of a discrete – or disparate or separate – paragraph,
but I am no chump and do accordingly reckon with the
cost of paper and the wear and tear inveighing on (or,
if you would, weighing on, bearing a weight upon) the
tools of free speech and the limitable resources of time. It
drains, you know. Time drains, you know, flushes right
out of your hands irrespective of how hard a clutch you
have come to believe yourself to have got a clutch on
it. It goes. Take the Brokaw kid. Has the time for us to
take full account of – or even passing account one – of
his impingementation in this – under the considerations
anent 'the road' or 'the whiteness thereof' or, heavens,
why it's never down it but up it – has *that* time, which
may have already once been a future time now forever
lost to us by reason of its having, or it having, slipped,

more or less, past us mentionless, or, as once suspended in a state of futurism, lost, thus unmemorable to us in virtue of its time having come and then gone as a function – this may prove to be over your head, but I beg you to bear, for a nonce, with me noncely – the speaker whence speaking interdicting, or interpellating, via the expression, or maxim, uttered, axiomatically perhaps, I quote: 'not to mention'. Lost? I'm lost.

Jesus.

Lives lost.

People – their dreams, their fortunes, their honor – obliterated – by, face it, expression, speech, written, spoken, even just evident, ever so nearly undetectably, by a shrug, a shrugging, a careless, a carefree, an all-too-human act (or action) of beshrugment.

Anyway, to harken backwards a little, whence you hear me say, or have heard me say 'you', in the manner of address most probably, when this happens, when you hear me, or have heard me, speaking thus, be aware, please to be aware, I am not saying it unsubstantively. Believe me, I am not like other people engaged in speakage with you who say 'you' to you. You see what I'm saying? Wrong, wrong, wrong as I (as a citizen) am, I am, nonetheless, all about substance, presence, sincerity, other words, such as enteric, troilistic, exilic, and, quite naturally, the Eliotic 'phthisic'. Are we clear? You are, without impediment, following me? Nay, coming along with me? Well, do it! Keep on doing it! For I am not without a sense, however stochastic or (Christ Jesus!) aleatory, of obligation. I mean, I owe you. You're, as has been said, as I am not the first to say, you're, you've been paying your dues. Listen, I am a from-the-heart type of person – as to me being a member of society, that is. Which (hint! hint!) I happen to have not always been. Look, I'm decent – humane – no kraken on a bet – not any of it! – I'm, as has been said of me, remarked of me, opined about me, despite no little professional palaver to the contrary, okay. So let's make an end of this skepticism I can sense, intuit, discern issuing unto me from your consciousness, lest it be better sited (or cited) as to be radiating, concentrically speaking, in waves (*waves!*), from a core source situated in your subconscious, or subconsciousness, or, if I might be permitted to venture this excursively, subconscience, assuming that extenuation in nowise proves offensive to you. No matter. What I just laid out for the indelible record is, I give you every assurance (reassurance?), no more than a glimmer of *my* subconscience in geriatric action.

We were where?

We are, if you will excuse me, yes, exactly where?

Ah, the road – the white road, is it?

You're, to be certain, curious as to … wait, we pause. Let me tell you, you are going to be pretty glad you made the decision to stick it out with me – when we get to where the publisher has elected to place the photograph of me – this (taken, snapped, made ready for the attention of posterity) produced when I was [REDACTED] years old and was standing, as will be evident, on a road in the foreign city called [REDACTED], famous for its arcana of medical activity in the nation known to American citizens as [REDACTED]. At all events, or at any rate, wait until you get a load of the suit. All I can ruefully say, yet utterly truthfully, is this: some suit!

Bought it myself. Acquired it with my own money, or with – who's ashamed of it, am I ashamed of it? – my own stealth. That right there, that was a prima fascia example of my humanity, the socially acute nature thereof, or of it. All right, the prima thing, I'm not in the least squeamish about it – i.e., did I spell it wrong? If no, then fine, the gods continue to see to the figure I cut in society, the impression I give. If otherwise, if I muffed it, then let me in all decorum say fuck it – I come before you minus a major experience in education, learning, the propaedeuticism enjoyed by my peers and various and sundry contemporaries, me having, my regretfully having, often been yonder in the formative years. Also, to be regrettably recklessly open about it, in some of the formed ones, too.

Anyway, all this is, if you would be so good as to accept it, a further compilation of the accruing of the masses and masses of evidence concerning the stripe of patriot – you are, may I put in, at liberty to check with the State Department, unless it's the Department of State – I have always, eximiously, been, and, to this instant, right up to this very instant, am a chap who's stood hidden in the lilac bush, a chap who's commuted (back and forth) into the terrors of Worcester, a chap who has departed these shores for the shores of a land not his own nor of his choosing but, goddamn it, because he was 'suffering' a 'condition' and fucking had to, God help him, go in search of the therapeutic surcease from itching, itching, itching.

Oh, the fucking itchment, goddamn it!

Or suffering *from* one, if that's what is contemporaneously going down among the so-called cognoscenti, extemporaneously, if you will be so kind, speaking.

Hey, spelt okay enough for you?

Take it easy, take it easy! – we're getting there.

'Up the White Road,' is it?

Fine, I can handle it, I can handle it.

All I'm doing is testing you for me to commence to establish a working, a practical, an adequately thoughtful, or thought-out, estimate as to whether you're (i.e. you are) up to it. Because it just so happens that, in my life, that all upon a day in my life, that a time was going to come up in my life when I came – as a child! as a mere shaver of a child! as a tad of a lad tucked well out of sight behind the lilacs, goddamn it, that I, an American still mounting an American mein, unless it's mien, had come to know the day would come when they would come and get me – and that when they came and got me, that when they had come to get me, and not even called first, had not even shown the simple common courtesy to call, or to phone, first – that's right, that's right! – they would come and take me to a place where the people who were there were all in rubber there and all in mats and screaming for the perfectly understandable purpose of defending themselves – defending! – against the roar of the water running tub-wise everywhere there, while – wait a minute, wait! – while every last one of them – people, the people! – they would all every one of them turn out to be the Brokaw kid, which I know, which I totally *know* is totally ridick, because it is known, it has been studied, deemed, been deemed, that the Brokaw kid, whatever stunts he, behind your back, might have been practicing working on, very possibly has been practicing working out, none of them could conceivably encompass the art of passing yourself off as more than one person.

You see?

So now so you see?

Or as a one-at-a-time person, if this appears to furnish you with enough supplementary guidance.

Forget it. I spoke too soon. Clarity, and that other word, lucidity, lucidity – there's no substitute for not thinking things out first. I got it wrong. I *said* it wrong, although as to me *getting* it, believe me, I get it. It's just that converting, that when it comes to the business of converting the chthonicism of your thinking into speaking (e.g. speech), you run smack into the age-old conundrum of translating, or the quandary of it, meaning: of translation. Look, the essence of the thing is that I know – chthonically – whereof I speak. On the other hand, this adverts to or reverts to or goes back or is ushering us back to the bygone era of the lilac bush (or of the lilac *bushes*) which you could stand in when you had made up your mind to take, or take up a stand on the Brokaw side of the house, where I – still tracking this, still keeping to the tack of the track in this? – the house wherein, I, your victim, I trust you needn't be tolden, grew up. With respect to, or concerning which, the side on the *other* side, on, namely, the non-Brokaw side, as to that, relative to that shit, to the who and the what and the which family and so forth and so on, this is where I am obliged to say I have no information for you, that as to that I draw a complete blank as to that, to coin an apt and fluent expression. Yet this is okay. This is no indication, no indicator, no index of any lapse here. Jesus, people, it was eras ago. It was the age of the lilacs, are we clear about that with each other, or with one another? Yon lilacs, or, more comprehensively to say, yon lilac bushes, they were the oldest friend I ever had.

So, yes or no, are the blinders coming off? Is the haze falling away? The veil, it falleth for you? The miasma, it's retreating for you, shrinking, condensing before the power of yon transparency, kowtowing to the impending bite thitherto dormant in the latently hegemonic tooth of the declarative, fugitive, fugitive, fugitive, given inroads achieved in virtue of the notorious swayage prompted by the resultant recoil arising from the spreadance of the clear, of the limpid, the lucid, the limpet, the liminally limned and courageously portrayed?

Are we approaching the nub?

Are we, as one, inching upward, ever upward, well enough positioned, me and you, on the phthisic thoroughfare to it? The approach, to your mind, it's sound, is it?

Because next – next, fellow travelers, trekkers, pioneers – next comes the building. Or the first of these edifices – are you hip to it? – the mystery of the edifice formatted as a building, inseparable from it, fused – I would venture so far as to say intessellated, unless this last is less lavishly spelt with only, no more than, one el.

Definitely peculiar, this 'structure', or 'construction'.

You want to hear something? May I tell you something? You are in a mood to take on more information?

The thing was definitely peculiar-looking.

Okay, back to business. Yes, I was going to put you in-the-know as to someone I know who has the gall to say 'definitively' when a person possessed of a mere modicum of grammar-school learning should know the word she seeks, the sense she seeks, it's not – oh, skip it, forget it – you don't care and I don't even know her that well and, besides, no interruptions, agreed?

No frigging interpellations, agreed?

Look, you see the photo yet? Did Latimer (I warn you, ignore this, don't make a big deal of it, it's just a name is all, one with a conducive array of syllables, if you please), but did he, the man Latimer, place it (the photograph) anywhere into view yet? Alas, you've never been made privy to how blind I am. Am I right or am I right? Anyway, no matter, no matter. So long as my mind is situated healthfully. The eyes, we can, with no admission of irony, I say, yes, yes, yes, we can piss on them. But the mind, the brain, the cranial exorbitance, I guarantee you, this is where the issue is, this is where the payoff is, this is the seat of the cathedra!

Ah, Latimer acts!

Great!

At fucking last!

Good fellow. My amanuensis (no, she's scarcely the author of 'definitively', she has just murmured to me the road photo, it's in sight).

Not bad, wouldn't you say?

Can't make it out with even a magnifying glass but the mind, the mind, it's not without its measure of dependability. I remember a suit. A lad visibly thickened from the treatments, eh? But a stalwart, for God's sake, an American patriot, a well-tailored boy American-born, erect in a roadway where the foreign-born roam. Unless Latimer and the amanuensis, they've devised a bit of pranksterism fit for the quality of fun to be had at the expense of the lord of the page. Unless it's the page back before this one and I'm just another victim of victimology on this one. It's, hey, it is indeed, to be sure, yon lad in the picture, it's, I accuse no one, but it's definitely, even definitively, it is, by thunder, positively a pic, in fact, of none other, no other, save me?

Fair enough. The conjecture that anyone, let alone Latimer and Company, that the bastardos would dare to horse around with me, it's, the very conjecture, done what it might to wind me, snatch the wind from my sails, unsteady the old fellow, give him to wonder are the foreign-born sending, as his inferiors have, in the parlous climes, been heard to say, *sending*, I said, or quoth'ed I, as it's said, the old boy up?

Dastards!

You toy with the wrong boy!

Listen up, if you dare!

I used to go to Worcester twice a week. That's when I first saw one. That's right. That's when. Back behind me when I was on the stairs and the girl going up the stairs alongside me, or alongside of me, she said for me to turn myself around and to take a look at what's up on the hill back behind us.

'You see that building?' she said.

The same girl. How could it each time be the same girl from somewhere? Twice a week. That's twice week-ly, do you understand this, are you comprendo-ing the chthonicistical crux of this? Because I demand to be tolden if you and yours are getting anywhere near to the drift of what it is I am sitting here next to the aman-uensis disclosing to you!

I demand!

Going up there to get a jar of it and come back home with it and when empty – emptied! – I would have to go back up there back again to Worcester again and take back the emptied jar with me and get a new jar for the coming interval for me and then come back home again with it and resume with it the interval again and no, no, no, it was never enough for me, it was never enough for me – my whole body and so on and so forth – over and over – *for a long time*, in case you and yours are sitting there counting.

And here's another thing.

Here's something else as to other things.

Forget it! – not a word for any of us as to what it was which was *in* it, no!

But as to the lid, ahah!

Adhesive tape, a white strip of tape, made to adhere to the lid of it, from lip, in a manner of speaking, to lip. With numerals inked on it and alphabetical entries inked on it.

And an equals sign!

Every time.

From side to side!

'Oh,' she said, 'go ahead, turn, look, don't be afraid.'

I was afraid.

Some suit, eh?

It had better be me in it!

Are you listening to this? Is she getting all of this down for you word for word for you in accordance with the denouement of it long overdue for you? Well, I didn't look back behind me not ever again, okay? Never ever again on those stairs, ixnay, no, *nada*! Even when I was coming back down them, I never looked over to across the road to see anything more of it up the hill.

This is reminding me of something, if you've still got a minute.

Yes?

Maybe all of two minutes?

Get this.

When I was little, when I first (etc., etc.) came to the conclusion (sensation) which I am taking my very life into my hands telling you about, I used to – then, then, at that time (during that period), in the course of that era – I used to wriggle myself inside of the lilac bushes which were over on the Brokaw side of our house and go ahead and hide myself in there and keep myself in there altogether hidden in there (amid the lilacs, in the midst of the lilacs), hoping and praying nobody could see me standing in there getting more and more worn out from it, weary, wearied, going crazy from the wear and tear of it wearing me down, just me standing there staring over at the Brokaws' place, exhausted, spent, spent, fucking ausgespielt just from me standing there staring, but – oh, yes, but – listen, listen to me! – nothing ever came of it.

Do you see what I'm saying?

Well, let's just go ahead and elide everything more after that whole part of it. Some things just happen, or have happened, and that's the long and short of it. Except me being blind, I'm thinking. Or, truth to say, not yet all of the way sightless yet. Except like there's a sort of hoverment of a sort of connection, you know what I mean? – which, let's not you and me and yours kid ourselves, let's not any of us kick back and commence to take it so easy on ourselves, which there certainly was – a connection, a connection! – with regard to the adhesive tape, with regard to the girl, the hill, the town of Worcester, the city of Worcester, the community, the municipality, the precinct – nay, province, the province – of, you know, of Worcester.

Oh, it's so great for me to be getting this pretty darn close to me getting the gist of the whole affair, if it's jake with you and with your staff for me to take note of the time, the duration, of all of the longeurs of it, hurrying the whole affair along and be, how they say 'brief' or 'terse' or compact or compressed about it, off – I turn now, or return now, to me in the coinage mode – off my chest, out in the open, dragged up from the chthonical essence of me out into the light, as it were, of day. As per me knowing.

As per me having knowledge, being knowledgeable as to the foretelling which was tolden unto me right from the first, from the start, from the once-upon-a-time of it beginning. Take, for instance, the ride into the city in the taxi, or into, let's say, into city central, cabbing it, b'suited, thickened, swollen from the various and sundry treatments. Man oh man, talk about a hill! Millions and millions of them, it all of a sudden looks like out of the window to me, not to mention the windshield, all of them there milling all around the thing – yon edifice, yonder Jesus edifice – like, you know, like fucking crazy people in that movie thing, like slowed down like, like milling around and milling around it in that type of slow-motion moving type of thing, deranged people, if you please, all of them, every man jack of them, don't they all have to be all of them foreigners – to a man, if you please, deranged, if you please, screwy and scary and – like hatters, like hatters – loony, nuts, mad?

Let me say no more than this to you – it's terrible.

You hear me, are you hearing me? – it's plenty darn unbelievably terrible.

So I says to the driver, I says to him, 'Up that hill up there? You see it?' Which I take myself to be saying to the man in his low-born language. 'Good fellow,' I says to him, 'what's what with yon chaps up there?' I says to him, 'Are they feeble, these people? Are we not ourselves to remain cabbing it in on the central highway city-ward city-wise?'

Nodding my head at it – gesturing with my nose at it – this, this too, in another language.

You comprendo what it is which I am saying to you?

It doesn't matter.

What was wrong with the Brokaw kid?

It doesn't matter.

We have no alternative but for us to acknowledge it's a worldwide topic, tropically speaking.

The answer is definitely.

My God, you think I am not giving every diarist unfettered credit?

The prying eyes, the prizes, the translations, the praises internationally sung from the rooftops sung – induction, induction! – definitively grounded. It's making me sick, it's making me crazy, kooky, wacky, cuckoo, batty, daft, tetched, unglued!

But – sure, sure, you said it – credit where credit is due.

Except Jesus *Christ*!

Anyway, the point of this being, or the fundament of this being (which I am sitting here with her amaneu-endowing beside me), blind, blind, a nickel-phonecall from really fucking blindereno, her making for me a clean slate of it, her making for me a clean breast of it, despite the risk of it, the riskiness of it, in spite of the danger notwithstanding standing in the lilacs.

O peril, peril!

Prior-wise.

Even prior to the lilac!

Me catching heard of them, the devilish wicked dyad of them, all a-whisper like witches, like witches, ain't it time, don't you reckon, how as it's nigh to high time yon child were put down for a nap?

Yeah.

But, no shit, that was some suit – ladies and gentlemen, is there a rebuttal to be recorded among these notes?

On the other hand, didn't have it on me when the bailiff came.

For yon bailiff did come.

For yon water did run.

Forget it. Don't knock yourself out. When I talk about people milling about all around, what it looks like when people all around you do it, milling like that, the way it looks to me in my mind, a thing like that, everybody all around me doing it, it's all off-course for your sort of human being and for all sorts of human beings who happen to be anything like you and your sort. I'm sorry, but in all the world there is only the one person I'll ever know about who I know I can count on to show she knows what I'm talking about when I talk about everybody all around you all milling all around and that's – that's Shirin Neshat. She's the one, that's who once did it, I swear it. Besides, I bet she wouldn't talk about it anyway or ever again betrouble herself for her to show anybody more than the once she did. No, I'm positive she wouldn't, or that she anyway couldn't, not unless she happened to have a camera with her on her for her to do it with and not unless she happened to be in just the mood for it. That's right – Shirin Neshat, all right. She's like from somewhere like maybe Iran or something. But no chance she'd go along with her being willing to show you what I mean unless she was in the mood for it, which it is my belief she wouldn't be. You know – like tough titties, all right? That's her, Shirin Neshat, I'm sure of it.

Once had in me the faculty to hear, didn't I?

So that about sums it up, okay?

I mean, okay, okay – you can see it if you can see the sunset in the direction of the bottom of the page.

One meaneth, you know, we're there.

Thus super-secret been all tolden – yeah.

JOKE-TIME, OR THAT OTHER WORD, JAPE

Listen, believe it or not, I was not always the free and easy individual you have come to familiarize yourself with. Believe me, it wasn't always like this – fame, money, the admiration – nay, awed attention, plus plenty of envy and resentment – paid me by my peers, not to mention (yes, yes, I know, I know – that's one of my tricks on parade, one, it's said – here's more – I invented) awards when the awards season comes screaming around for another round of national and international acknowledgments (not too much yet? – more, more? – sure, sure!) rendered unto me at your topmost level of the literary game. Believe it, by gum, I had to overcome the snipings so vilely cast me-wards from the bile-ridden ranks of not a farthing fewer than legions (legions!) of your so-called VICIOUS DETRAC-TORS, this, Sirs and Mesdames, before my books could break out through the broken-through back-biting escaping from the ersatz fore-teeth of THOSE WHO WOULD DETRACT AT ME, bastardos and malefactors, every last sot of them, *there*! *there*! liberated from the injustice of it, my typings were thence catapulted into THE LIGHT OF DAY, delivered unto the OPEN SPACES where they (my works, my creations, tailings of entail-ments) might BREATHE THE AIR OF AMERICA THE BRAVE and commence to get busy monetizing the crap out of the marketplace (whilst plucking the odd coin for to not a little fill the cavernous coffer of my agent, a cute guy and a honey of a personality in his own right – I might add, a sweetheart, very sweet, very nice, not too agenty a gent, if you take my meaning, which is how I personally like it, you know – well, sure, of course you know, how could you not know?). Well, time's money, as the man says, so why not get to the nitty-gritty of this rags-to-riches sasquatch of mine (and of yours, of yours – you not being denied a stitch in your assistatory part in things) right off the bat, in a manner of writerly speaking? Yes, yes, yes, there were, I am not in the least ill at ease to admit it to you both openly and that other word, candidly, there was, or were, years and years of therapy (therapeutic appliqués) beforehand needed, and naturally I would not be the brand of humanity which I am was I not (were I not?) therapized, and that's the man in me himself speaking unto you, so take it from me, get help, this is my advice to you, plus that other word, counsel, of which (about which?) I would not be being this forthcoming with you if I was not (were not, were not!) wont to take advantage of this opportunity to recommend to you young guys and young gals (out there) which are, the good Lord love you, still sniffing around the old byways rushing hither and thither pell-mell and helter-skelterly from pillar to posthumously in hopes of emulating me and my example as far as your acquiring the acquisition of your cue from an American guy who's gone (out there) and made something of himself elbowing his way inward through the door of the high cenacle of what has come to be referenced as THE WRITING GAME or that other word, you got it, that's got it, LITERATURE, that one, indubitably, THAT

ONE, yes. So, yeah, you bet, definitely, or definitively
– get help. Get therapy. Not for a zinc not working the
connections and the networkings and the internet like
all get-out, or that other word, internecinely. So go
ahead, gnash your pathwards skyward, waste not a tick
of the clock not grabbing admittance for yourself by,
first and foremost, laying your hang-ups off to the side,
or onto that other word, BYWAY. I repeat, get yourself
some professional advocacy, plus that other word,
activism. So ask yourself (REALLY SIT YOURSELF DOWN
AND SERIOUSLY ASK YOURSELF, or that other word,
EARNESTLY), what did GORDON do? Did he mope
around feeling sorry for himself? Did he consider
knuckling under that his dream (purpose in life, goal in
life, yon youngster's gotcha among the hotshots) might
taste of the fateful kiss goodbye? Did the fellow take to
the drink and that other word, THE HARD STUFF?
Worse, to narcotics? (TO NARCOSIS-INDUCING
NARCOTICS?) Because the answer is NO. I took myself
in hand, SIRS and MESDAMES. I sought (out) HELP.
Seeked it – yes, seeked it! Believe you me, it paid off (see
Screen Romance, Jan. 1958. Check that: Jan. 1978). Well,
face it, FACE IT, time flies when you're lounging around
reviewing the SCROUNGING PERIOD erstwhilst the
longed-for arrival of the long overdue gravy train.
Thus it is why I always personally suggest GET THERAPY
first and foremost, then thereafter, or that other word,
THEREAFTERWARDS, get staff. Get a staff. But first,
before you go out there and start assembling staff, get
some jack, you hear, or that other word, mazumah, not

to mention, A WAD OR TWO OF CASH, assuming you're
not too high and mighty to turn your nose up at larceny,
or at that other word, theft, let alone the sophistications
of BURGLARING. Okay, so what was my problem?
What was it which was holding me back? Tell us, I can
hear the mermaids singing, WHAT? WHAT? Look, you
want exhortation, no problemo, it's exhortation you'll
get! Back down, right back down we go to the nitty-
gritty again, unless it's BACK DOWN TO CASES that's
said. Here, compadres mios, here's one of the major
cases in my case! We moved to this different block and
the first thing which I as a potential wordsmith do
notice, or that other word, which COMES TO MY NOTI-
FICATION, is this: to wit, that these twelve houses on
this block, or that other word, residences, they can boast
of the PRESENCE of NO MORE than ONE FIRE HYDRANT
among, or that other word, AMONGST, them. PLUS,
FIREPLUG. Believe it! But, HONESTLY, can you honestly
believe it? So do you still have the nerve (cheek, gall,
CHUTZPAH) to sit there and ask me what was it which,
right there from the FREAKING get-go, what was it
which was HOLDING GORDON BACK! You see the
picture, do you? This, or that other word, THAT, it's not
right. And I, as a TYKE, am newly installed on this
'block' seeing this, noting this, taking this deeply UNDER
ADVISEMENT. It's unjust. It's disequal. It's an ONUS ON
MY SELF-CONSCIOUSNESS, is it not? I mean, I
(GORDON!) am barely in kneepants yet! BUT AM MADE,
BY REASON OF THE MERE ONSLAUGHT OF REASONING,
TO COPE WITH, TO DEAL WITH, TO STRUGGLE TO, OR

STRAIN TO, NOT IMAGINE THE NOT IMPROBABLE CONSEQUENCES THEREOF! Can I sleep? Doth I go sleepless? Doth I not, night after night, AS A CHILD, AS A CHILD, lie wide-awake CONSIDERING? (Not to invoke, or to convoke, *various and sundry other* PARTIC-IPALS? Or, that other word, PARTICIPIALS?) Pay attention to me – even with this drawback drawing me back, so to speak, do the arithmetic, as the saying goes. Well, okay, in my situation, what is it but the division? This, by the way, means you take one and divide into it twelve and you get an answer which would BLOW YOUR MIND even if your mind was the mind of a CHILD. Speaking personally, I personally, AS A CHILD, AS NOT EVEN OUT OF CHILDHOOD YET, I, GORDON, was scared shitless. But you think I could communicate this ANXIETY to my family? Tell me, do you think for two seconds I COULD? Forget about it. I was frozen in fear, or that other word, TERROR. Do you think I could even think for one minute maybe I could take a chance and try APPROACHING them? Are you crazy? Are you OUT OF YOUR MIND? And all night long I am interminably lying there in my bed – IN MY BED, if you please – wondering TO MYSELF what if there should come a BLOCK-WIDE CONFLAGRATION, what then? I mean, DO WE GET THE WATER? Well, do we? Or does all of the water go to quelling the FIRESTORM consuming the houses which are CLOSER TO THE FIREPLUG? It's just logic, isn't it, or like LOGISTICAL? Now look at me! Go ahead and TAKE A GOOD LOOK AT ME, me, GORDON, who has to risk his life night after night taking, or, fine, swallowing his HEAD OFF taking SLEEPING PILLS! It's not good. It's definitely not a good situation. The fear, the terror, FROM YOUTH, FROM THE TIME OF MY YOUTH, from this I, AS AN ADULT WHO IS NOT A CHILD ANY MORE, I have to suffer because of the fact that my mother and father had the total lack of foresight to move me LOCK, STOCK AND BARREL to a block where one fireplug, where one fire hydrant, is supposed to protect the whole block which has on it HOUSES GALORE. And I'll tell you something else. No, really, I am sitting here thinking it's high time you were taken into my confidence and immiseration and HEARD WITH YOUR OWN TWO EARS what who knows, do I know? I mean, is it FIREPLUG or is it FIRE PLUG? This is the texture of the ANXIETY and IMMISERATION which is, HEAVEN HELP ME, my lot! Which one is it, which one is it? Tell me something, answer me something, make a reply, FOR PITY'S SAKE, do you know, or that other word, what is it, what is it, HAVE ANY RELIABLE COGNIZANCE OF?

Look, who's got the time for me to sit here and go through the whole thing WORD BY WORD with you kids? All I want to say is, if you have heard about EMOTIONAL SCARS, if you have heard about PSYCHIC TRAUMA, if you happen to have heard anything at all about THE SINS OF THE FATHER and so on, NOT TO MENTION THE SINS OF THE MOTHER and so forth, this which I have had to UPROOT from the MUCK OF MY PAST, this is what is confronting you in this day and age and is asking you, or that other word, BESEECHING you, or begging or entreating or – ah, FORGET IT. The other guy's TWISTED KISHKES, it doesn't even interest anybody even if he put a gun to your head and asked you who ERVING GOFFMAN was. I mean it, they come along and they pull out a gun on you and they say to you, 'Okay, for the last time, who was ERVING GOFFMAN?' Because this, this is what happened to my COMPADRE, or that other word, BUDDY or SIDEKICK or PAL-O-MINE, a boychik who's already half-nuts and EMOTIONALLY ALL SCREWED-UP just from having the terrible name he has, which, my hand to God, MY HAND TO GOD, is, don't laugh, you'll laugh, Wayne.

Did you hear me?

Were you listening?

WAYNE.

I swear to God.

It's crazy, this world we live in, a person who has to GO THROUGH LIFE with a name like that, another person WHO HAS NO CHOICE BUT TO LIVE on a block where it makes NO SENSE for a child to live and expect to grow up into manhood MINUS PROBLEMS and DIFFI-CULTIES and horrible episodes of NERVOUSNESS.

Wayne.

Jesus, it's not easy not to laugh, God help you if you heard, or that other word, WERE TO HEAR what the other name, THE SECOND NAME, is.

Now you know why I have to DISTRACT myself with telling stories ALL OF THE TIME in order for me to CALM myself from the TENSIONS I have WELLING UP IN ME on account of me having had such a MISERABLE childhood.

Okay, like there's these three guys at a bar and the first guy says NYARNYEEP, NYI WUD NYIKE NYU NYAV A NYRASSNYOPPER, NYEEZE, and the barkeeper he says okay one grasshopper coming up, and the guy says NYARNYEEP, NYI NYUST NYOO NYOW NYOW NYOO NYAKE NYA NYRASSNYOPPER, and the bartender says sure, you take some crème de menthe, you take some cream, and so on and so forth – so NYOKAY, NYOKAY, says the fellow who ordered the grasshopper, NYI NYESS NYU GOD ID, NYANK NYOO, whereupon there's another fellow sitting at the bar next to the first fellow, and this second fellow, he says to the bartender NYARNYENDEH, NYEEZE, NYI NYOO WUD NYIKE NYU NYAVE NYA NYRASSNYOPPER, NYEEZ, and the bartender says sure, sure, got it, a second grasshopper coming up, where-upon the first fellow says to the second fellow NYAT'S NYOT NYICE, NYIT'S NYENFINYITNY NYOT NYICE NYU NYAKE NYUN NYOF ANYOTHER NYUMAN NYEEING, whereupon the second fellow turns to the first fellow and he says to the first fellow, NYOOK, NYISYEN, NYAY NYATTNYENNYION, NYI NYOT NYAKINH NYUN OF NYOO, NYIT NYUST NYO NYAPPENS NYIS NYIZ AN NYUNNYUNYUNATE NYOYINNYDENCE NYAT NYEE NYOTH NYHAPPEN NYOO NYEE NYITTING NYAT NYIS NYAME NYAR NYAND NYEE NYOTH NYAPPEN NYOO NYALK NYIKE NYIS, and so thereupon, it's wacky, but there's a third fellow there and this third fellow, he says to the bartender BARKEEP, PLEASE GET ME A RYE AND GINGER AND, IF YOU DON'T MIND, GO EASY ON THE

ICE, AND HOW ABOUT A WATER BACK, AND MAKE IT
SNAPPY, OKAY?

So the next thing that happens is that the second
fellow calls out to the bartender, HEY, BARKEEP, SKIP
THAT GRASSHOPPER, HOLD THAT GRASSHOPPER, I'M
SWITCHING MY ORDER TO A RYE AND GINGER WITH A
WATER BACK AND, IF YOU PLEASE, DAMMIT, MAN, GO
EASY ON THE ICE!

So the first fellow taps the second fellow on the shoulder and he says to the second fellow NYI NYOO NYOO
NYERE NYAKING NYUN NYOV NYEE, and the second
fellow, he turns to the first fellow and he says to the first
fellow, NYEEZ, NYET NYA NYOLD NYOV NYORNYELF!
— NYIM NYOT NYAKING NYUN NYUV NYOO, NYIM
NYAKING NYUN NYOV NYIM!

So how's that?

Not bad, right?

That's my latest.

You just heard my latest.

Told it to WAYNE only just yesterday.

Fella's so messed-up, he didn't even laugh.

Jesus, PEOPLE!

What are you going to do? I mean, they ALL NEED
THERAPY, am I right? Or that other word, NYICHO-
NYOLNYICAL NYEATMENT — am I right or am I right?

That's right.

That's what she said.

Exactly.

I would not have installed it back up there as the title for this (*of* this?) if that were not what she – exactly, exactly – said.

Have I tampered?

Did I tamper?

Word for word (apropos of which claim, you have my word).

Whereupon I, startled, probably stupidly startled, or startled into an instant of stupendous stupidity, said, 'That deserves to be a title for something, or is it of something?' which statement (mine) naturally – naturally! – provoked my antagonist into her saying, 'A title? Why a title?'

To which provocation, I (myself!) replied, 'Why the dickens not a title?'

She said, 'Oh, you! To you, everything is a title. It's sickening.'

I (myself!) said, 'Very nice. I'm very impressed. You must be proud of yourself, your being, as is evident,' said I, 'so very verbally – verbally! – impressive.'

She went to pick it up, gave every indication of applying herself to doing so, or of *her* doing so. I, however, beat her to it.

Old as I am, I beat this personage to it.

But just, you understand, just barely.

'You notice?' I said, laying the napkin back into her lap, this after first flouncing it out, of course.

She said, 'You needn't have flounced it out.'

'Floor's dirty,' I said.

To which she said, 'Bullshit.'

'Have it your way,' I said. 'It's your house,' I said. 'So you are perfectly, unassailably at liberty to have it as you wish it,' said I.

'Apartment.' she said. 'Besides which,' the woman hurriedly put in (*put in*, can you honestly believe it!), 'I don't know if you were paying attention, but older as I am, which is fucking older and plenty wiser than you, pal, I came very near to snatching it up before you fucking did.'

I said, 'First of all, you had a headstart, didn't you?' Then, by the instrumentality of my fork, I hoisted a particularly repulsive (loathsome) mushroom off my plate and off-loaded it, this rather (if I say so myself) handily, onto hers, declaring, as I did this, namely, as I accomplished, with finesse, this act of self-administration, 'Second of all, inasmuch as the floor is part and parcel of your apartment, does this not inure (is it, instead, spelt *innure?*) to you as an advantage?'

I took it that this closing bit had put the lady in her place, but could not, would not, of course, say as much inasmuch as this might be – by her, of course – construed (wrongly, of course) as a pun.

(Not that I can claim to be all that certain concerning the issue, if issue it is, of what a pun, definitively, is.)

I want you (a neutral, one trusts, presence) to know:

never, ever, would I conceivably let myself appear to be making my way, in society, in incontestable combat, by adverting to puns, a pun, punning.

The woman spoke – but not as yet – no, not quite (if you are keeping yourself well up on your impartial readerly toes) as yet. One saw (I saw) – first, first! – that she was positioning herself for speech in virtue of one's having seen, or seeing, her touch the vagrant napkin, ever so viciously, to her cunning (come on, it's in the literature – check your Spillane) lips.

'You are no punster,' she was heard to utter. 'Don't we all, doesn't the whole worldwide worlding, know it?'

I was, of course, ready for her.

'We will dine,' said I, 'on the advent of the evening of the morrow,' said I, 'at my house.' I said, 'Cheese, my friend, out of a can,' I said.

'Apartment,' the woman said, advisingly, then called to the cook in the kitchen. 'Margaret!' the woman called all too intemperately, 'would you please be so good as to open the canned cheese for dessert for Mr Lish? A double portion, if you would!'

The cook called back, 'Unless you want to cough up for overtime, how am I going to get it chilled enough to satisfy such a fine schmecker as him!'

A stitch later, I saw – what I imagined (pegged) to be the cook (perhaps a comma here, I think, but amn't one hundred percent) show up in the dining room doorway.

'I suppose I could, couldn't I, serve it with ice,' she (another woman, let us justly acknowledge) said, promptly taking herself away from her occupation of the doorway and, presumably, restoring herself to what we may come to classify as the joint's scullery, thereafterwards (at full tilt) shrilling (it's in the thesaurus, you got it?) from this redoubt (no doubt), 'If that would possibly be in keeping with the Barthelme-esque character of this – what, what? one wonders – this esquisse!'

I'm telling you, it all of it caught me flat-footed.

Unless that's not hyphenated.

Okay, unprepared, then – correctively amended.

'And all,' my hostess said – and not a dot unhaughtily, let me put in (PUT IN, Jesus), 'on account of your coming in here armed with felonious intent. To the teeth,' she correctively hastened to append.

It was then I who spoke (did the speaking). 'Madam,' I poochily offered, 'I, Gordon, do importune you, do not trouble yourself to deny nor to affirm this, but I, with all due respect, remind you,' said I, 'if you will do me the favor of taxing your pertinent faculty, it was, in fact, you yourself who said ...'

'My napkin, it fell!' I heard the cook (Margaret) shriek from the interior (or, anyhow, from within). 'It's poetry!' the cook (Margaret) screamed. 'Positively poetical!' screeched she.

'Quite so,' I (Gordon!) murmured to the figure in seeming – to be fair, official – charge, thus creating, for this dignitary, an opening wherein I might be taken to be ceding to her – magnanimously, magnanimously! – the last word.

But fuck it.

No!

No in thunder!

Did I ever let Carver have it?

Canned cheese, for pity's sake. We all of us sit ourselves down to gorge on fake cheese. And you know what? Better cheese spooned onto one's plate from a can than for one to be utzed into one's beholding the slime becoating these coddled mushrooms of hers, or of Margaret's, all of them all too fraudulently (unconvincingly) alleged to have earned a mealtime place for themselves on the menu in a household of any quality.

Well, yes – Barthelme, yes.

But where anymore's the big payday in that?

Whereas ...

Shut, if you will, your yap.

You bet – too late, too late! – for any more of your belated whereases!

The napkin fell.

Therefore is (cannot but be) irredeemably, plus nonhypothetically, soiled. Or, anyway, its folds made, by the most stewarded floor, askew.

DECLARATION OF DEPENDENCE

Tell you what – I am going to sit here and keep on talking until it feels to me that what I have said has come to something finish-like or finished-like or like whatever that's been said has come to appear, in sum, or in the aggregate, to have come to the finish of itself or until I am too tired or too wearied or too fagged-out for me to keep on talking anymore and then, when that's become the state of things, which is to say, if talking *ad libitum* comes to such a state of things, then, at that turn, then I'm going to, at that turn, turn what's been said over to a publisher and if the publisher goes ahead and publishes what's come of this undertaking – which is going, in truth, to be no more than what it occurs to me to say – but then, at the end of that – at the end of which, at the end of which meandering, I mean, which end (or ending) will occur when I have come to become aware that I have run out of steam, at that point, at that endpoint, the finish, or at the finishing, of it – namely, of this meandering (or, better said, meander), then you'll find, at the end of it, or at what amounts, one way or the other, to the, you know, to the 'end' of it or, at my having come to a halt and therefore come to the end *to* it, or *of* it, then, there, at that point, at that site, at the point of that conclusion and so forth and so on, you, the reader, O cherished reader, there, then, I'll go ahead and put an end to the thing by telling you my telephone number – honestly, I will – to wit, tell you what my home phone number is (fact is, it is not as if I have possession of a phone number other than that of my home one) – so, anyway, what I'll do is that – viz. what I'll do is I'll tell you what my telephone number is and then you, O coveted reader, might, may, can, are, assuming you feel like doing it, you are invited to phone me, which is to say not only if you feel like it but swear to me at the time we talk that you, as an uncommon reader, won't share my phone number with anyone not designated, or not indicated, a likesome reader of this very act of meandering, which is, as you surely have by now surmised, already underway, or under way, but feeling like it, earnestly *feeling* like it, rather than your calling me intent upon your carrying out a vicious piece of horseplay or of meanness or of malice (maliciousness) but are, instead, thoroughly 'up' to it and 'up' for it – in other words, phone me only if you feel like it for whatever result may come of it, which is to say that you are to do so only if you are so inclined to, truly feeling 'up' to it and 'up' for it, and, further, are not you yourself too tired or too wearied or too all fagged-out to bother yourself with the bother of phoning a fellow human being, let alone the person who has, and who has continued to, hold (or make that 'held') you in a state of attention (to this point, anyway, to this stage, let's anyway say, or say I said 'let us say', up to now, up to this very instant, said nothing less than to signify how peerlessly I esteem you in peerless esteem – nah, forget it – oh, well, it appears it doesn't take all that long for the best of intentions to give a person a bellyache. So, shit, shit, shit, I guess I'm convinced to quit.

Not such a hot job, anyway. But didn't I tell you I was exhausted to begin with? Yeah, sure, fine, fine – it's 212-348-6443, here in the U S of A, okay? Fuckheads, both of us.

Oh, if you've seen *Satantango* or *Gummo* or read Jason Schwartz, we'll have plenty to talk about, not to mention sat through *Aurora*, another movie, which it wasn't so easy for me to spell, fair enough?

TRANSCRIPTION 6

Material assembled by Patient 9 [s]

Excerpted from the study 'Nice Hat', funded by a grant from Scripps Bros. Worldwide/MGM Outreach; interviews conducted and recorded, in 1974, at San Francisco State Hospital, under the direction of S.I. Hayakawa, chief research officer in psychosemiotics. Typed by Mrs Carol Atkinson. Bracketed matter indicates uncertainty in determining utterance intended in voice signal. Publication protected pursuant to articles 4 through 17 of the Fair Use Act, pertinent provisions revised June 2015.

[i] Do the best you can.

[s] The best I can is say there was a dog in it.

[i] Good. Big dog? Little dog?

[s] I [don't] know.

[i] How can you not know?

[s] It wasn't anything I was paying attention to.

[i] Then what was it you were paying attention to?

[s] To standing at the sink. To getting the dishes washed.

[i] What sink? Where sink?

[s] Oh, come on – this is such bunkum.

[i] Of course, of course – yet isn't it your bunkum? But agreed, agreed – so a [dog], a dog. Was it Paco?

[s] Paco! Where'd you get Paco from?

[i] Where do you think? Where possibly?

[s] I told you?

[i] You told me.

[s] Jesus Christ. Good old Paco.

[i] And Rusty. Months ago. First thing out of your mouth – your dogs, your dogs …

[s] You're kidding. I did that?

[i] You did that.

[s] Crazy shit, all [this]. Isn't all this stuff just the craziest shit?

[i] Bunk, bunkum is what you said. Crazy or fake, which is it?

[s] Whichever I pick, you'll say there's no difference.

[i] There's [never not] a difference. Difference is the essence.

[s] Who said that?

[i] Didn't I just say it?

[s] Fine, have it your way. Anyway, crazy's more like it.

[i] So which was it, Paco or Rusty?

[s] Beats me. Just a dog – nosing down there around my ankles, me in my bathrobe. Whimpering.

[i] My, my – whimpering. Now *there's* a word. Why whimpering?

[s] Why whimpering? I'll tell you why whimpering! Because it hadn't been fed, is why. Everybody'd forgotten to.

[i] Who's everybody? Or [do I] mean who're?

[s] Whatever wife I had at the time. Yeah, that's right, that's it. I had the distinct feeling this was an instance of inhumanity perpetrated by whatever wife at the time. I was entirely in shock, shocked, let me tell you, thoroughly furious, scandalized, heartbroken. How dare

she! – and so forth and so on. Whoever, whichever. The crassness, cruelty, the thoughtlessness. And worse, worse – washing the dishes, what with the water running, that's when it dawns on me – thunderously, like a torrent, torrentially – it dawns on yours truly she hadn't been given any water either.

[i] She, you mean whichever wife, right? So if you meant to indicate whichever wife, then shouldn't you have said she hadn't given, not been given? Because if not, then, ergo, Paco.

[s] Right, right, right, right – inasmuch as Paco was – you're right – a – what [do] they say? – female.

[i] Let's say is. For our purposes, is will get us farther than was.

[s] Make it is, then. You say farther, I'll say further.

[i] The pencil's yours.

[s] Check, I'm [the one who's] got the pencil, and in virtue of which I'm [saying] further.

[i] And we're saying female and therefore Paco.

[s] The dog?

[i] Of course, the dog. What ever else but the dog?

[s] You know the song 'Frankie and Johnny'?

[i] We all know [the] song 'Frankie and Johnny'. Quit stalling. The dog went without water because she, whichever wife, hadn't given the dog water. Stalling counts, you know.

[s] What doesn't?

[i] Right you [are]. Stalling, however, the thing of it is with stalling, it counts extra.

[s] What's to stall about? The dog – Paco, Rusty – it was unfed.
[i] Nor given water.

[s] Hey, man, it *hadn't* been fed. Hadn't. And where was the water bowl? I search the kitchen [floor and] nowhere, nowhere do I see the dog's water bowl.

[i] Say Paco's. Say Paco's water [bowl].

[s] Listen, bub, I'm not exactly ready to relinquish Rusty yet.

[i] Agreed. We'll hold the dog's identity in abeyance for the while. Are we agreed?

[s] Why not? What's it costing me? You bet we're agreed. Christ Jesus, man, it's only a fucking dream.

[i] What is?

[s] What we're talking about.

[i] Oh, well, indeed – that makes all the [difference], doesn't it? I see that now. Thank [you] for your being such a sport about it and pointing that out.

[s] Look, I want to say something. May I say something?

[i] Please.

[s] Fuck this, okay?

[i] Irked, are we?

[s] Yes, irked. Quite [naturally, quite] reasonably, irked.
[i] Tell me if you see commas in there when you write it out in your head.

[s] Who's writing it out in his head? It's maybe what you and your pals sit here doing, writing it out head-wise. Me, I'm just talking. Me, I'm just [in] sympathy with your invitation [to] recount …

[i] Recount? To recount? There's no recounting. You don't still think there's any recounting anywhere, do you?

[s] Fine. We have to talk. In order for us to talk …

[i] Where's it written that we have to talk?

[s] Okay, fine, fine, if anything tears it after all these [months], that, my friend, what you just that instant said, my friend, that, pal, that tears it, darling.

[i] You see commas when you [say] that?

[s] So now we're talking about punctuation. That's great. That's really great. I feel we're really getting somewhere. I really for the first time feel it. Fucking goddamn commas – terrific.

[i] Well, yes. As a matter of fact – or let's just relax that – [uh], that object of the preposition – let's just decalibrate it to opinion, mm? Because, mm, I do indeed think so, yes. For instance, it interests [me] to wonder if, when you say 'a dog', you have some sense you've succeeded in eluding [your] saying 'the dog'.

[s] That I have some sense of relief in that? Is that what you're sitting there tediously asking [me]?

[i] Testy, testy.

[s] Oh, manners, is it? Moods? Yeah, I'm pretty damn exasperated, you betcha.

[i] Not aggravated? Everyone says aggravated nowadays, don't they?

[s] Obviously not. Because you just heard me not. Jesus! Isn't this turning pretty incredibly petty? Which if you actually want to get into it, you said everyone equals they. How's that for annoying? Fucking goddamn know-[it]-alls!

[i] Well, is one not fond of the conjecture petty is as petty does?

[s] Holy shit, what in Christ is that supposed [to] mean?

[i] Aggravating, was it? Or do you reckon you're ahead of the game by reason of your uncovering an opportunity to disapprove of my diction?

[s] Your *diction*? *Your* diction? Hey, are we not well wide of what petty measly point you've got the [gall], or, piss, say the mental inacuity to insist …

[i] Inacuity? Is there such a word? Oh, and mental, is it? Would you perhaps be prepared [to indulge me], mentally, as it were, speaking, as it [were], and expand on what you imagine you gain by writing, 'Did you say a dog? Or say the dog?' as compared with, say, your writing, 'Did you say a dog or say the dog?'

[s] Hang on, hang on – I took it we were talking. My God, what's wrong with [people]? Is it that you've been practicing these crapfests of yours for, woe be to the inexpressibly diseased, for far too long? Is this one

of those dreary bits where, lo, [lo], sites are transposed, reversed, as in trans, [you] know, posed?

[i] Loci, you mean?

[s] Want some water? Let me go get you some water.

[i] Not any [of the] kids?

[s] How's that?

[i] It wasn't any of the kids' responsibility?

[s] Fuck no. [The] wife, a wife. One or the other of them.

[i] Not a girlfriend perhaps? Not your sister, eh? Mother?

[s] Hey, how about not my *Aunt Tillie*, okay? Fuck, will you people come [on], for godsakes. You're prodding and probing and I'm meanwhile losing the drift of it.

[i] Oh no you're not, old sport. You? You're not losing, nor getting rid of, anything. No chance of that, stout lad. Which encourages me to query – that heartbroken you said heretofore, just curious how now you would say you imagine you were, in your mind at the time, if you don't [mind my] inquiring, writing it when you said it back then – heartbroken, was it, the parts hooked-up,

conjoined, or was it [heart-broken], parts, by a hyphen, separated, divided, broken – like, if [hyphenated], the word?

[s] Who's writing anywhere? I'm talking. This is talk. All this time you haven't noticed this is talk?

[i] Don't try to dodge the question. You're eluding. [Don't elude.]

[s] For [what] profit? It would bear on conceivably what?

[i] Could bear – *could*.

[s] Come [off] it, will you please? Who's getting mulcted here?

[i] Now *there's* a word.

[s] Okay, conned – say I said conned.

[i] But you didn't, did you? You said what you said.

[s] Skip it, let's skip it – I'm sick of this shit.

[i] Has it not been [you who's] been insisting words don't figure in any of this? You have to be kidding me, right? So, sturdy fellow, is it hyphenated or not?

[s] Jesus, how can anyone say – or guess? Situation's passed, context's overwritten – I'd be feigning, faking, making it up.

[i] Make it up, then. Don't you think what you make up is just as notable as what you don't?

[s] Notable, note-worthy – get off my back. Bunkum in, bunkum out. What happened to Rusty? Where's, you want to talk about talk, let's talk about Rusty.

[i] No thanks. All talked-out about dogs, dreams, water bowls. How about we nose around elsewhere some more?

[s] Not interested. Fed-up. That's hyphenated. Hey, didn't [know what mulct] meant, didn't [know] what mulct meant!   Bigshot [know-it-all] doctor, hah!

[i] Scientist, you churl. And the word would be means, not meant. Want [to] inform yourself of something else?

[s] Which would be what?

[i] Which is that, in this racket, there's [no] past tense.

[s] Where is there any in anything?

[i] You on the scent for bonus points now?

[s] Like so you'd know.

[i] That's one. Want more?

[s] Isn't there always more, and who would be who if we didn't live to want them? What have you got?

[i] You're saying you're not concerned to want any more?
[s] Did I just hear right? Was it you who just said it that way?

[i] Which way?

[s] Any more, not anymore?

[i] How is the stenographer to know how to record that? How can it be known what you're saying?

[s] Aren't we talking about what you're saying?

[i] Both said. Both.

[s] Was that the past tense?

[i] That a C in there or an S?

[s] Combative, aren't we?

[i] Does it amuse you to mock me?

[s] Yeah, but not gigantically. I mean, I think I could maybe get along and live without it.

[i] You really are a shit, Mr [name redacted]. If you were not a patient here, I'd smack you.

[s] You think such a tack would prove productive?

[i] When's candor not productive?

[s] That's confession, is what that is.

[i] Speaking of which, let [me] compliment you on your hat.

[s] What hat? Where hat? I have a [hat on my] head? What, for pity's sake, are we talking about? You sit there and suggest we unpack the terms dominant in the foreground of some dream of mine fairly fresh in memory … shit, man, there was never any hat in any of it. Where in it does there occur any mention [of any] hat?

[i] Exactly. My point exactly. When was there?

[s] Excuse me, is there?

[i] My heart breaks [for] Rusty. Breaks no less for Paco.

[s] Hang on. Time you heard about Big Foot.

[i] Another dream?

[s] No dream. Real dog. Dead, died. Some great beast, by jiminy!

[i] All regrets, Señor [name redacted]. Hat's great. Tape's running [out]. Take [it up next] session. Should sess – [?]

TRUE, OR, BLOOMINGDALE, WESTCHESTER DIVISION, NEW YORK HOSPITAL, DR WALTER MCKNIGHT, PRESIDING

Every utterance in this book has been coddled, eggs in a pan.

It's all been bent, deformed, calculated, a swindle. You can trust it a little, but only, as admitted, a little. In the end the end is for me to have my way with you, get the better of you, not so knavishly that the result's a scandal, but enough to show myself and the sentences which accrue toward that disclosive effect – see me here, I'm here! – are accordingly false, falsified, a matter of everything and anything: sound, music, manner, device, this last betimes reflexive and practiced in such supernally rehearsed order that schemes might be enacted without my being all that in charge of them, the fraudulence thereby to seem indivisible from innocent speech, an element no more notable than, nor less than, the 'unconsidered' electing of this phoneme in lieu of this sidling – no, sinister, sinister – casting aside of that one. No writer of experience may honorably declare otherwise. But honor, it needn't be emphasized, as with other of the occasions endowed with value on the diapason of virtues, if deemed a prompt to be respected, falls, as it must, to the judgment of the beholder.

What follows, I aver, is proposed as a departure from all that. Not that this, any of these sayings, was composed while my senses and habits were disarranged by the available substances or by the dread hysteria known only to the irremediably diagnosed. I am, please believe, keeping a promise I made to the psychiatrist who came to my room on the day of my dismissal, or does one say discharge, from a mental hospital, where I was, while a teenager, held for eight months as I gradually was retrieved from a psychosis whose seizure of me was, according to McKnight, and to S. Bernard Wortis, MD, given the advantage over me by dint of my having received six or so injections of ACTH, this to determine if so drastic a measure might succeed in staying the march of a disabling and intractable metabolic disorder to which I had been subject since the age of seven.

The ACTH worked, oh so strikingly – and delivered me to a state of indisputable derangement in no time flat. The day in April when Dr McKnight came to me to bid me goodbye, he made me promise to say a true thing to take a certain prominence among the lies by which my being among others made my being among them manageable for me. It also happened that on that day I was treated to an exchange with the poet Hayden Carruth. I was making my way around the side of the institution's central housing unit, my having been released – for discretion's sake? – through a back door. Ahead of me there waited an automobile borrowed from my father and driven by a minion of his, my brother-in-law, Shepherd (hah!) Zinovoy, later to be divorced from my sister Natalie when his liaison with Bess Myerson, a figure of some attention in that era, became known. Calling goodbye to me through a ground-floor window was my tutor and mentor the poet Hayden Carruth. It was difficult for me to hear Carruth because the window was constructed of various layers of high-security steel mesh in place on either side of sheets of chicken-wired, double-glazed Corning's top-line shatterproof glass, this, of course, to allow the smallest likelihood inmates might not be kept in. I couldn't be certain of anything Carruth was saying, and I know there could be nothing worth reporting among my thin, confused replies. I only know Carruth was crying, and that if I were to answer with suitable emotion, I risked our keepers coming to rule it would be better, in that event, were my course homeward to be canceled and a return to incarceration be reckoned before I'd made it to the car. Evidence of emotion was evidence of unchecked disease. I was fastened upon the business of not slackening my pace. There was one task to get done: get where I knew my brother-in-law would be waiting for me, gain my place in the passenger seat, and no matter how violently I despised the fellow, and how outraged was I by his having been appointed to the role of escort (not implausibly because it may have been deemed he'd all too cheerfully be up to the job were I to fly out of control), I suppose my comportment betrayed no particular sign of truculence, the strictest silence succeeding in covering my wrath. I was free – conditionally, at least – consigned to a sort of house arrest until I was attested a safe enough bet again to take up my post as a staff announcer at the Panhandle radio station, in Pampa, Texas, KPDN.

Natalie took pills and, by such means, did away with herself when she was fifty-six, this after two bouts of cancer and, if it's not concluding too much, by reason of vexations suffered at the hands of a pair of troublous children. Some years before killing herself, Natalie took up treatment with the same S. Bernard Wortis who had exercised his rather extensive authority as chief signatory to the committal papers that had me remanded from a mental hospital in Florida (Miami Retreat), shackled there for a brief while, then sent to University Hospital in Manhattan (in which hospital, several months previous, I had been the youngest among five candidates selected for a trial regimen of subcutaneous dosages of ACTH), and then ambulanced from University Hospital, as I've already remarked, to involuntary status at the White Plains institution New York Hospital, Westchester Division, a redoubtable lock-up informally referred to as Bloomingdale. To be sure, Carruth's long poem considering his residence therein bears the title *Bloomingdale*, a species of inside joke to the familiars. Before killing herself, Natalie, while engaged with Wortis in a therapeutic inter-lude conducted in his consulting rooms, witnessed, from her site in his embrace on the physician's couch, his succumbing to a fatal attack of a cardiac nature, an event whose general shape was described to me by Wortis' once-secretary, the historian Barbara Tuchman's niece, as a matter of fact, Tuchman a contributor of articles to *Esquire* magazine, where I by then had fetched up as fiction editor. That rounding completed my relations with Wortis and, shortly thereafter, with Natalie, leaving only Zinovoy's destiny to account for in the comings and goings of my life. He married the daughter of the top dog at Federated Stores and, with the lady's connivance, brought about the births of two offspring, both of whom I one day saw him, hand-in-hand, walking within my neighborhood as he chaperoned the youngsters to Diller-Quaile, a nearby school for developing skills in the playing of various musical instruments. The second and last time I had any touch with the fellow occurred at the estate, in Scarborough, New York, of Brooke Astor, to which grandeur I had been invited to lunch by Astor's next-door friend, a man named Richard Schwartz, yesterday reported deceased among the obituaries du jour deemed to merit featured status in *The New York Times*, syntactically an amphiboly, damn the snares of unplanned speech. We sat at a big round table, waiting on Zinovoy, who had been golfing, to shower and get himself into a change of clothes. Zinovoy arrived, took up the place that had been set for him, reached his hand across the table to greet me cordially but, to my prejudiced surmise, a trace warily, and, after the usual preliminaries, asked me – I thought archly, surely knowingly – after the state of Natalie's health. I said that I hadn't been all that up to date with her affairs, but that I understood from an afternoon's fling I'd enjoyed with a former associate of her analyst, that she, Natalie, was dead. Oh, that's too bad, Zinovoy said, or produced words, not, I'd to allege, litigably dissimilar to those, whereupon we all proceeded to eat the species of light summer lunch I took it the rich and well-golfed eat.

There's one other point to be made – more a strand of narrative to be set alongside the foregoing account. Carruth, himself long gone to dust, would, I think, think it not too cumbrous a detail.

It's this.

That I came to hear, in the course of the lunch, that Federated Stores had recently bought – or sold – a reigning interest in Bloomingdale's.

The department store.

And now for what I promised Dr McKnight, a shamefully belated statement of truth offered towards a partite dilution of the lies I have lived by. Here are the names of the people I have loved mightily, strangely, not with a day of it lost any day of my life. Notice, dear shade of Dr McKnight, each entry is entered without a word of why.

Wanda and Marsh.

Ruth Hirsch.

Atticus gazing.

Elsie Weidenfeld.

Tante Adele.

Jim Washington.

Dr Raymond Jackson.

Maxine B. and Bill O'Grady.

Hayden Carruth.

Edward Loomis.

Val at Weatherby's.

Harold Hayes.

Hart Day Leavitt.

John Kemper.

The preacher who came to preach three Sundays in a row.

Rochelle Stein.

Mary-Louise Parker.

Binnie.

Louis Calhern.

Yow dancing, singing, cracking wise, being wisest.

Oliver Sigworth.

Miss McEvoy.

Neal Cassady.

The townie who leant herself back against a low cold wall.

Will Eno.

Sandy Dennis.

The mother's helper in the woods behind Rabbit Pond.

Reuben Barkey.

Robert Ryan.

Becky gazing.

The Chasid teen in Geronemus' waiting room.

The physiotherapist in Fort Lauderdale.

George Andreou, seeking to seem unbemused.

The harlot, pantyless and patient in red brassiere.

Child on the bus on her father's lap.

Grace.

Ethan frantic to be let loose.

The occupational therapist who fired my clays.

Lee Marvin.

She who peddled neckties door-to-door in Dallas.

Patricia Anne Marx.

Elaine on the boardwalk.

Barbara first beheld at her drawing board.

Jack Palance.

Jonn Meyer Greenburg Greene.

Dr McKnight, I am still not in my right mind. Nothing is any different. Nothing has ever changed. I am very ashamed.

I am very afraid. Not in an Adorno formulation, taking the world into account – for, no, I do not take the world into account. Just in the way of a coward less able day by day to consider himself intact as a state of intelligible coherence. But that's okay. It has to be. What is there for me to do? I laugh a lot. I like to laugh. Doctor, doctor, it's kind of an accomplishment, isn't it? I suppose it wouldn't be the worst outcome if I could cry sometimes. It's just I don't seem to have a talent for it, or an inclination. But I guess it won't be all that long before I turn out to get pretty good at it. I guess it's just a matter of my letting down my guard some more. The death of dogs has done it to me – and of certain moments in certain movies. Well, I well up, you might say, especially probably when fathers and sons are, you know, caught up in an embarrassed overcoming, a release, say, of the famous strain, as I have seen, in theaters and on television, incorporating actors such as Kevin McCarthy and Fredric March and, not all that unrecently, what with Gene Hackman and Melvin Douglas. It gets me. It gets to me. They hug, or they don't. But there's weeping, or no weeping, but plenty of feeling – and of facing it, if you know what I mean. I mean, it's not a whit different from how it was between Ethan and me, and between Atticus and me. No, there's nothing anywhere anytime different going on in you as you give yourself away to the gigantism of the experience. I'd say it's ditto the world over. I'd say it's definitely great – a hedge against death, a fugitive, virile denial of it – a swooning, a thrill – lasting maybe a couple of terrific curative instants – and then it's back to the norm again, but forever better than that, tipped-off, as you both have been, reminded, as it were, of an uncanniness, for the rest of your days, it has saved you, as men, to share.

What I meant to do was first to fasten your attention on
the base of the lamp that stood on my mother's (Mother's) night table.

The night table would be seen as it's standing close
against the side of the bed Mother slept in, or really,
make that, worked in. One would, surmising from the
writing (if I had written this) but not by my making a
direct statement, reckon that my father (Father) occu-
pied the other side of the bed. No object is presented (or,
that is, *would*, were this written, be presented) as one in
his (Father's) purview, as one pertinent to his (Father's)
domain. He is not heard from, remains unspoken of,
until the composition comes (you understand that I
mean by this *would come*, or would have come), to its
close, or to a close. Much notice is given to the base
(plinth) of the lamp. One is told fanciful creatures
(dwarves, knaves, scamps, rascals, rapscallions, this sort
of lingo, that sort of being) in period garb are seen
capering (pictorially, of course, for I have said 'seen') on
the base, clogs, earflapped caps, snoods, pointy foot-
gear, that sort of thing, overalls, occupationally aproned
(you know, words like *ferrier*, and so on, come to mind,
etc., etc.). In a sense these depictions are made to seem
unearthly, somewhat fierce, given to abandon, lively in
their gambol over the surface of the glass, a little too
lively perhaps, mildly menacing perhaps, unsettling,
sure, I can live with that, unsettling. It is claimed the
glass is porcelain, and that it was fashioned in a faraway

place. It is my mother (Mother) who enforces, endorses, this claim, which the writing hints could very well be unfounded, issuing from a need to affiliate herself and, by implication, or extension, my father (Father) in this unschooled belief of persons made (me too, me too!) subject to the desire in them (Mother, Father) to cling to the esteem conferred upon those who appear improved by embracing such a belief. (But, of course, between you and me, as it were, who – unless it's 'whom' – is not subject to his, to her, to their desire?) It is then proposed, graphically, what would the probable result be were the lamp to fall from the height it enjoys from its station on the night table that stands alongside Mother's side of the bed. Would its draped linen (or, as you like, gathered silk) shade protect it from its being damaged? My reply is yes, certainly not impossibly, for the room, it is then disclosed, boasts (or can boast of) carpeting from wall to wall. (I happen to prefer the expression, just developing in my consideration of the tableau, 'baseboard to base-board', but will stick to (keep to) 'wall to wall' by rea-son of the latter utterance arriving belatedly, so, you know, too pitiably bad for it, for tardiness, okay? Par-enthetically speaking, I despise those who fail to surren-der themselves as slaves to the punctual; may this senti-ment be extended to words? Sure – why not? Fucking words, they're no less guilty than people are. In other words (ach, there's no escaping them, but must we con-nive with them?) in these procedures the rule, to my mind (*my* mind, as if the contents of another mind could conceivably be consulted, or, for that matter, matter to me) is this: fair is fair. Good grief, fair is more than fair! Never mind. (Or is it nevermind, quotation marks unmarked because mustn't someone speak up for impenetrability, and won't every stroke unstroked help?) But to revert to the object, and to its milieu, the context in view, or under review, is, after all, a bed-room. Indeed, it is shown, or will be shown, that the occupants of the bedroom have taken to referring to the attached toilet thereto (thereof?) as the en suite toilet. (Never you mind: there is indeed a key on this key-board that will render a letter in italics, unless it's in ital-ic that's properly said, but I happen to have made my way up from my bed today not feeling myself quite up to the business of my putting my back into conceding I'm prepared to permit any portion of my time to be taken from me insofar as it's appropriated by the for-mality of my giving way to intensifying the grip for-eigners have succeeded in seizing with respect to their perpetuating tranches of petty victories in their inces-sant pursuit of pummeling us into our observing, or knuckling under to, particular shows of ceremonial hospitality to their covert incessance to get more and more, or greater and greater, control of our idiom – of their, oh, you know what I mean, of their having made inroads, incursions, essayed unresisted forays into it – oh, scratch all that out, erase all of it, forget it, it's plain I'm all balled-up already – it's either because the words won't come or I'm just not up to, never was up to, mak-ing any brainy enough headway with stuff as – shit, shit, they're both, those alibis, aren't they – yeah, yeah, the

same damn thing, no difference, no differential, if that's
the word, no sense in any of it, or to any of it, Jesus, all
I've – well, I haven't – so never mind, then, or nevermind, okay? – although, still and all, I do think I sincerely feel something sincerely pending, so to speak, it
feels like – I mean I do, I'm pretty positive I do, there's
not the least, I don't think, question of it, I do have the
sense that I do, or that I do, or am feeling that I am feeling something which feels pretty authentic to me, or at
least marketable, not that I mean marketable in that
sense, as to the marketplace, etc., etc. – look, firm
ground, firm ground, getting grounded, or reground-
ed, if you please, toes are, the gods be praised, they're
giving me to think they're just about in touch with,
touching, or retouching terra firma – firma? Did I just
say firma? – that en suite, yet – oh God, yet, yet, this en
suite facilitation of theirs was somehow constructed
such that it, believe it or not, that it lacked a wash basin.
An implausible oversight, a builder's incomprehensible
error, but adjusted to, adapted to, 'put up with', as the
saying went (and perhaps, for all we know, or for all I
know, still goes). Ah, man oh man. Compensating for
this infelicity (defect, better defect, dammit!) is there
being, in the bathroom (in the en suite toilet) a good-
some window, whose dimensions are so generous that
one entering the 'space' cannot but behold the whole of
the backyard, or, if it's clearer to say, say that I would
say, or would have said, 'the yard in back'. Anyhow, as
I had meant to produce the piece, and have not much
tried to do so (this either owing to my having lost

interest in it somewhere along the way toward meeting its demands in its continuing – and exasperating – continuance, or (lost) the confidence in my ability to bring it into being (Being, if you like it, with that capital letter inaugurating the inflation of the notion, if you like it) – oh, to be sure, the window, the en suite window, its glazing gives onto a shabby backyard, one whose low degree (wait, wait – is it backyard or back yard?) is set off (or would be set off if I had got, or gotten, myself this far) by the grotesque presence of an ill-made manmade fishpond. Goldfish fetched from a five-and-ten-cent store are shown (would be shown) struggling to make their heart-breaking way through the untended murk, sludge, goo, creature-deep shallow at best, too little depth for its tenants to accomplish much other than to strive to hide themselves beneath rotted plant-life (flora, floral – wordings to this effect, or in this category, or of this, or taken from this, chosen, elected, from among the many such of that stripe, is it?) or to shoot themselves, or scoot themselves furtively (unless it's 'fugitively') from here to there in search of food. (I probably would have exploited the value of the word 'listless' or, alternatively, 'listlessly' here or somewhere in this vicinity of this exertion if I, in my decrepitude – I'm old, have I done anything to convey – wait, were you informed of the fact? – have you thus far been put on notice that I am – well, yes, over the much-mentioned, over the much-fabled hill, for fucksake, I mean, I am no spring – wait, wait – you have or have not read Joy Williams' story, or short – well, short, if we must, fiction 'Chicken Hill'? – fabulous, fabulous! – read it, for fucksake, or Kelman, what'shisname – Kelman, James, James, James? – fabulous, fabulous! – but these people, these are young people – I mean mustn't they be? – that spring, like unto spring chi – fucksake, fucksake, which didn't I, did I not get from, well, is it or isn't it James, or Ed, or Edward? – stealing from the kidlinks, taking from the kinderlach – Jesus! – but Joy, Joy, yes, yes! – and consequent indifference, or lassitude, lassitude – alas, who (whom?) can be said to really give a hoot about any of this in the first place, at any, I don't know, rate or anyway? You see what I'm saying, not what I would have said, inasmuch as no, no, no, I would not, had I made it this far, 'said' anything of the kind, no! I mean, there was a time, there definitely, I think, was a time. Anyway, (say I realized better for me to have said, or say 'anyhow') do we wonder who it is who supplies the food, or, rather, provides for its insufficiency? We are not told by who (or whom), but are urged to infer feedings are irregularly offered, the estate of the pond's denizens undisciplined, undependable, unless it's independable – is it independable? – disorderly, disorderly, haphazardly, sporadically, sporadically (all the foregoing – forgoing? – for the sake of alliterative expectations being in receipt of a certain occasion of occasional satisfaction). The fish, in any event, are shown each winter to perish from the ice that overtakes what constitutes the idea of the pond held in mind from our beholding it from the en suite window. A rock garden, improvised on the site to the far side (the window in the en suite toilet being our vantage point, unless it's just, as Don himself, Don Himself, has written, vantage alone, just vantage solo, no point, pointless: all that, that's all been, it was written just as a reminder for your benefit, yes?) of what we might as well now reference (vile word, atrocious, putrid, putrid, a putrescence – is that a word, is that now not a word?) what has befallen 'refer to' – as the pond, is presented, that is, would be, as ill-organized and predominantly rubble. The reader is informed that a decision has been taken in the house: the fish will be rescued from outdoor doom by reason of removal to an indoor redoubt, this a tank into whose less intemperate 'winterized' water (the basement being where it is believed fish should show themselves adept at surviving, at making it through, the unwelcoming (shitty, pitiless) conditions coincident with the season … hold it, think I've somehow, or, rather, that the composition (the which was not actually composed) has, you know, isn't the expression 'gotten ahead of itself?' Or got – got! At any rate, I apologize – am – deeply, inextricably, nonrestaur – skip it, can't spell it, all balled-up.

Let me, I'm going to, try this for a sec.

Get, regain, my, you know, my bearings.

There might have been a draped linen shade, or gathered silk shade, overtopping, or o'ertopping, the bedside table lamp, its base formed of what Mother, in perfect certitude, proclaimed a fine old porcelain handmade in a faraway place. Capering figures of roughdrawn, or rough-hewn, ruffian-like dwarves, turned out in dark clogs and earflapped caps and other stuff,

their array of outer garments flared in rashly decided pastels of a rusticity recording what one felt oneself encouraged to concede as yielding irrefutable evidence of the freer pastoral fashion in fashion in another time boundlessly gayer and wilder and in every wise
livelier than was the time of one's time, or is the time
of etc. of one's own etc., etc., a veritable horde of rascals, of rapscallions, of imps, knaves, jackanapes jigger-
ing themselves all about in sportive exploitation of the
strangely interwoven columns of soft grisailles of glass,
if in fact it were glass the plinth of Mother's night-table
lamp was made of. That's right, made of. I must tell you
that I did not know then and that I expect I am going to
persist in the likelihood of my never knowing ever what
materials and procedures needs must have been brought
together for the affair (come on, dope it out for yourself,
I'm already, am I not already dizzy from these bootless
pointless peerless confusions?) to conclude the phase of
its making such that the result to be relied upon would
eventuate in porcelain, or into what might be passed off
among persons of my family's grade of persons as same,
or *qua* same. Not that it amounts to a hill of beans, but
for a piece to be pronounced a porcelain piece, must it
not be constituted of components conducted along a
fairly exacting avenue of intent, the thing contrived by
acts performed in accord with an approximate template
of chemical technique, or is it technology I mean to say,
or ought to have said?

Well?

Did I not say, have I not said fair is fair? – which it is, which if it isn't, then where, what, tautologically conceived?

Or portrayed?

We need know only that, were the base of the lamp to fall from the night table on which it rested in profitable adjacency to the far edge of Mother's side of the bed, and were it, when it (hypothetically) fell, to fall to the floor so that it were not superintended by the draped linen, or gatherment of silk, constituting the givenness of the shade ... no, skip it, forget it, we can do very nicely without any more of that. What say we instead jump to 'its utility shattered all to jags and to shards and to irrecoverable smithereens, especially were a collision to occur on an uncarpeted region of the room reserved for the slumber of Mother and Father (progenitors, forerunners – forrunners? – more words in this vein)?'

All right, we'll do that, then.

Skip, jump, etc., etc.

Let's take a look outside – to the prospect rearward of the residence, and thus to a fishpond where in it the fish left there for them to endure, if endure they can, the winter, didn't. Or phrases to this effect, but contrived in such wise as to exhibit rather more in the way of clarity, lucidity, etc. – true, affective feeling. The murk too shallow, scarcely creature-deep. No, they froze, or got cold enough for them, in effect, to perish, be dead, to become dead.

No, they couldn't make it.

Every winter.

Winter after winter – or, in other words, winter upon winter.

So Father (the father in the unwriteable – unwritable? – piece), he, the man, he decides (in his mind) the fish shall be taken from their habitat and placed indoors, this in a tank (a pretty biggish 'object') brought into the house for said purpose, conveyed (the fish, that is – or, viz. the fish) thereto, or therein, as it would turn out, if it were, or was, to turn out, by means of many family-sized mayonnaise jars, or by one such jar, several trips (circuits?), from the far reaches of the backyard (back yard? yard out back? rear yard?) to inside the house, therefore required.

No luck.

Not one relocated fish makes it through the unendurable season.

In the event, a thermostat setting etc., etc.

Who knows?

Never got to that 'phase' of 'things'.

You know how it is – or don't. Nor am I ever to know, really truly sincerely or earnestly to know, in what we might reference as a comfortably confirmed terra firma-style of knowing to know, what 'in the event' means. No matter. What, if anything matters does, in the ensuant (resulting?) stench, which stench Father, Mother (no? first Mother, then Father!), and I (okay, right, yes – all the time we've been at this) this, one supposes the word is 'confusio', it's been I who's been addressing you in the form of the one best-informed of the goings-on that have, in theory, gone

on, or would have gone on, and so on and so forth,
Gordon.

Okay, da capo, whatever Father, Mother, and I do to
rid the basement of the ... stench ... of dead fish (that of
quite a lot of them, if you must know) availeth not.

Probably jars, not jar.

It's wretched.

Next bit we would have had, had we had a bit next,
would be this: a cousin (Eugene) is brought into this
business by dint of his having (at another time – before
or after the occurrence of the foregoing – when? when?
when? – it's not known, not said, and is anyway, virtually, of no consequence, of no pertinence, none, anyway, two anyways, a pair of anyways, this, you can
count on it, would have been written composed put
together just as just shown in order that emphasis be
imparted, or inconsequentiality underscored – I don't
remember which the intention was, or had been, have
(or having) lost my place in these imaginings since,
as imaginings, they've, you know, not been reified,
word.

Cousin Eugene, it would be revealed, let us say as to
how the 'known' comes to be known, via a revealing,
to wit, has sent war memorabilia from a battle in which
he committed the deeds of a soldier in combat, killing
this one and that one and then, having survived, made it
through, lived (obviously – for the sake of Jesus!), strips
the defeated (wounded or deceased or dead) enemy
combatants of choice articles of a martial kind.

Insignia galore.

Packaged them in corrugated cartons, which cartons have been shipped, received, stored, or would have been, where convenient, stacked – or, rather, expressed to have been assembled in such manner – stacked-wise – in the basement, but oh no, not in Cousin Eugene's mother's and father's basement or just mother and not mother's but mother and father's basement (but in ours!), or did I already say instead back there? – or not said it? – as a curse might be, as a voodoo root might be, laid off in a corner of the undercroft, tucked away where nobody entering the cellarage would ordinarily, in the course of 'things', go.

By the by, got those tasty words from Joy Williams, but wouldn't, had I been capable of doing the job I'd set out (to do) for myself, by myself, have used them, written them, indicting them – no, no, no, stealing being what stealing is : theft.

Oh boy – instead left unsaid?

Eliot, Bloom – no sir, no pace from the likes of me, sirs, not any, no! Patience, please! – we're almost to the end of what it would have been terrific for me, as per a feather in my cap, even maybe as a bodkin in it, had I, you know, been able, been up to it, had what it takes … such as would one who knew what bodkin meant and, finding out it means nothing of the sort of what he had guessed it meant, using it thus – inasmuch as, fuck fuck fuck, does it, in the event, matter?

Fucksake?

But, man oh man, we are – where we now are – we are so far from that lamp with its vicious grinning daimons – nay, aren't we, are we not? I mean the base, eh? The quirky silly scary figures all a-leap a-lope all about it. Oh, you can't, you absolutely can't have possibly forgotten – wasn't it grisaille? The plural of it? It was. It was! Sure, sure, I get it – where's the progress, has there been a progress, a progression, one shred (shred?) of anything getting anything anywhere? Let alone – anyone? But so, okay – the boy, a boy (I, son of Reggie and Phil) lures into the basement a girl. Well, they (the boy and girl, as to age? – I don't know – make it 'that' age, okay?) – like just about their making it to that stage of 'things' when, okay – you 'know', you can work this out for yourself, the matter of age-wise and so on and so forth. Enough, as the poet says, said. And there occurs, or there would occur: a scene.

In the undercroft, in the cellarage.

She's great. Joy? Joy's great! Joy, forgive me – had to, absolutely had to.

So – with respect to the scene!!!! – the execution of it, the, you know, the making of it, it would be made something more or less like – like kind of along the lines of these lines – like this – it being said, written, many were the girls who could be ushered into the basement on the assurance no monkey business needs must be countered, fended off, afraid of. I'd say, or, one would say, come see my cousin Eugene's stuff. 'You want to come down there with me and see my cousin Eugene's stuff?' All sorts of connotations of the fleshly laid in stacks in the bleak light pointing the direction for us ahead. Ah, here she would come, coming along, going along, feeling with the toe of her shoe her way (incautiously, however) down down down the slatted stairs, not a trace of hesitation in her stepping ever so gamely as she makes her way behind me as she comes along with me keeping herself just rearward of me following me in my mad advance upon the darkest corner where lying before us we were, we are, to come upon carton upon corrugated carton lying before us in this, you know, it would be like this helter-skelter torn-apart state (laid open, laid open!) of things, or 'things', treasures, treasures, foul fucky treasures.

I'd say, 'See this belt, moi charmant?' I'd say, 'The buckle, its buckle – it opens, it can open, or be opened up, Cousin Eugene has confided this potentiality, this capacity, a capability in me,' I, Gordon, would say, as if it mattered what I'd, the boy would, say, says – then, then! 'So what, chérie, cometh out of it thereupon, do you think, mon ami puella? – dirk, dagger, code, tablet of toxic teeth, duet of bullets shrieking to the captor's head, paired ordnance striking their target, both of them, at once?' I'd say, 'Oh, ma pet, ma pet, so tell me what it is, what is it, you are thinking, do you think? Because I don't know, because we shall never, the two of us, the pair of us, ever of us be given, it has been spoken, said, murmured, for us to know – but, you know, tell the truth, aren't you pretty plenty scared? The enemy, the enemy, it's all of it right down here with us where in this dark dismal grisly corner – together, together – where we silently in this bewitchment stand.'

'Oh, God,' the child would whisper into the thickened air. 'How awful, how bad – and oh my God, the smell of it – yeah,' she would whisper, all hushed-like, 'Oh, Jesus, the smell of it, it's so awful, just awful – I mean it really, it's terrible, my darling Gordon – it stinks!'

'Yeah,' I'd say, 'it's death,' I'd say. 'That's death for you, sweetheart,' I'd sort of oodle into the murk, tactically, expectantly, longingly, yearningly, all those words of want. 'Can't you,' I'd say, 'tell?' Then answering myself, I'd say something along the lines of, 'You bet,' I'd say. 'Chickadee, that's what death smells like, it really reeks of a lousy reek,' I'd say. 'Every bit of it, death, death, and worse,' uttered into the maze hymnally, implorishly, in gatherment, let us say, even, in the event, breathing, if you will, gotchally. Then I'd say, 'It's all, you know, it's all this thing of this thing of death, you know?' all the while reaching for what I knew my need entitled me to see, to have, to actualize, right? – a look at her naked heinie, the sight of her naked heinie, getting a hank of my hand up under her underpants and maybe even touching it, just maybe even touching it, just touching the very nature of it, very notion of it, oh the amazement of it, her, of this girl, skin, her skin, echt.

I don't know.

The next thing I'd do is I'd probably veer the thing back torquely to the lamp for an instant's peek at it – or of it, yes? The base, I mean. Then go on and close it all off with a quick squint at or of Mother laboring all the hours through, with needle, as would be her wont, with thimble, with thread – not forsaking her object until Father, recursively, had smacked the crap out of his besieged pillow and snarled from his glaring portion of their imperium: 'For pity's sake, make night, Reg – I beg it of you, mon petite, please!'

Oh no, the recursion goes, or would go, or have gone, not there exactly but more or less elsewhere – or make it everywhere, have gone, or would have gone – oh yeah, oh yeah, say, everywhere.

Well, come on – I'll bet anything you understand.

MR DICTAPHONE

I'm telling you now so there will be no questions later.

The name was Rigamarole before it was Dictaphone. It was my grandfather, Morris Rigamarole, who effected the change. There is probably a word for name-change, but I don't know what it is – if, of course, there is one to be known. If there were one and if I knew it, I would use it. Interpellation? It sounds right, but you can't necessarily go by sound, can you? Or can you? No, not interpellation, I'm almost positive of that. No, I really do not think so – but perhaps, perhaps. If I had the energy to consult the big book behind my back, I'd make my way up from my seat, turn with care, and do it. Consult it. But no. I do not have the energy for so exhausting a task any more. Or, rather, the strength. For, behold, I appear to be in possession of energy enough for the undertaking at hand. Namely, the writing of, the recording of, my history. My years as the last of the Dictaphones. As for the Rigamaroles, they had their day. Two generations' worth. Or does one say one and a half? For inasmuch as it was my paternal grandfather (my grandfather on my father's side) who shed the name Rigamarole in favor of Dictaphone, yes, there were not – I'm counting, I am doing the arithmetic. No matter. No, there cannot be a half generation, can there? It's not one of my strong points, arithmetic. Let us forgo any further historiography of the kind. It is no great thing, the counting of generations. As has been said, 'What's in a name?' Mark me, if this be true, then is not the generational perdurance of this or that name not also dismissible? I mean, if what's in a name, then what's in a number, true? You see what I am saying? So, anyway, prior to Rigamarole, the family name was Geebonee. Odd-looking, eh wot? I agree. It was doubtless this that convinced a prior Geebonee to take on, or to take for himself, the name Rigamarole, which sustained itself in the family line for one and a half generations. Or so my calculations would have had it had I carried them out to a favorable conclusion. Time you were told, unless the writing thus far written has already done so. I am not at all handy with the practical sciences but am terribly able with the metaphysical ones. Words – and their extensions, relations, affiliations, not to mention their interiorities. Ideas and the like. I am terribly excellent at words. Were you to ask me a question having to do with words, I would have the answer for you not only with promptitude but with speed. Or haste, if you prefer. Alacrity! You see what I mean? This is my forte. Plus ideas. These are my fortes. Words and their consorting, or consortium with ideas. This is what I was born to be terribly excellent at. And with flare and flair too. I would have for you the right answer reposing in the right words if you were to put to me a question that solicited and so on. Or were so disposed to. Dispositive. This word is not, I must make all alacrity to tell you, my word. I cannot claim it, or lay claim to it. It is the word, leant upon rather, for my particular taste, far too often and far too greatly, by my best friend, Georgie. A lovely fellow, Georgie.

Positively lovely. In every respect. Except, as I have already implied, if not said in so many words, in his tendency to make use of the word 'dispositive' rather more often and with far too much stress than the case calls for. To my mind, that is. Still, a lovely chap. Also to my mind. Quite altogether nice, save for that singular regrettable tendency. To be sure, I imagine the word 'tendency' is not the best way for me to cite the practice Georgie overuses. Later perhaps. We'll perhaps review the matter as to him (Georgie) later – when I have had time to catch a breather and consider the question in a calmer clime. At my leisure. Or at our leisure. In a leisurely state of mind. Just now, at the moment, as must be evident to you, everything is at sixes and sevens. One makes a start at the writing of a family history ... no, erase that. My error. Entirely my error. And for shame, for shame – insofar as was it not an error with words? Well, yes, it was. But does it not, this error – with words, my God, with words – prove my point? For when one makes a start at the writing of one's history, one undergoes a certain period of pressure. An episode of it. At all events, this is scarcely the occasion for us to look all that deeply into anything not central to our declared course onward, or ahead. You take my meaning? We must concentrate our attention. We must focus it. On the object, or, if you will, our objective. Do you see? To be sure, mentioning Georgie was a woeful, a wretched, an execrable mistake. Monstrous. Yes, Georgie is, indeed, a good friend, one of my better friends, a fellow more or less dear to me, an estimable chap, even, in a certain fashion, one might, in that fashion, say an inestimable person, but my life is my life. I like Georgie, really I do – but this book is devoted to the telling to you the tale of me. It's my story, you might say. Yes, that's good. My story. Perhaps the title should take firmer notice of this. We can review the matter, if you would find such a review interesting. Perhaps later. Perhaps when we've both had occasion to settle down a bit. Yes, later perhaps. When the pressure has eased, or been eased, or been reduced, or lessened. Mark you, I brought him up, I brought Georgie up, we took hold of his name, as it were, only to remark on his tendency to dwell upon the word 'dispositive'. Prior to this, did we not dwell upon there being, or there not being, a word that might be made to replace the word's name-change with? Or, at any rate, words to that effect. I believe we did. Did not the word 'interpellation' arise in the heat of that consideration? Or, if you will, context? I believe it did. Yes. I was making, was I not, mention of my dwindling strength. Yes. I was reporting to you, we might even say we are certain of this, apropos of the existence – behind me – of the big book. Yes, of course. It is a terrific book, its exhibiting, as it does, an incomparable compilation of words as to the meanings thereof, or a vast compilation of incomparable meanings as thereof to words – as well as, mark you, an equally vast repertoire of, how shall we say this, synonyms? Sayings of like intent. Ah, how like a bad penny! Intent. Good heavens. I cannot recite the precise saying, no, but the sense of it is, the intent of the saying is, that such and such keeps turning up in the manner of a bad penny. Which is to say, as a bad – oh, you know, as a penny bent or a penny no longer terribly shiny – as one of those pennies forever to be found, the very penny, among the coins to be discovered reposing in one's pocket. A moment, if you will. It's entirely my fault. Getting a shade confused, am I? What set me on this course? Intent. The word 'intent'. This is what happens. The very thing. It's the pressure. Did you not just witness an instance of it? I let my thoughts wander ever so slightly and, by this irruption of momentary inattention, an instant of my letting, if you will, my guard down, if you will, I said 'intent' and 'tendency', words an interval ago used and discarded, however long or less long ago words made altogetherly presentable use of and ever so gently, if roughly, discarded, when – all right, that's quite enough of that. One grows unconcentrated. It's been more than enough of it, focusless nattering. I am, in a word, confused. You talk, one talks, and then *wham*, or *blam*, or what have you, the resounding, it resounds, or, as is said, resonates. Terrible, terrible. You see what I'm saying? One is turned around. One is confounded. And hardly, scarcely, barely realizes it. Talking in circles. If you will. Or willn't. What one is saying is in the grip of what one has said. You see what I am saying to you, don't you? It's a question of control. One has none of it. The words themselves, they have it all. Time one came to one's senses and took this senselessness into account. I mean, whatever properties the word possesses take possession of the word to come. Did you get that? Fully?

Thoroughly? Let us pause to make sure. For surely there is no reason for one to soldier on if one is made to march round-wise and rounder-wise and thus be never in prospect of confronting the enemy, which is death. Or say I said the future, which is death. It is in this sense that there is no next. You do see what I am saying, don't you? Personally, I find this, dare I say, mazelike. Like a maze? Dare I? It is terrifically depressing, no? Discouraging? Deeply. Utterly. No, you know, progression, or progress. I mean to say that what one says jogs, or jiggles, what one has said, ensnaring one. Is this the gyre one's heard one's fellows make mention of? It jolly well could be, would you not say? One is trapped in the trap of the trap – lest one not speak. Are you taking all this in? The vertex, the vortex, the cortex, yes? No history. Just Geebonee onward to Rigamarole onward to Dictaphone, or, elsewise – Dictaphone back to Rigamarole back to Geebonee – and that's it? Yes, yes, to be sure, of course, there's always recourse to one's adverting to some perfectly workable Georgie perhaps, but after that, *after that*? – then what!

Georgina?

Time for one to say oh Jesus and quit yon curse, yon grip, yon snare of yon bullshitting.

LEVITATION, OR, MY CAREER AS A PENSIONEER

Say, do you think you could make believe you're a real pal for a tick and sit yourself down for two minutes or maybe as many as more minutes than that while I noodle around in search of opening up a topic worth the while for me to talk with you about which, who knows, it could work out to maybe jack you up onto a higher plane of entertainment whereby you'd have a chance to come away from the elevation with a degree of some solid moral improvement in the sense of your having gone and lent yourself to a little bit of some quality tale-telling of the old-fashioned snitching-on-the-ogre-and-his-covey-of-coattailers-slobbering-drool-under-their-snoods type, or maybe it's, all-in-all, not likely to prove any more of a consequential timeout for you than what you've already so charitably been not too awfully unwilling to throw up your hands in ceded concession to, not demonstrably in praise of and delight in, not especially, but not without your prospering well enough along towards the goal of sharpening your reading skills without any of your having to, for prac- tice, cram the cupboard with cartons of breakfast cereal that are, by law, forced to come accompanied with footnoted instructions as to how to protect your eyes while reading them, or is it while eating what's tasty- good inside of them?

Shitfire, I don't know what I'm saying.

Just don't you go quitting on me now that we're getting to the assessing of litigablities, their surprise packages and their dogged indifference to work out the rogue impasse, to gingerly kick the kinks out of inadmissible ramifications beforehand.

You with me?

Be with me.

I hate it when I have to fight a fight without advantage.

And this, oh, it was a fight, all right.

The scene's *Esquire* magazine, where, among other odd jobs required of me, the riskiest task assigned me was my being expected to pick the fiction month by month. This was from sometime in '69 to sometime in '76, and under the governance of Arnold Gingrich, founder and publisher, Harold Hayes, editor-in-chief, as the preferments of hyphenasia had it back in those time-takingly fastidious days, and managing editor, Don Erickson, all first-class fellows but with acutely varying views with respect to, uhh, the business of perching yourself on the left or right wing of fiction's flight – to the moderate left: Erickson, graduate of Yale and Oxford across America: to the far-ish right, Gingrich, fishing buddy of Hemingway, wed to a lady Gingrich finessed from Hemingway in the course of a Key West weekend of bone-fishing, his, Gingrich's, all the years going off to the side of this matrimony with, as they might still be saying, if not all that exactly declaratively, owing to the intractably stricken status of the purloined, with the altogether healthy mother of Rudolph Wurlitzer, a writer at the time toilsomely stirring the literary pot. Yet never once did Gingrich deign to say okay to me in respect to any of the Wurlitzer stuff I sent up to him up via first Erickson and, as the protocol then had it, thereafterwards to Hayes. I had scored the job by my first proffering a pledge to collect for *Esquire*'s pages instances of The New Fiction's flare, a mode of writing my employers mistakenly thought me in intimate touch with, if not the inventor of, this perhaps not just because I might have intimated I was, but because I had come to them from the fecund-famous city of San Francisco, had organized a couple of litmags out thataway, could point to the presence of a staggeringly pretty wife, and knew of Wurlitzer for his having brought out the novels *Nog* and *Quake*, though I am sure I'd not investigated all that many pages in either of these books, nor those pages in other long forms of Wurlitzer's troublous labors tending to be brought out with titles no less known for their penchant for quirk. Well, there was a Richard somebody whose work was all the rage, my phony intimacy with the reasons for which I wore like a hanky draped from my public pocket, but what his claims to fame were actually buttressed by, in what regard he qualified for tempting notice, there, with that question I couldn't, I'm sorry, help you a whole hell of a lot with, aside from my saying that I excelled at my hiding behind the allure attributed to me on account of my disseminating the effect that, with prompting, I'd probably recognize the man's name, which, as you can see for yourself, if I ever did succeed at that test, I would now, damn my eyes, fail to be awarded a passing grade for facing my duty in its precincts. But, come on, to retrieve the name Richard, isn't that a triumph enough? Ah, wait, *Trout Fishing in America*, there we go, wasn't that what this Richard was being feted the most frantically for? In a sense, it might have been said that he was thought smart, cool, hidden, hip, and, in that same sense, a taciturn version of the program David Foster Wallace practiced in his day, nothing up the sleeve but a first-aid kit of the latest make. Does this help? It's surely woefully dumb. But I'm trying to help, be helpful, at whatever personal cost to myself. Not that you really need better preparation for you to get the echt heft of what comes next. Anyway, it's just that I want you to be sensitive to my endeavor to seem tremendously keen to make my way, and to make my way my own way, cultivating writers who, for the most part, or for not part enough, had yet to be cultivated. My job called for me to put out the call for The New Fiction, and this I was devoted to doing, disguising myself as a fellow who couldn't have been more in touch with adept acts of shopping for writing in aisles not much anticipated to carry the store's stock in displayable prose. It was in the course of such an off-course ramble that I was to come across the fictions of Cynthia Ozick, and cheekily ran them in the magazine, work such as 'An Education', 'Usurpation: Other People's Stories' and 'Bloodshed'.

Then came the essay 'All the World Wants the Jews Dead', and, thereafter, the furor the piece stirred up having lost enough of its top notes, I planned to run Ozick's 'Levitation', a piece whose closing effect, the saving of social errand by reason of the Jews assembled as guests in attendance salvaging the dispiriting progress of a roof-top cocktail party, as they, the foregathered Jews, are lifted, Jew after Jew, into the night sky, the other revelers less buoyant by reason of their being less captured by the vivifying dislectics of the day, are left behind earth-bound below, while Jews, buoyed aloft, levitated into the realm of the hyperium above, lifted en masse, still biting the backs of one another as they maintain, sustain their attempt, while floating above out of reach of their ungeschichte counterparts. That's right, in Ozick's 'Levitation' the foregathered Jews are by the power of their highmindedness taken up into the night to hover on high, while from below they are witnessed in disbelief and disgust.

Hidee-ho!

Some piece of work for to draw everybody in for a stellar performance for the Christmas edition of a magazine circulated, nation-wise, wall-to-wall, goodwill among men, and so forth and so on.

And there we have it: Ozick's story slated for its place as the fiction to be featured in the upcoming number. December, it was, the Christmas edition, by gum – the story to be laid asquat in that fateful issue – in order that it entice the merry mood of the seasonal consumer. Did you hear me? 'Levitation', which title was made the title of the next book of stories Ozick was later to publish. Hey, did I tell you yet? That one there, that December number right that there, that was the last number of *Esquire* I was ever at liberty to have any truck with.

Guess why.

Well, here comes the episode I've been edging towards getting it told to you. Gingrich retires. The magazine is sold to Clay Felker, bankrolled, as it was not left to go to unprominent notice, by a Lord Harmsworth, who seemed to have something to do, or whose money had something to do, with a chain of pizza parlors called Pizza Huts. Well, Hayes gets canned, takes off for California, assumes charge of a magazine of that name, and presently enough drops dead from cancer of the brain. A great loss. A great man. Never reported to a boss I was prouder to do the bidding of. Not that Hayes ever bid me to do much of anything except schlep back to his attention fictions he could roll out as demonstrations of the magazine's incontestable affiliation with *Esquire*'s boast of the evidence of its tightening private ties with the phantoms of The New Fiction. These, not entirely, but for the most part, were fictions that exercised the suppression of information, favored placelessness, namelessness, the absence of motive, denouements abrupt and muffled. Hayes doted on such forays. He didn't get what was going on in them, but he was glad their covertness was noted as his province. Erickson was sympathetic, supportive, all for it, but careful to proceed with caution. The thing to be was hipper than *Harper's*, hipper than *The New Yorker*, and as hip as Ted Solotaroff's *American Review*. Gingrich? He was complacent, aging-out, convinced that wantons had hijacked good sense, and did what he could to keep the lid on the leftward drift (or is the proper figure slow the speed of mental

breakdown), which policy included keeping the belli-
cose writings of his 'son' excluded. On the other hand,
I did run, got away with running, the magazine ran,
with much hoopla marking the matter of a periodical
publishing the filmscript of a yet-to-be-filmed movie. This was *Two-Lane Blacktop*, which a most spotty
memory seems off and on to have it Wurlitzer wrote.
All I'm certain of is that a Monte Hellman directed the
thing and that its principal players were five good actors
whose names I could have recited for you a week ago
but can't this minute, thus witness the swift decline of
mind. No, wait a sec – one was Alan Vint, and maybe his brother R.J. Vint (*v.*, or is it *vide*? – Didion and
Dunn's *The Panic in Needle Park*) and the other War-
ren Oates (Malick's *Badlands*, a corker), is all I'm right
now remembering. Anyway, it was a big step, printing
a filmscript, and it didn't go over. Was it around then
that everything began to slip? Gingrich retires. Hayes
gets canned. Tries Buckley's gig with TV hosting, flubs
it, his having never been cut out for the cross-hatched
methods of crossing swords with real cutters. Didn't I
say he went out to California to take over a magazine
of the name? Then died of cancer of the brain? I'm all
mixed up. They've just made the first fissure in the ceiling of the apartment beneath mine: there's a yearlong
gut-job of renovating slated to kick off this morning.
Notice went around. They're taking it all down. Walls,
walls, everything! That's not renovating. It's not even
demolition. JESUS, YOU HEAR IT? SHITFIRE! BLAM!
BLAM! IT'S A JACKHAMMER TURNED UPSIDE DOWN

FOR IT TO DIG FOXHOLES IN THE CEILING! Lucky thing I've got me my sack of my lucky chips to keep nibbling at and keep calming me but SHITFIRE, THIS IS NO JOKE, BOYS AND GIRLS, THIS IS WHAT THEY CALL DESTRUCTION. CAN'T YOU HEAR IT? Anyway, where I am is I was going to get myself all set to tell you that it was somewhere in this vicinity of (excuse me – lost touch with time) that I get the go-ahead to run Cynthia Ozick's 'Levitation' in the December number, the belief upstairs being, I suppose, that our Christian sisters and brothers are going to love having their Christmas reading JESUS NO NO NO HEY COME ON DOWN THERE TAKE IT FUCKING EASY ON ME UP HERE I'M TRYING TO THINK A LITTLE UP HERE. But then he's fired, let go, goes, after a brief try at doing a TV thing mimicking Bill Buckley's TV thing: pretty positive I told you. Hayes, he's gone, Felker's – that's Clay Felker – he's got *Esquire* all to himself, keeps Lish and Erickson but oh so very tentatively, it feels like, puts in as our master a man named Byron Dobell who's sitting in Hayes' office and relaying orders to the crew, these piped in by telephone while Felker remains onshore presumably looking around town for the right suit of clothes for him to show up in and see if they work anywhere well toward his clearing his name with us.

I CAN'T BELIEVE YOU DON'T HEAR THEM DOWN THERE!

THIS IS MERCILESS.

THIS IS GROWN-UP STUFF.

I, GORDON, I AM DEFINITELY NOT READY FOR THIS SPECIES OF SHIT.

Ah, here – Felker phoning in – there comes an exhibition of the kind.

To me. For me. WHERE'S THE FRITOS, GODDAMMIT?

The man Dobell toddles from his corner office down along the hallway to my office-like office to tell me Clay has just phoned to give me to know the Ozick scheduled for December must be killed so that room will be opened to accommodate, in the space for fiction, a bulkiness from the book that Nixon's John Ehrlichman had developed during his creative writing exertions performed whilst his person was being held for punishment levied at the chap in exchange payment for his commission of high crimes, etc., etc. Ehrlichman had, as Felker had made himself the happy harbinger of, yes, gone to prison, yes, but had come out from it, yes, yes, a goshdarned golldarned good writer. Well, there's plenty of precedent for a conversion of the kind. On the other hand, you didn't need to look at the MS for as much as a wink for you to know this conversion wasn't one of those high-type conversions. At any rate, Dobell gets up from his corner office, you see, makes his ungainly way along the hallway to my office-like thing, tells me Clay's plan and, to set it into motion, kill the Ozick, ready myself to receive into my hands the Ehrlichman manuscript, prepare it for excerpt, and wait, wait, phone Miller and tell Miller to hurry up and make haste such that he gets to me the fiction he'd promised to work on for me.

Hah!

OH I CAN'T CANNOT WON'T BELIEVE IT'S NOT DRIVING YOU AS CRAZY AS IT'S DRIVING ME – PILEDRIVERS

DO THEY CALL THEM, DERRICKS, BACKHOES, YOUR
DOUBLE–A–TURN–A–PULL.

Clay wants.

You hear this?

Clay, who's never anywhere to be seen, wants.

I say to the man Dobell stay here, better you stay here and hear first-hand how I handle this, indicating to the man Dobell for him to do his best to seat himself in the chair wedged between the other edge of my desk (provenance: a discarded typewriter stand) and the very immediate mouldy (or is it moldy?) greenishly coated wall. I take up the Ozick manuscript and move it authoritatively from one edge of my training-desk to the other, then take up the telephone to dial Miller, indicating to the man Dobell, with a squeeze of one eye and, since I'm no good at winking, probably this guy-to-guy gesture involved the scrunching of one whole side of my face, that he is going to welcome the hell out of witnessing the carrying-out of his opening command's issuance to my person.

Arthur, I say, it's Gordon, I say, then saying, Hey, no reason for you to knock yourself out getting me that story and setting aside other pressing work because, hey, the new administration here, in its decision to cancel an Ozick piece to make room for a piece by John Ehrli-chman, gives every indication that whatever fiction you send me, the new owners lack the standard to see that it will be viewed by any measure you and I hold in common. So, I say, skip it, Arthur, sorry to have been a bother, okay?

It was terrific.

I mean, shitfire, the Dobell guy, he's going ape-shit.

The man Dobell's going nuts.

He struggles to get himself up out of the chair, bustles himself out the door, screams as he goes, 'I'll see you in my office!' and then is to be heard, his having made his way back along the corridor to back behind his desk, calling to Erickson, 'Erickson, come in here and fire him!'

Erickson wouldn't, didn't, told Dobell, Erickson's having heard the tale of my misconduct, well, that's Gordon, whereupon Dobell takes me by the shoulder, escorts me to the way to get out of there, cooing hey, guy, come on, guy, just don't, you know, do it again, the force of which injunction I flawlessly heeded until the dawning of the next day.

So I'm fired, let go, am free to join myself to Knopf, from which site, after eighteen years of damage-doing, am made jobless again, this round by displeasing (what ho!) another surrogate, if you will, and time, as it will, hurries, hurried ahead, bringing it to – wait a sec, hold it, GODDAMMIT, THEY'VE FUCKING RESUMED DOWN THERE – JESUS SHITFIRE JESUS! – they, the crew of demolitionists, they've just started in AGAIN making a MIGHTY resumption AGAIN tearing down the very fundament of COHERENCE. Oh yes, boys and girls, the circular so alerting went around among those dwellers to be the more violently affected, THE WORK WILL TAKE ANYWHERE BETWEEN NINE MONTHS AND TWELVE OF THE TEAM OF RENOVATORS TO COMPLETE

THE REARRANGEMENT OF THE PLANET EARTH. Oh, Jesus, hey, hey, they've just this instant begun beating the piss out of the ceiling my floor is on top of – so that the typing chair under me just shifted into the lees a little bouncing me off of it A LOT, gained an inch or two in its project to shoot itself up from the floor and rush the ceiling with my head head-ward, not to mention the FRITOS HONEY BBQ SACK I'M NIBBLING FROM, it's been ripped off the table and tossed onto the deck somewhere rearward of me BOUNCING THE FLOOR'S BOUNCING – I AM BEING BOUNCED JOUNCED – THERE IT GOES AGAIN, HERE IT COMES AGAIN, ARE THEY KIDDING, THEY MUST BE KIDDING, A YEAR OF THIS SHIT, HOLY MOTHER OF CHRIST! Dope that I am, had thought it was widely known what a delicate dumb type I also am, such as to FLY OFF THE FIRST HANDLE crumble and crumple under the pressure of my HAVING MY FRITOS KNOCKED FROM MY HANDS and the sack from which I have been nibbling them from SPILLING FRITO CHIPS FRITO CHIPS FRITO CHIPS JESUS THE SLAMMAGE THE SLAMMAGE IS MY CHAIR REALLY SLIDING HAS IT SLIDDEN SLIDDEN ONE OF THE WHEELS THE ROLLERS IT'S COME OFF HAS IT TRULY COME LOOSE AND COME OFF THE THUNDERING OF SLEDGE-HAMMERS THUNDERING STACCATO-ISHLY CHRIST ALMIGHTY I CAN'T I CAN'T NO ONE COULD TAKE ANY FUCKING WHOLE FUCKING YEAR OF THIS!

Wait, wait! – hang on for a bit, wasn't I going to, I was going to tell you – the subject was pension, my pension, isn't it, the subject, isn't it pension, pensions?

Yeah, my daughter Becky, the younger daughter, she's always, isn't she always, discovering discoverments ONLINE, as is said? Bec, Becky, onlining it?

Dad, she says to me, it says right here, *Esquire* owes you the money it accumulated for you in a PENSION FUND. Okay, it comes to $1,050.10, but it's yours, all yours, so go on and get it Dad, go!

Go on and get it, Dad, go!

One thousand fifty dollars and ten cents.

Well, sure.

It's mine, isn't it? Been ever so patiently awaiting my taking POSSESSION OF IT while meanwhile down there they are chopping existence into manageably uniform pieces. But, sure, fine – it's been decades, but am I a sucker, I, Gordon, shall have my pittance! – meanwhile finding for my trouble the corporation that owned *Esquire* and that owes me the – hey, come on, that's no pittance, that's $1,050.10 of money – that *that* corporation has been sold to *that* corporation which was acquired by that, you know, that *other* corporation which – fuck, fuck! – but then the other onlining daughter, Jenny, she phones, Jen phones, says Dad, the outfit you want, it's Viacom, Viacom.

Hang on!

There is a company operating under the … it's called VIACOM!!! Oh yeah, it's the sledges again THERE'S LIKE THIS ARTILLERY BATTERY BLAMMING AWAY AT THE CEILING DOWN THERE HOWITZERS HOWITZERS ROCKET FIRE there's Becky again, good old Bec, she's onlining the hell out of it for her good old da

LOOK, LOOK, Dad, it's a guy named Redstone, Sumner Redstone, born Rothstein, Dad, a landsman, Dad, Jen's just emailed me his home address, Dad, he's the guy who owes you your *Esquire* pension, Dad, it's no dough to sneeze at, Dad – you get it, you go get it! – you know how good you are at writing letters BASHING THEY'RE JUST FUCKING BASHING IT ALL TO SMITH-EREENS DOWN THERE – HANG ON – I BELIEVE I JUST HEARD A DERRICK THING MANEUVERING, TRAC-TORS, TRACTORS, DAMN DAMN IT'S WAR MATERIEL BEING FUCKING OFF-LOADED – and I try, I do, I write letters, I do, I know how to write a doozie of a letter, can"t I break steel itself with one of my goddamned great letters?

Entreat him, Dad!

Beseech the bastard!

Dear Sumner Redstone,

My name is Gordon Lish and many years ago, back at the time when they were shutting down the sixties, I went to work for your magazine *Esquire* as, well, as its fiction editor, and one of my kids was fooling around the way the kids do – I mean on the internet, unless it's Internet or Inter-Net, and she just happens to come across this item about, well, the magazine and its editors and various and sundry unpaid pensions thereto and everything and so okay, I'm not hard-up exactly, I grant you that, but, after all, it *is* my money right-fully due me because earned by me and it's only, okay, not a fortune or a windfall or anything, it being only ONE THOUSAND FIFTY DOLLARS AND TEN CENTS, but

I would definitely appreciate you talking with your people and seeing if you fellas could see your way clear to making out a check (cheque?) to me for the amount, or *in* the amount, of …

There's a flotilla of DUMP TRUCKS ROARING AROUND DOWN THERE NOW HEAVY-DUTY WAR EQUIPMENT ARMORED VEHICULAR SHIT SOMEHOW MILITARISTICALLY INVERTED SO IT CAN USE THE CEILING AS THEIR STAGING GROUND eloquent, I'm telling you the letter was eloquent, plus which it must have torn at the man's heartstrings, him a Rothstein and me a bar mitzvah guy, shitfire, that letter must have fetched the heart in him right out of the man's chest, so tender, so needy, so needful, and mild, a measly, lousy $1,050.10 and every nickel of it legit I mean check the files check the records (cheque them!) OH, GOD, THEY HAVE JUST COMMENCED HEAVING NUCLEAR SUBMA-RINES INTO POSITION asking for what, FOR BUPKIS, the man's got millions, billions, God knows how much gelt am I asking for what is not rightfully mine am I seeking to break the bank of what is it what is it what's Viacom I never heard of anything called Viacom it's what it's a *Star Trek* thing it's a hit isn't it it's TV smash for pity's sake don't I have to lay out for taxes on it for heaven's sake plus the ten cents I'll be a sport and write old Sumner (Sumner?) back and tell him me and the wife we've thought it over and he can go ahead and skip the ten cents what the hell to hell with the ten cents let's be human beings about it forget the ten cents even the fifty bucks fuck it fifty fucking bucks just go ahead and write the check (cheque???) for a lousy stinking grand make it it's more eloquent isn't it we'll call it even we'll work it out between ourselves as gentlemen as hell you know as Hebraic gentlemen call it even-steven with a you know an even thou and everybody's got a load off their heart and it's the right thing to do let's just call it square with a check (a cheque!) for what for bupkis a thou even okay okay?

I guess you don't have to guess what I get in reply.

DO YOU?

You got on you a kind of real-world way of looking at things, am I right or am I right?

Hey, I bet I know what your WELTANSCHAUUNG is.

None of this, not a spicule of it, it's no news to the likes of you, is it?

SILENCE, A SILENCE, NO ANSWER, NO REPLY, NO, AS THEY NOWADAYS SAY, RESPONSE, NOT EVEN THE LETTER SENT BACK SO THAT I MIGHT PASS ALONG TO YOU A SAMPLE OF MY ELOQUENCE PAR EXCELLENCE.

The chips, the Fritos, they've been skidded into the corners, are dusty, fuzzied, made filthy by the filth HE SAW ME IN HIS OFFICE, ALL RIGHT, AND THEN I FILLED A CORRUGATED CARTON WITH A STAPLER, GOOD STURDY STAPLES, BUSINESS ENVELOPES FOR ALL OF THE BUSINESS I WAS GOING TO BE DOING PEOPLE PEOPLE THEY'RE BANGING THE CRAP OUT OF MY HABITAT. Dear Mr Redstone, I write to you in your capacity as the custodian of $1,050.10 your holdings in Viacom indicate you owe me, are the steward of, the caretaker of, to whom there has inured a fiduciary responsibility, not to mention the expectations desires needs of my four children and of their four spouses and, Sir, there are grandchildren in the picture as well, GRANDCHILDREN, COLLEGE KIDS WITH WHOPPING FEES TO BE PONIED UP FOR THE ACQUISITION OF, YOU KNOW, OF EDUCATION, OF ERUDITION, OF WISDOM AND CIVILITY AND DEPTH OF VISION AND GREAT FUCKING LIVES —

Please.

Please.

IT'S ABSOLUTELY ALL-OUT WAR GOING ON DOWN THERE WHICH I DO NOT HAVE TO REMIND YOU IS ALL HAPPENING IN THE MIDDLE OF, IN THE MIDST OF, AMID ME TRYING MY TRYING TO FUCKING THINK STRAIGHT UP HERE.

Fleered.

Have I ever used the word before?

Boys and girls, I'm not positively certain of its meaning, but I think that's what was done to me.

Was fleered.

Been fleered.

Let go, released, exiled, made exilic, readied for fleerage ON THE FLEERING TABLE!

Shitfire, yeah, yeah, it's put to me — I'm telling whoever's still listening that it's forever being inquired of me, unless it's enquired of me — why is it, young fella, *why is it*, that you have turned out to be *an old fella* so quick, so unseasonably, so NOT NICELY to hasten to make of yourself, so quick, so irrationally, so reprehensively, SO NOT NICELY such a terrific pain in everybody's ass?

Nobody's looking for an answer.

Because nobody's any different from me.

That's what I just this instant figured out – and another thing: that question mark up there after the bad word, does it or doesn't it, grammatically speaking, rightly belong up there? Which question invites a reaction whose ensuant consequentia regarding the interrogating of which is, or are, worth well more than any pension payment or any pension pay-out or any importuned pensioneer's settlement IN A WORLD MONEY CAN'T MAKE – especially, *definitively*, even as handsome a sum of it as is one thousand fifty dollars and ten goddamn cents of it.

That's right: SHITFIRE, BOYS AND GIRLS, IT'S GOING TO BE A LIFETIME OF HEAVY-DUTY BOMBING DOWN THERE – AND ON UP THERE WAY UP THERE TOO!

ON ALL OF THE CEILINGS AND INVOLVING ALL OF THE FLOORS EVERYWHERE!

HEY, got a notion for you, maybe a nostrum for you, hurry it up and you GO GET YOURSELF ANYWHERE ELSE in the gorgeously irresolvable realm where you are going to get better and better off – UNCANNILY, incommensurately – livin' and talkin' la vida loca all of YOUR TOTAL ALLOTMENT of money-free days.

Oh, God, is it subconsciousness or just subconscious?

Well, for one thing, my neighbor – this is on the one
side, on the other side the setup is different – it's a psychiatrist. I'm going to start, or say that, again. Got it
cluttered back there. Wasn't really ready yet. Or then,
say I said then – the moment having moved on, thus
calling upon us to view it, that moment, via a word
devised to condition, or oft meant to deal with, the
mish-mash of temporality, not that yet – the word, got
it? – does not obtain (itself) untouched by its own, not
unrelated, alities. Ach, let's quit this. There's tons of
talking for us to get under our belt ahead of us. Why get
all meshugeh now contaminated now with the this and
thats of it, you appreciate what I'm saying? There comes
a time for the untimely. Now, this minute, we'll both of
us feel a hundred percent better if, as the bard himself
was not unaccustomed to saying, we get, in a word, on
with it, unless a hair-splitter would look you in the face
and say to you that's three words. So you're not a
hair-splitter, are you? The psychiatrist I was not so long
ago telling you about because the man occupies an
apartment on one side next door to me, he's probably a
hair-splitter. Maybe he even would resent it being spelt
with a hyphen. Who knows? The man might look you
in the face and give you an argument on whichever topic it was your pleasure to have an argument with him.
I'm not saying this is the case – I'm just saying, for crissake, the man is a psychiatrist, emes? Not that there is
not a little something on this subject which I am going

to shy away from taking up with you. So, okay, on the one side there's the psychiatrist, right? Which to me, to my mind, is, to my mind, intrinsically interesting or diverting because it just so happens I have happened to have spent certain periods of time (ach, time again!) in a psychiatric hospital, or hospitals, but not in this city. None of them were, these hospitals, or, if it suits you, asylums or sanatoria, in this particular city from which I am speaking to you from. Neither of them was located in this particular metropolitan area – let's get that straight right from the outset, since I am not taking a chance on it looking like I am implicating the wrong area, or say instead that I didn't say outset but used the words the start. Is this fair? Does it make sense to you? The word outset, it can confuse people, whereas the words the start, this is a concept nobody on this floor of my building should have, if they happen to come along and, you know, happen to read this, should have any trouble with. Because listen to me, the one thing at my age I am not looking for is trouble with either of my neighbors. From the outset this, and this alone, I promise you, it should be clear to you. The farthest thing from my mind (ach, my mind again!) is starting up with people, let alone cultivating differences with people – with decent human beings, I want to interrupt everything at this stage of the game to say – which live right next door to me. As far as I am concerned, these people, they should both live and be well. You know what? The same goes for you. From my heart to your heart, I wish you the best. Believe me, nobody is looking for any trouble. What with the world so confusing just to begin with, who needs a complication or a confrontation or conflict on their front doorstep? This is my sentiment. Maybe you, it's not your sentiment, and along with you being a hair-splitter, you can't wait to stir up a war – you heard me, a war! – with the people on one side of you and the people over on the other. This is a thing which comes under the question of *social relations*. Some people, even the scholars in this department, they prefer to go with the word 'relationships', but I personally find that word disgusting. You notice? I didn't even say it a second time! I said 'that word'. That's as far as I go. So long as you know which word I am referring to, we can continue and, like citizens of the same country, get along with each other and appreciate what the other person is saying and, as the saying goes, live and be well. This is my philosophy. You didn't ask me what my philosophy is, I understand this, you posed no questions, you didn't raise your hand and say to me pardon me but it would make all the difference in the world if you would take a little timeout (ach, Jesus!) and explain to me and my colleagues what exactly your philosophy is. I get it. A person is seeking to get their bearings. A person has a civil right to orient themself and determine where they stand with regard to the national conversation and with regard to the point of view or the vantage point of the individual which is addressing them. We can, howsoever, go into more of this later, if you, the arbiter, desire to. Right now at the moment there's much indeed to tell you of so that you, still as the arbiter, can grow familiar with the crust of this as promptly, as expeditiously, even as quickly as is practicable à la the art, or the knack, of storytelling. By the way, none of the times (is there no end to this!) 'away' was for anything you might mentally be imagining as serious. Nothing like psychosis or psychomania, to cite the two biggies in the mental arena. These 'awayments' were, if I may be permitted to say so, more in the realm of the venereal or the venal. Aphasia, remarked by Freud in his famous paper on the marmoreal, played no part in my, what is the word for it, incarcerations. I'm not saying I was wrongly handled, or that my case, or cases, were. I'm just saying you'd be better off, as would history itself, were you to keep an open mind (ah, Jesus, Jesus!) on the subject, which, damn my eyes, I was rash, I think, to make mention of, or to have mentioned, so early in our entering upon the crust of the situational material currently existing between, or among, or amongst, me and my neighbors. Or having accrued – yes, accrued – that would be the more telling, the more explanatory, the more clinical word. Yet I myself am not, as you must by now be critically aware, a clinician. I have a daughter who is. I have a son who is. Two of my aunts were, not to drag into this – as well – my uncle once-removed, Uncle Harry, no word of which, I swear, shall ever be thrust before you again. Or of whom. Did you make note of that – *of whom*? Apart from these admissions, acknowledged without the suffering of stress, I also have had, you may as well be so informed, my share of various and sundry experiential comings and goings with people certified, licensed, and duly documented to enact the commerce associated with the fraternal – nay, and also with the sororiological diagnostic panels set up to interview those citizens *on the ground* whose complaints smack of the fraying of nerves believed to, or thought to, or posited to – that's got it, posited to! – develop from a surfeit of enduring the vicissitudes of life. This I say to you without the least sphincter of embarrassment. Experiments have been conducted. There is a record of results. For all I know, there may be not just one record but records, all of which, it has been affirmed, or confirmed, are on file. Look, you know what I always say? I always say *fons et origo*. That's right. Now you know my motto, which has, since the first, been my mainstay. My, you might even say, my secret sharer, which is, I do not waste your time (Christ Jesus, honestly! – did you ever?) in freely admitting, derives from the years of my reading – namely, from the epoch in my history when, face it, I was reading like a madman. Unless it's mad man. It's trivial, the difference, but, let me correct you, not trifling. Unless it gets, or takes, or is knitted up with, or by, or by the instrumentality of, a hyphen. No matter. We have more important fish to fry. Is it Harry? Wait a sec. Back in a jiffy. There was – it's lodged somewhere in memory – no, not Harry, scarcely one's uncle Harry, the momser, the clinician, but wasn't there a Wayne somewhere? The name is not without its resonance. Again, the trivialities, the trifles, the not unbecoming sweetmeats. Onward. We're getting nowhere. You're not even familiar yet, you've yet to be familiarized yet, with the situation à la the so-called adjacencies relative to my residence in this building. Excuse me. Yet another atrocious interruption, but I'm telling you, it's been plaguing me, it's been night and day pecking at my sub-consciousness, the word 'resile', does one know it? Or of it? Is it, in fine, known? Namely, to *be* known? Or, rather, a word to be kept well away from the lexicons of man? It's not, I refuse to let myself linger a fig longer with the hypothesis, a word that I, in fabled subconsciousness, made up, is it? It strikes no chord. Resile. Interesting. Virtually intriguing. Neither you nor I, however, must submit ourself to loitering, to a moment's daydreaming, or day-dreaming, especially with respect to rumbles well off to the side of things and their convokings, invokings, what with their Harrys and Waynes and, yes, this too, this 'resile', if it is not, in reality, no more than a figment of one's whatsis. To get back to basics, the diagnosis for which I have been, in all discretion, searching is altogether likely to, or bound to, at any instant pop into my mind (yaah, it's no joke anymore!) as we go along with me telling you about the situation confronting me here, right dab amidships where my habitat is, which I do not mince words with you when I impart to you the estimation, if you will, that the thing is damnably of the essence. At least to my – skip it – or better said, in my opinion it is, very imperiling and not unprospectively expected to worsen, or get worse, even *out of hand*, as is not uncommonly said. There are, as you are yet to have been told, twenty units in this building – well, there are *exactly* twenty units in this building – as of the most recent time (aah, all right all right) of their counting, or of their being counted, or of their having been counted. That's official. The what-do-you-call-it, the uhhh, the real estate company, or the company agent, or agency, puts the number of units (a.k.a. apartments) at precisely twenty, one of which, to one side of me, is in the hands of, is owned or rented or whatever, by a professional psychiatrist, or, as has been rumored over the course of the years, a psychoanalyst, of which distinction you might very well do honor to yourself to make a note of, or, otherwise put, note, simply note, or jot down a reminder (eeeh, the devil take you!) of, so that we might proceed, sans any Harry, sans any Wayne, or, excuse me, pardon me, sans and sans, okay? *Fons et origo*, okay? Jesus. How does a chap talk anymore? How, on earth, does one speak? Unless it's any more? It's akin to a minefield, n'est-ce pas? As to the count, if we might rejoin one another at the juncture where we were obliged to take leave of one another in order that a digressive intervention might be made room for, it was as recent as either yesterday or the day before – this count of twenty I mentioned during our fact-gathering phase. That's how recent this fact is, in case you were wondering, or are wondering, or have been given to wonder, about the recency of the count. Anyway, yes, the place is full of them. I personally like to say *clotted* with them. Even, on occasion, 'cluttered' with them. But mind you, there seems to be a perfectly elementary explanation – hold it, not mind you, if you please, but mark you, yes? – that's 'mark you', thank you – a perfectly straightforward, probitive explanatory reason for this phenomenon or, if you prefer, happenstance, which I will also get to later on, if time (fuck, that's it, that takes the cake, does it not?) enough remains, or obtains, for the basis of the factual material to be discussed. Unless, of course, the matter is of no consequence to you, or of no consequentiality to you, but be warned: let yourself not incubate any anticipation as to any such eventuality, for, at this stage of the game, the future and its conditions cannot be known, nor relied upon, not even hypothesized or prophesized or guessed at. Okay? We are, may I hasten to hope, *on the same page*? Who can say, or forecast, what will be of moment to us as we pass from now, from right now, to some as yet undetermined, or indeterminable, or shall we say aleatory or stochastic endpoint? Who, for pity's sake, can? Is it undeterminable, then? Do you laugh at me? Are you *laughing* at me? Am I, in speaking openly, without notes to which I might cagily refer, without forethought, without *malice* aforethought, do I, in this regard, or by reason of this probity, do I transform, have I transformed myself, in your estimation, into a figure of fun? You think, you have come to think, Uncle Harry, or this Wayne, if you will, have not beaten you to the punch? Very nice. This is very nice. It's wonderful for a human being to find out, to be made to see, or take in account, the kind of life forms one inhabits the so-called planet alongside of. In other words, when the worst comes, and, not to worry, it is *on its way*, this is what one might expect to enjoy as one's companion in death. Nay, nay, I go too far. Hardly companion, nor companions, hardly even neighbor or neighbors, no! But co-tenant or co-tenants, yes! Yet I am willing to set all of these vicissitudes aside. No, really. Honestly. Even, if I say so myself, cheerfully, and without lingering, or any lingerment of, recrimination, this in favor of, or on behalf of, a shared humanity – i.e. the humanitarian aspect, facet, consideration (among our species). I do not sacralize! I hold no hard feelings! I am pliant, considerate, a follower of the give-and-take mode, its various and sundry dictates, covenants, fiats, and teachings, not to mention various and sundry *related* modes of the humanitarian disposition. Look, I'm a regular guy. No reason why you should harbor any doubt on this score. To be sure, I happen to be 'saddled', so to speak, with certain vexing pressures concomitant with, or resulting from, the texture of my residence insofar as its locale is concerned, or location is or locus is in relation to the rest of the building. That's the size of it. There's nothing radical here, nothing hidden, no mystery or subtext calling for your sleuthing or, you know, your volunteering yourself for any covert or undercover investigatory digging, or interpretating, unless it's no more syllablized than 'interpreting' is. Or, that is, the *word* 'interpreting'. Oh yes, oh absolutely, absolument, yes, everything must be virtually insanely examined. You know what I mean? Are you, as they so incessantly say, sensitive to what I am getting at? Hinting, if you would, at? I hope so. I insincerely do. Please do what it's in you to do and *work with me*. It is definitely not in your interest for you to sit there and work, in a word, against me, be it one word or three words, for it all comes down to the same apprehension, which is that you are either with me or against me, unless there's indifference. Personally, I cannot stand indifference. I really can't. For instance, I said, not in jest, mark you, but in all seriousness – with respect to the nation's inquiry into the hazards endemic or innate or native or embedded or effluent from this or that occupation – so I said to this particular personage (I am taking every care not to tip you off as to the gender thereof), I said to him, 'Harry,' unless it was 'Wayne' which I said – I said, 'Listen, I'm interested to know, to, in a manner of speaking, hear it right from the horse's lips,' I said, 'when you are in the course of administering to one of your clients, or analysands, as they say, unless it's customers or patients, do you, over the course of the interview, or session, if you will, shift, if you are seated, from buttock to buttock, namely, Sir, or Uncle, from this buttock to that buttock, that is, from side to side, the assumption of course being you render your services whilst seated and not standing up, or,' and I believe this last bit is what it was which provoked the chap no end, so that she (ah, no fooling you, is there?), so that he screamed, shrieked, went ape-shit on me, turned untethered, became livid, downright unhinged, okay? – 'Get the fuck out of my consultation room, get the fuck out of my treatment room, get the hell out of here!' Just because I brought my interrogative, posed to him from my office as an American citizen sensing myself to be carrying out the responsibility of those taking a rightful part for themselves in the national conversation, just because I added or appended or stuck onto the (yuck!) closure of it, just after, if you will allow me to err a trice in my reaching back into memory for the words, 'unless you conduct your business in the manner of your respondent arranged in such wise as to be lying down?' Well, it was terrible. There was a scene. Hideous, hideous. And what do I sit here and say to this, well, look to the source, the origin, which is a translation, moderately loose-ish, of course, of you-know-what. But do I shrink from the feedback when a citizen has been called upon, empanelled, recruited as to government business? Not on your life! With me, it's all out in the open. Naught spared. No shrinkage. Where the national conversation is on the line, is it something to be taken lightly? I say again – and with fervor – keep it, get it, if need be, drag it out into the open, godamnit! But sorry. Terrifically sorry. Got caught up in an excursus. Shame on me. Distraction, I am, in a word, too subject, too susceptible, too *nice* with respect to making way for the distractive, that which is lacking the constructive, or which is deficient in it, or under par as to it. Yet perhaps, there at the bottom of this, the causality of all of it is that, in my role as a member of the human race, it's all out in the open with me! So sue me, shoot me, see to it that I am made to be 'away', but do not sit there in some flight of anticipation, or expectation, or belief that I am going to change. Let the world do it! Let it change! I, for your information, have no recourse but for me to remain changeless! You can, if you so wish it, set your clock by me, your watch by me, your handheld device by me. Is this enough for you? Has my statement proved itself sufficient for you? Do you need to check with Malcolm, with Mrs Dalsimer, with Dr Harry, with whomever – Wayne, for godsake, with wherever, whatever, the man, be it that and not some errant essence or haint or meme, for shitsake, hovering in the hauntings of a proper man's mi – helpless, hapless, yet ever so staunchly American subconsciousness or subconscience or, we may have yet, as twain, for us as confederates, come face to face with it and face this thing and deal with it, some fucking, you know, subterranean subtext? Or of it? Or of something? Please to lend me your complete attention, yes? As I have already made all too abundantly clear to you, I sacralized nothing! Listen, lest it shock you to hear this, my mother is on the table! My father is on the table! There was even, I'm almost entirely convinced of it, a sister – and *she's* right there with them – on, as it were, the table. Fair enough? I trust so. Believe you me, if I were in your shoes, I'd be glad of it – to wit, or viz., to have the attention of a totalized human being addressing me without even a fig of limitation, limitlessly, illimitably, person-to-person, heart-to-heart, let the devil, or the Devil, take the hindmost. I promise you, that's the crust of it insofar as I am concerned. Let it be true that as much, that no less than as much, that not one jot of as much, might be expected from – nay, invested, invested by! – you-know-whom. Very well, then, back to him, back to Malcolm, or to Mal, as he urges me, or encourages me, or gives me to, or commands me to, even demands that I do, address him or refer to him or, in the current parlance, reference him as, first and foremost I should like to preface my remarks with a word or two touching upon the population of psychiatric workers, therapists, therapeuticists, analysts, alienists among the psychos (joke, joke!) living side by side as practitioners and residents *in this building*. Parenthetically speaking, I take it that you can take a joke. God forbid I should sit here and give myself permission to embark on another one of my sublimely *lawful and natural and humane* digressions, but in taking it for granted you do not require from me counsel or instruction or commendation, if not a down-and-out *directive* to the effect that a sense of humor, unless in your precinct the going expression is H U M O U R, which, I want it known, is entirely all right with me. People have their ways. It is perfectly consistent with their nature as people. Customs vary. This is why we have the saying 'various and sundry'. One must be aware of these things, sensitive to them, uncensorious of them, the luxurious diversity of – or say I said lavish, as in 'lavish', leaving no room for misunderstanding, or misprision, and the conflictual element so often arising therefrom. Mores, manners, distinctions in comportment, deportment, and what is felt to fulfil the requisite components in the idea, or ideation, if you will allow, of decorum, these *variations* worldwide, are, without question, discoverable universally and, albeit not infinite, quite staggeringly numerous. Even, so to speak, innumerable! (Emphasis mine.) Or, rather, imagine, please, brackets, for I have, in speech, or in what is called chalk-talk, no means of indicating them (that is, brackets) when it is necessary they be deployed, as in first bracket, or bracket the first, or bracket prime! emphasis mine, then second bracket, or bracket secundus! Problem solved. No problemo. Slate, may the gods be praised, cleared. At all events, our topic was, if I am remembering aright, Malcolm. Or Dr Malcolm. Namely, as he himself would wish it, Dr Mal. At any rate, or in any event, not my preference among forms of address, ono-mastically speaking. Yet one must allow for these things. Variances and variations, as I am certain I have already taken up with you, *fons et origo*, okay? Hereto-fore. The man secures income by dint of the purvey-ment of therapeutical services, this for hire. Next door to me, I might add, which is fine, with which I have no argument – this being America, I being, thence, an American, as, I take it, is he. Mark you, the building houses many (no few) of the kind. My wild surmise, after eons of my living here, as a resident, is this – not a floor lacks one. In words of one syllable, if it is to be known as a floor here, there is, on it, one of them on it. Not impossibly even two – or, taking my floor as an instance, as an example, as an exemplum, if you will, actually a total of three, although in the case of my floor, this floor, the floor on which my apartment is on, though there be room for three occupants, only one of such manner of human being is, in fact, operating on the

premises as a fully fledged psychiatrist, or psychoanalyst, *fons et origo*. Well, he's a grand fellow, let that be, or
stand, as my first word bearing on the matter, or
brought to bear on the matter. Mal is okay. Again, to
advert to another wild surmise, Mal has been my neighbor *on that side* for forty years or more. Arithmetic not
being my strongest among, or amongst, the disciplines
taught me at school, or in school, I think it best for me to
shy away from putting the finest point on it – i.e., how
many years – discretion being, as I have maintained
since my getting about in kneepants, the better part of
valor. Unless this is unignorably unoriginal of me to cite
as an axiom, or maxim, or guidepost of mine, or of my
own. Now that I set my – now that I review the question in my – now that I give the question some thought,
yes – I'm wrong, off-base, far out of line, or far out-of-
line. Apologies. You arrive at the age I've arrived at,
there arise errings in 'things'. The same-wise, I might
hurry to make it known to you, would apply to Mal
himself, not to mention my neighbor *on the other side*,
who would be, as you might have adduced or deduced
or intuited or guessed by now, Mrs Dalsimer. That's
Mrs the widow *Dalsimer*. To be sure, Mal's widowed.
I'm widowed. The three of us, it's strange, is it not, all
on the same floor, all widowed, or widowers? Viduity,
as somebody recognizable, or recognized, has, I'm certain the case is, said. Just so. Isn't it, when you give the
state of things – by that word, convoked, or invoked –
all the trials and tribulations, to coin another very apt
expression, doesn't it say it all? I mean, one means, the

state of things, *fons et origo*, the nature, the deep nature, of, as they say, the whole shebang? Whoever it was who made a tsimis of this, my hat is off to that individual. Viduity. I mean, please – why say more? Yet with diligence and with dedication to survival, to the pursuit and to the pursuing of existence, the being of being, as Wayne may have put it, we must bind ourselves. Tempting as another *road* may appear, forget it, skip it, keep to the *road of life*, are you listening to me? Because believe you me, I would not for an instant give you a bum steer. This is in what respect yon therapists, throughout the building, from floor to floor, have my vote. They stand for life. They are advocates of life. They advocate for it. It (the psychotherapeutic cathexis) keeps the wheel turning, underpins, undergirds, is ballast for, is buttressing for, balance itself – God bless the national conversation, and while we are at it, shall we not reflect for a moment on the matter of 'recycling'? That's right, you heard me right, I am suggesting, I am recommending, I am thoroughly in favor of our, *fons et origo*, undertaking an examination of, a reconsideration of, indeed, a reexamination of, the practice of, the very praxis of, this thing called 'recycling'. Are you with me? Do I hear a nay? Am I, as I sit here, however remotely, entertaining the prospect of a prospective repudiation? No.

And no again! Mal notwithstanding. Dr Mal to the contrary! All right. There's no place for overstating things. I oppose the pose of the agitator. I want no part of it, or in it, the protagonist of what can only be described as one's surrendering allegiance to a brand of activism that runs counter to engenderment of neighborly relations. Mark you, I eschew it. Boy, do I eschew it. They know I do. Not just the co-tenants on this floor, or at least Mal himself, anyway, but I would venture to say throughout the building it is well reputed that I eschew contributing to any growing excrescence of out-and-out divisiveness. We must live together. Together we stand or together we fall. There is no option but harmony. You know what? I have heard it sing to me, the well-played harmonium. All I ask, both as an American and as an American citizen, is this tenor be let to ring in every corner of the building and that the occupants therein take note, or notice, that man is happiest when harmonious. Surely this is a tenet that finds favor, or that shall be made to find favor, with all who reside herein, and that agitation specifically conceivable to turn this one and that one vying, how does one say, against me, speaking critically of me, readying himself or herself to decry me at the drop of a pin, this, and this agitation and this agitation alone, it must be, it shall be, I have every hope, nipped in the bud.

We, with common interests and with common disinterests must be led into the light by the calm, cool, gentle touch of the avatars best-suited to do the job by virtue of their grasp upon the steady hand of reason. When I advocate for this approach, I am giving you the very best of my concern for the welfare of not just the renters and owners on my floor, but for what's best for the denizens in residence on all floors, or on all *of the* floors, regardless of race, religion, and related points of the conflictual. People, human beings, the living, we are all God's children irrespective of those grudges ensuant to, or pertinent to, or germane to, matters of higher and lower – matters of whether the apartment under lease or deed faces the front of the building or, contractively, gives onto the back, or whatever. We must set aside these vicious exceptions. They are, in a word, deceptions! When I say this, when I sit here taking into account these provocative, yet evocative, differences, I am – please attend to this point with particular vehemence – those areas in the building, those insets, if you will, one to a floor, I assume, and have no choice but to assume, inasmuch as I have yet to visit every floor and to garner the data from a direct and personalized inspection of that floor, going, as one would be obliged, up and down by courtesy of the freight elevator, taking due notice of the limited hours of its operation and of the on-duty or off-duty schedule relevant to the operator thereof, his 'hours', as they say, making very specific allowances for the various and sundry changes flowing from the onset of stormy weather, rain days, snow days, not to mention rain *nights* and snow *nights*, plus emergencies calling for a surge in staff to be focused on a particular on-floor or off-floor but nevertheless hopefully *temporary* but *necessary* downside situation erupting, or irupting (let, Wayne, if you will, or Uncle Dr Harry please to be the party who checks that for orthography, please – since I simply cannot, at my age, be held responsible for everything which goes on, or which is going on, in the building). Sorry. Lost my place. No matter. We'll just take it from here and, as heretofore recommended, we're going to let the devil – nay, Devil – take the hindmost, is this tack, or tactic, not, to the majority, agreeable? In the name of reason, of equinamity, or equipoise, etc., I say plod on, slog on, soldier onwards, avant, avant – else be picked off, one at a – well, singly, then. Yet we – and I can feel this, I can sense it, I am intuiting from my vantage point as one of the original inhabitants, or habitués, of the building – I say we are hesitant, are shifting the general load from foot to foot in our hesitating before us, which I needn't report to you is the central, even to say centrifugal – no, no, centripedal – question of WHAT POSITIONS, OR POSITION, is or are to be adopted, via democratic procedures, with regard to RULINGS covering the current wrangling (rankling? – again, Wayne, please? Harry? thank you, thank you, prompt or tim – nay, speedy attention much appreciated) whirling around – nay, nay, *raging* around – the BINS or CANS situated on each and every FLOOR with respect to HOW THEY ARE TO BE DEALT WITH regarding the latest notification as issued, or having issued from, the building's MANAGING AGENT with regard to the issue of RECYCLING. Again, apologies. Not one hundred percent positive as to whereabouts – the devil, Devil, take it, these digressions, you know, everything circumlocuitous around a man, who's to keep track of it all, what with the building in such an uproar – no, sorry again, mea culpa again, guess I was vying, trying, conniving to – or with, *with* myself, as it were, to shunt the brunt of the matter most vexingly at hand off to yon wild blue yonder, you know, instead of, rather than to taking the bull by the horns, which is not the worst of coinages, and come clean with you as to where the 'eye of the storm' is raging as to the current moment anent (some beauty, eh? agree, disagree?) the BINS, the CANS, the area, or ANNEX, if you please on THIS particular FLOOR where there is in residence, or are in residence, Mal himself, MALCOLM, Dr Mal, ME, yon ACTIVIST, yon AGITANT, yon AGITPROP, albeit I might just as well as instead put it as per – viz. NON-ACTIVIST, NON-AGITANT, NON-AGITPROP – seeing as how I am strictly opposed to assuming the role of TROUBLEMAKER, unless it's better put TROUBLE-MAKER, making use of the tradition, the ti – the historically honored HYPHEN. And, of course, of course, I am not forgetting, geriatrical as I am, I promise you, I do not for an instant forget, or fail to be terrifically aware of my neighbor on the OTHER SIDE, namely her, namely MRS DALSIMER. Lord no. Jesus no. I give you my word that not for an instant, that not for a minute, is this individual far from my – let us say subsconscience, or, for compression's sake, efficiency's sake, we'll adjust the onomastic to hereafter, or hereafter to, conscience, no? Because I do not have to tell you we three, we widowers three, we SHARE the 'space', that which the cans or bins or trash receptacles are to be found – *three of the foregoing*, THREE OF THEM, one for THIS, one for THAT and another, a THIRD, LET US SAY, for SOMETHING ELSE. So do I or don't I make

myself clear? AM I MAKING MYSELF, TO YOUR SATIS-
FACTION, PERFECTLY CLEAR? I trust so. And that, my
friends, is, in a word or three, the CRUST of it! Or ought
I say THE FUCKING CRUST of it? So I ask you, in all
cordiality, in all geniality, with all deference to the
various and sundry amenities, WHERE DO WE GO FROM
HERE? Is it a question simply of *fons et origo* any more, or
anymore? The answer you await, it's no, it's definitely,
DEFIANTLY, fuck no! – there is no longer any room,
God help us, for any question subject to any resolution,
or to any denouement, or to some all-purpose apolitical
nonpartisan UNDER-REACTING. Yes, I seek to raise, to
lift aloft, morale. Yes, I seek to bolster obedience and at
the same time underwrite the human longing, the
humane yearning, the homo sapient's needfulness for
the exercise of freedom. But do I condone lawlessness at
the expense of conformity, or VICE VERSA? Of course I
don't. It would be insane of me, I'd deserve to be ranked
among, or amongst, the irremediably non compis, or
compice, or compeace were I to throw in with those who
inveigh for violence. Plus which, at my age? Whereas
Mal's even, by my reckoning and without the aid of technology, or direct interrogation, or inquiring from staff –
Mal is even, *to* my reckoning, older, more aged, than I.
Mrs Dalsimer, you ask? As to the accruage of her, the
accumulation of yearage relative to her, please, the
woman's at least as geriontated as Mal is, unless the word
I felt inspired to, or felt myself inspired to, deploy, unless
you, as yon witness to these affairs, or to this 'spiraling
dive', if it may be described thus, down into the diverse

185

stands, or positions, or pledgements of a trio of tax-paying, rent-paying, monthly maintenance-paying, or by-the-month-maintenance-paying citizens of this nation, not to mention of this metropolis, is, in a word or three, too much for you. Fine, that's four, then. I see that. Mark you, I am not entirely unalert to the seductions of tripping up. Be it even tripping-up. These conundrums, these perplexities, these stopping-blocks, or stumps, of the everyday, or of the quotidian, they are wide-spread, widely spread, very nearly everywhere, and, however petty-seeming, however inconsequential-seeming, however superficially accounted for as dismissible, and are, by the masses, by the multitude, by the madding crowd, let alone the lonely crowd, simply dismissed, fleered at, sneered at, blown off, as goes the colloquium of the man (and woman, and woman!) in the street, the prittle-prattle of the mob. I shall have none of it! I want you to know, posthaste, that I, your docent in the elucidating of the whole affair, do adopt a stand well apart from others, from, in a word or two, Mal and Mrs Dalsimer, however many, if one were to be so petty and narrow-mi – so petty a person and so shallow a person as to enter the fray governed on all sides by a parti pris or personal or, for that matter, IMPERSONAL opinion, this is the nature of me, this is the cut of my jib, this is WHAT I AM, residentially speaking, not to mention speaking with complete impartiality – IMPARTIALITY – this here, that there, something else of a different variety – *fons et origo*! 'Mal,' I say. I say, 'Dr Mal, you are a practitioner, harken to reason.' This is what I say to the man when we just so happen to run into one another or to each other in THE ANNEX, or WHERE THE BINS ARE. Whereas as goes MRS DALSIMER and her partisanship vis-à-vis the cans and the packaging and depositing therein the throwaways, the garbage, the trash, how the CRAP is to be SEPARATED and PREPARED for its trip down the FREIGHT ELEVATOR and thereafter, or thereafterwards, RECYCLED, I tell you, I am a HUMAN BEING WITH A CERTAIN AMOUNT OF TI — WITH GOD KNOWS HOW MANY FORGET YEARS THINK MONTHS AT THE MOST OR WEEKS PROBABLY GOD FORBID DAYS NOT THAT IT COULD NOT BE HOURS EVEN MINUTES EVEN ANY SECOND NOW IF YOU PLEASE and in this condition, with the prevalence, with the PREVAILING of this PREVAILMENT, go figure, GO FIGURE, I AM EXPECTED TO, I AM BEING ASKED TO, nay, COMMANDED, ORDERED, INSTRUCTED, GIVEN A PRINTED DECLARATION TO, AN EDICT, AN EDICT — are you ready, are you listening with both ears? — I WHO HAVE ALL I CAN DO TO MAKE IT DOWN THE HILL AND GOD HELP ME BACK UP AGAIN WITH A CART ALREADY WITH THE HUMILIATION OF EVERY PURCHASE IN A CART IF YOU PLEASE ONCE A WEEK ONCE WEEKLY ONE DAY USUALLY THURSDAY PER WEEK FOR GROCERIES FOR GOD'S SAKE WITH MAYBE MILK AND CEREAL AND WITH PERSONAL TISSUE GOD FORBID THERE SHOULD NOT BE MAYBE ONE YOU HEARD ME ONE LOW-COST TREAT LIKE OKAY COOKIES LIKE CRACKERS I'M THINKING NEXT WEEK MAYBE FRITOS OR DORITOS OR HEAVEN HELP ME OREOS WITH THE DOUBLE FILLING THE

BIRTHDAY OREOS — and that at this stage of the game that I should be told by the MANAGING AGENT OF THE BUILDING I am expected to — nay, REQUIRED TO, DIRECTED TO package and package and distribute and distribute and do this THREE TI — THRICE — not to mention BEAR IN MI — BE AWARE OF — this goes there and that goes there and this other thing in the bag, IN THE BAG, God forbid it should not go THERE, and this, I want you to know, comes after I have expended what little, what MINUM, what BUPKIS I HAVE LEFT IN ME AFTER OPENING UP THE DOOR ALREADY, God forbid I didn't remember to get my pants on that instant or am not already in my bathrobe or IN A HOUSE-ROBE and SOMEBODY IS ALREADY AFTER I OPEN THE DOOR AND AM STANDING THERE WITH THE VARIOUS AND SUNDRY BAGS ALREADY AND THE DOOR IS WIDE OPEN AND THERE ARE THE CANS THERE ALL THREE OF THEM AND YOU GOT TO HURRY UP AND FIGURE OUT WHICH CAN GETS WHICH BAG PLUS THE FACT THAT SOME-BODY EITHER ONE OF THEM IS ALREADY STANDING THERE WITH THEIR BAGS and you, ME, you're in effect, in essence, as a practical matter NAKED, UNCLOTHED, UNSUITABLY ARRAYED, or garbed, or covered, even nude, NUDE — this, my friends, this situation is to my — in my opinion, personal and otherwise — UNACCEPT-ABLE, VILE, PUTRID, AN OUTRAGE. Listen to me, treat me with the respect I believe I have a right to, and am fully delegated to, expect me being treated like an American citizen, in the manner of a patriot, i.e., A PATRIOT. Do I have to put up with this shit?

Am I, considering the circumstances, not to mention THE NEWS OF THE DAY, supposed to, obliged to, tolerate this shit? Excuse me, but, all things considered, do I? Whilst meanwhilst there remains the pressure pressing at me from MRS DALSIMER for her to have entry into my apartment, my house, or household, not to mention, additionally, habitat and residenciality – fucking PROVINCE, godamnit, THE WOMAN WANTS TO GAIN ENTRY TO MY FUCKING PROVINCE TO GAIN FOR HERSELF A LOOK AT THE TILES THE WALL TILES THE TILES SURROUNDING THE SHOWER BODY IN THE MASTER BATHROOM THE MASTER TOILET IN THE EN SUITE TOILET OR RESTROOM WHICH STAFF WHICH A CERTAIN STAFF MEMBER REPLACED FOR ME REIN-STALLED FOR ME AT NOT INCONSIDERABLE NOT IMMODERATE AT NO UNDER-THE-FUCKING-TABLE DISCOUNTED EXPENSE TO ME OR IF YOU PLEASE COST TO ME, which work was executed, enacted, done years – YEARS – ago – YEARS! – and which afterwards, and AFTERWHICHWARDS, the master bedroom CARPET, NAY, CARPETING! was replaced – REPLACED – at FABU-LOUS COST, wall-to-fucking-wall of it, of brand-new RECARPETING, unless, for all I know, unless it's RECAR-PETTING, if you understand me, assuming, presuming, you are continuing to accord to me the patience and regard and respect due me and are preparing yourself to be INSUPERABLY NICE TO ME in the continuance, or continuation, to dispose yourself to heed me – that's HEED ME! – WHICH IS, okay, ECRU-COLORED, which means it (THE CARPET) is colored ECRU, which you

189

can look up and see the hue of in a book concerning the various and sundry hues and naps and whabs and whorfts of AMERICAN carpets, which such a book, or directory, or compendium may, for all that matter, be on sale ALL OVER THE WORLD EVEN — AND NOT inconvenient for you — OR FOR MRS DALSIMER to consult — that's right! — look into, unless it's in to, and to thereby, or thereby to, preserving, if you will, the integrity of the infinitive — of, namely, the VERY TISSUE OF THE INFINITE — come to be informed of the fact — THE FACT! — that when a carpet is ecru-colored, its color, or hue, is particularly fair or light or CLOSE TO WHITE IN NATURE and that therefore, *fons et origo*, likely to discolor, become discolored, darkened, shmutzed the fuck up by the instrumentality of PEOPLE walking on it, treading upon it, crossing it, or coming across it, from the threshhold of the doorway, from the 'saddle', as the word happens to be, in place underfoot at the DOORWAY, thence thereafterwards, THEM! their, *they* having entered, set foot into, or in to, the space — SPACE! ROOM! MASTER SUITE! — and thus upon the ECRU-COLORED CARPET, they (MRS DALSIMER) would, one is imagining this aspect of the exercise, one is ENVISIONING IT, ENVIS-AGING IT, the woman's FEET, shod, am I right, SHOD FEET, SHOED, not unlikely, in lieu of their (THE FEET) being SLIPPERED, as MINE are, KEEP CROSSING ACROSS THE SURFACE OF THE FAIRLY NEWISH ECRU-COLORED CARPETING for her (for MRS DALSIMER, lest you disre-member, or misremember of whom — OF WHOM! — I speak), for that woman, THAT WOMAN, to get herself an eyeful of the character, THE CHARACTER OF, the

tiles NOT AT ALL RECENTLY BUT INSTALLED YEARS
AGO, YEARS, YEARS, YEARS — AND THEN, AFTER
THAT, AFTER SATISFYING HERSELF AS TO THE CHAR-
ACTER OF THE EN SUITE, OR EN-SUITE, TOILET, OR
SHOWER BODY, OR THE SHOWER-SURROUND, TILES,
if you will – thence to have to, for her to have to make
her way back again, back across the ALMOST WHITE-
COLORED CARPET back to the doorway to the master
suite, step onto, or on to, the saddle, negotiate, in the
act of retracing her steps, negotiate the threshhold, pass
along through the corridor, pass through the front hall,
or FOYER, thence into, or in to, the kitchen, and then
out THAT DOOR, into, or in to, the ANNEX, which has
come to be dubbed, by the managing agent, and by Mal
and by her and by professionals and laity, by psycho-
therapeutical types throughout the building (I know
this, I am positive of this! – sight unseen, word unheard,
I have no doubt of this!) and THOSE OF US among, or
amongst, the laity – nay, the very POLITY – who happen
to HAVE THE GOOD FORTUNE to be, or to ENJOY the
status of being their NEIGHBORS, dubbed, DUBBED, the
recycling area.

Did you hear this?

You heard me say, did you, THE RECYCLING AREA?

Ah, yes, thence, she, Mrs D. (MRS D.!), one posits the
scenario, returns to her place, apartment, HANG-OUT,
pad, ranch, CRIB.

But of course, I get it – the woman is a widow.

A WIDOW. IS, APROPOS of this, IS À LA THE REST OF
US re this, namely, MAL AND ME, that is, SPOUSELESS.
Is subsisting in a state of – right, right, very good! – of

ceaseless VIDUITY. Is all alone. Is old and alone. And only
endeavors to inform herself as to the quality, the character, the nature of my – Christ Jesus, forget it. I am
speechless. The craziness of this, the madness of this, it's
unique in my experience as a person who has twice –
TWICE! – been, as the expression goes, AWAY.

Well, I am telling you, I personally have never seen
the like. I mean, my heart breaks. I sit here, speaking
to you, appealing to you, prorating and perorating this
SITUATION as far as you, with my heart broken, torn in
TWAIN, ripped, as it were, ASUNDER, yet not even telling
you yet, yet not even murmuring to you, whispering to
you, THE LOCK ON THAT BACK DOOR, THE LOCKING
MECHANISM ON THAT BACK DOOR, the door that gets
you from the kitchen, with bags in your hand, or hands,
and thence into the – or in to – the ANNEX – YOU CAN'T
CANNOT LOCK IT. It's, the saying is, unlockable. Viz.
UNLOCKABLE. One, when I approach that door with my
groceries fetched from down the hill up the hill, thence
into, or in to, THE BUILDING, I am comforted to know,
to recall to me – to be made aware all over again that
the way ahead, once I have gained entry to the freight
elevator, lies OPEN TO ME, in whatever weather, in the
worst the meteorologists can THROW AT YOU, not to
fail to point out, your GROCERIES, some of which are
PERSONAL TISSUES and, if purveyed in a package whose
integrity is impaired, LYING OPEN TO THE ELEMENTS,
however harsh.

It's, at all events, this foreknowledge of what lies
ahead, the needlessness of a chap's having to rooch

around in his pocket for his keys, or worse, far worse, not at the moment his or he being uncertain as to which of his pockets he put, or deposited, or placed his, or the, household keys in, for one, for me, to be relieved of this prospective impetus, or prospective impediment, or bar to my unimpeded access, it being, one trusts, not beyond your skills, or not beyond the limitude of your 'skill-set', as the young-at-heart are nowadays heard fouling, if not befouling, the good clean air of our nation with, this being, I must hasten to remind you, America, the United States of America, access, that was the word where we left off, ACCESS, achieved unimpediently to the kitchen, via the back, or kitchen, if you will, door, whereupon I might off-load the cart, the FOUR-WHEELED cart, onto, or on to, the kitchen table with a certain MUCH APPRECIATED, EVEN DELIGHTFUL ease. It's wonderful. It's a boon to me in my old age, a gift to me in my decrepitude, or desuetude, a blessing to me from GOD HIMSELF, no offense intended to individuals of a different ilk, of which 'types' the news of the day tells me there is no telling how many. Or is it ARE? Back there. Take a look. Make up your own you-know. This is a free country, remember – it could be, IS, for all I know – yet, I ask you to remain alert to the universality of yon motto – which one thanks one's own God, unless one is cursed with the stain of the ATHEIST, which one is thankful to and praises ONE'S DIETY, unless it's, or be, DEITY, the saving grace immanent in the oft-required recourse to invoking the comforting recitation – nay, obeisance, or is it oblation I mean? – of one's prayer, one's mainstay, one's resorting to the sanctum sanctorum of – let's have at it, then, let's hear it for its calmative powers, then, as a nostrum, then – the ever-applicable *fons et origo*. But we have much to lead us into dismay, or in to it, when collecting our attention onto, or on to, the other side of that happy coinage, or coin – to wit, that she, that my altogether DECENT, IF NOT CHARMING neighbor *on the other side* of me may, with no interference interdicting her will, whim, or wayfaring intent, get through, make her way through, pass unchecked through that – well, the matter needn't be restated. To my, never you mind (ach!), to my mind (OH, JESUS, SHIT!), the matter, as far as I am concerned, need not be restated. It has been, more than adequately, in a word, framed. *Over and over again*, for us to put the finest point on it. Plus which, as to one's hearing, seeing, whatever, the news of the day and the effluence noted in the reportage thereof, there can be no gainsaying the fact that, to put the finest point on that too, there are more and more of them, whatever, in their multitude, they be. One further word on this score, if I am permitted to append it to the muchness already in view – that (this is that further word) it is surely the case that the manyness remarked, that the influx of that mob, if one might, in the absence of fear, essay saying, makes it all the easier, all the more readily, ever likelier, that the DICTATES of the MANAGING AGENT will be submitted to, surrendered to, made way for, authorized – or, shall we not say, SET IN STONE.

Fine, fine, fine, fine, fine – I have said it. Shoot me. Sue me. How long have I got left? How many more excruciations trundling down and back up the hill, down the hill and back up it, for foodstuffs, for minums of it, for mere staples, am I faithfully to believe continue (such circuits, the occurrence and recurrence, or even the reoccurrence, or reoccurrences of such circuitries!) to exist for me? Or unto me? Future-wise? And then what? One makes use of one's purchases, one consumes the consumables, which is, if you happen to need clarificating in this regard, or with respect to it, which is everything, *everything*! – and then, thereafterwards, one is *obliged*, OBLIGED, by reason of the directive circulated in the building, as an order to staff actuated and distributed by the minions of THE MANAGING AGENT to us, US, tenants, residents, renters, owners, to LEASE-HOLDERS and to LEASEES, thence backed up by, enforced by, entered into, or in to, inscribed onto (or on to) the pages of the BOOK OF HOLIES by, or is it HOLEYS by, such NEIGHBORS as DR MALCOLM, CALL ME MAL, yeah, sure, I'm going to call you Mal, yon practitioner thence monitoring, okay, the ANNEX, okay, located between him and me, okay, between us, okay, or, pardon me, let me be emphatic as to amending my statement to invite revision as to REFERENCING IT as this floor's RECYCLING AREA, the which we share with Mrs D. (that's MRS DALSIMER), to make sure, make certain, make it strictly obeyed that this goes here and that that goes there and that the other stuff, that it goes in THE THIRD BIN or THE THIRD CAN – are you with me? You are assimilating the crust of this? I could keel over in the next two minutes but should I be ready to engage in an act of discarding, I must first, somewhere in the next two minutes, I must first encase the discardable or discardables within a specific type of BAG, which bag, which type of bag, which STYLE of bag, is ON SALE, meaning which bag MAY BE PURCHASED, not meaning anything reflecting the idea of which bag might happen to be found among, or amongst, the store's DISCOUNTED, or AT DISCOUNT, and that's that. I am then at liberty to drop dead without my children and YON GRANDCHILDREN, without them being, BY LAW, made subject to penalty, fine, punishment, WHICH I WOULD BE THE LAST ONE TO PLEAD ON THEIR BEHALF IS DESERVED. This is America. I abide by its doctrines, principles, values, and legislations par excellance.

I don't know. The spelling of that, it just doesn't look right. But let's face it, we don't have all day. Neither, geriatrically speaking, all night, or even, impossibly, a fraction of it. So spelling aside, the crust of the thing being bandied about here, is that I am a good guy, a nice fellow, a man who is not afraid to take his lumps when the circumstances warrant. I am not a bandit. I am not a hooligan. But, Sirs and Mesdames, I protest! I say no. I say enough is enough. I say THERE'S A LIMIT. My question to you is this – which is which? How do you know? How does a mensch such as myself remember? Is there, you'll forgive the expression, color-coding? You know what I mean? But I will inform you, it will be my pleasure to inform you, because as to color-coding, I say stay the fuck off my carpet! Listen, to each his own, right? Meanwhilst, I am waiting for Wayne to weigh in, unless it's wade in. Dr Harry, or between us, Harry is sufficient – Harry, as I have heard a staffer here say, Harry is my witness. Thank God. I take sustenance in this. I feel strengthened, or I feel *myself* strengthened, in me sitting here and in me being freed of the load off my shoulders, or of having it lightened a little at least, to embrace, via remembrance, the words 'Harry is my witness'. Would to High Heaven that this saying was original with me, or were. WERE. On the other hand, Harry is one thing, whereas society is another. Or what if I WERE to delete, erase, elide that 'whereas'? Yes or no, you think the extraction of it would result in a better effect? Who, I ask you, is appointing themself in the monitorization of a matter such as this? Might I turn to Mal? No! Mal is SILENT when it comes to matters like this. Might I, in that event, turn to Mrs Dalsimer? Please, I am beseeching you to be serious. Not even Wayne, not even Harry, do I hear volunteering themself to be my witness something on the order of this. The man Latimer? Well, that's a thought. There may be, for all we know, something in it for us, resorting to the man Latimer for investigation, consultation, guidance when conumdrums like this come rushing to the fore front-and-center-wise. Let's face it, unless I'm mistaken, the man gives a certain degree of evidence as to him having what is known as a stake in questions of this type. Or variety. Or in this regard. I'll think about it. I'll give it some study. Check, I have never met this individual and there is little doubt that he is equipped to view affairs from what is known as *an American point of view*, not to mention from *an American viewpoint*, but you never know with these foreign people. Believe you me, they can surprise you from ti – let's just say now and then they can, as in 'now and then'. Which all of a sudden puts me in (ach, to hell with it!) me in mind of what the current condition is relative, or related to, *the neighbor on the other side of me*, whom, yes, I am not unaware I have made various and sundry mentions of, but have you been brought up to date as regards the latest? Again, once again, I have little choice but to answer unto you that the answer is no. Truth? The unvarnished truth? Well, I have been turning somersaults sitting here doing what might be done, or effected, to protect you from you being 'exposed' to what's been going on here as to the latest *incursions*, or, rather to say, *incursive* menace issuing to me, and to my property, by dint of me having *on the other side of me* the neighbor I believe I have already – no, no, there is no need of quotation marks, why on earth have I permitted myself to embark upon this bit with the introduction, if this be the way for me to best put – here, wait here, deep breath, we're going to amend, amend – CORRECT, CORRECT – which I do not at all (ACH, GODDAMMIT IT, SHIT), at all *mind* saying of the species of THING you would expect the man Latimer to exhibit him having a, or an, EAGLE EYE on. No matter, we shall shuttle the fellow along to the byway where individuals of the rank of WAYNE and HARRY (christened HAROLD) and other persons not immediately known to me by virtue, or in virtue, of their LESSER PERTINENCE to the larger purpose – I do beg your pardon! – THE LARGER PURPOSE of our developing the unfoldment of our inquiry, or consideration, or encounter with CRISIS, CRISIS, CRISIS lies. She's been, over the course of the last two weeks, phoning me, PHONING ME, daily, every day, weekends included. This is strictly from memory, you understand, and, I grant you, my memory is not what it was, but will you LISTEN, for shitsake, to an example, which, I admit it, *fons et origo*, may turn out to be, to its being, or to it being, no better than a COMPOSITE.

Okay?

You braced in place?

Here goes.

Her: 'Gordon?'

Me: 'Yes?'

Her: 'It's me.'

Me: 'It's who?'

Her: 'Lizzie.'

Me: 'Lizzie?'

Her: 'Yes, Lizzie.'

Me: 'I'm sorry. I'm pretty hard of hearing. Lizzie?'

Her: 'Yeah, Lizzie your neighbor.'

Me: 'Lizzie my neighbor?'

Her: 'That's right. Can you hear me?'

Me: 'I'm pretty hard of hearing.'

Her: 'That's okay. DALSIMER. Your neighbor for how many years?'

Me: 'Mrs D. Hi. Hello. Wasn't expecting your call.'

Her: 'I'm calling you. Do you hear me okay?'

Me: 'Yes, yes, yes – you're phoning me. Are you phoning me from next door?'

Her: 'I'm next door.'

Me: 'Are you okay? Is there an emergency? Do we need to get out of the building? Fire, is there a fire? Is there a fire in Dr Malcolm's place? Can you see a fire in front of my place? Have you phoned staff? Are you going to be the one to call the fire department? I can't be the one to phone the fire department. Did you try Dr Mal's door? Is he all right in there? Wait, wait – should I bring water or something? Listen to me, there's a fire extinguisher up on the wall by the stairs! Mrs D., do not, for heaven's sake, do not try to go down in the elevator! Don't be crazy, don't be crazy. You get in the elevator and you're taking your life in your hands! Don't do it. You still have years yet. You're no spring chicken, but there's plenty to live for. Do you have a television? I miss your hubby. It was a great loss when your hubby passed away on you leaving you in a state of viduity. Have you phoned your children? Phone your children. Phone your grandchildren. Inform the front desk. Call down to the doorman. Stay away from door-knobs. Whatever you do, do not touch a doorknob, do you hear me? Go down the fire-stairs. Don't run. You could fall. Stay calm. Take it easy. I'll be right behind you. We'll live through this. We have a lot to live for. There's plenty of fun ahead. You wouldn't happen to know what's on television tonight, would you? Wait a sec. Is this a joke? Lady, are you perpetrating some spe-cies of damnable prank on me? Have you any idea how old I am? Listen to me, lady, I don't see so well, I don't hear so well – it's not right to take advantage of a person like me. Should I run? I can't run. What should I do? Do you know what I should do? Alert the doorman if you are really Mrs Dalsimer. Hang up. Hang up. I'm calling Mal. I'm calling one of the doctors. Have you Wayne's number? Harry's? I'll take anything. I'd look through the peephole in the front door, but I can't see with that eye anymore. Which is it, one word or two words?'

Her: 'Don't pull that shit on me, Gordie-boy. You're not fooling anybody. There's no fire. I want to see your tiles. Let me in to see your tiles.'

Me: 'No.'

Her: 'Give me one good reason why not.'

Me: 'The carpet.'

Her: 'Fuck the carpet.'

Me: 'I love the carpet. I want to keep the carpet the way it was.'

Her: 'The way it was? How the fuck was it?'

Me: 'Pristine.'

Her: 'You know something?'

Me: 'What?'

Her: 'You're a wack-job.'

Me: 'I'm hanging up.'

Her: 'Everybody says it. Mal says it. The doormen all say it. The only reason the managing agent doesn't kick you out of here is because you've been here so long.'

Me: 'I'm hanging up.'

Her: 'What they're waiting for is for you to finally drop dead.'

Me: 'Don't make me hang up on you. I happen to be a gentleman and a gentle person. It is not in my nature to hang up the phone on people.'

Her: 'Gordon, you're a kook. Are you aware of that? Do your kids know how nuts you are? All I want is to get a look at your tiles.'

Me: 'Ask the super. Ask staff. They're no different from the tiles we had in here when we moved in.'

Her: 'Oh, they're different, all right.'

Me: 'Prove it.'

Her: 'You had them replaced. The super says you've got great new tiles.'

Me: 'The *super* says?'

Her: 'Yeah.'

Me: 'The super discussed my tiles with you?'

Her: 'Yeah.'

Me: 'You realize there's probably a law against that?'

Her: 'Quit the idiot act. Let me in.'

Me: 'No. I'd sooner take poison.'

Her: 'Fine, have it your way – for the time being. All I'm going to tell you is this. Dr Malcolm has reported you to the Board of Trustees for violating the recycling rules. Did you know that? Did they contact you yet? You are not forgetting there are fines involved, are you? You could be evicted. What would you do if you were evicted? Everybody at the grocery store says you've got a screw loose. Are you knowledgeable of that? They say that guy with the hat, he's a loon, he's a wack-job, he's probably a danger to the children in the neighborhood.'

Me: 'You talking about Food Universe?'

Her: 'I'm talking about Food Universe.'

Me: 'You don't shop there. I never saw you there. In all these years I never once saw you there.'

Her: 'Oh, I'm there, all right. You're just too far gone to notice.'

Me: 'Bullcrap. You're lying. You could go to jail for this. This is using the federal telephone lines to harass people. I could report you to the FCC.'

Her: 'Report me. I'm terrified. I'm going to run into you in the recycling area and beat the shit out of you.'

Me: 'I am not in the least surprised to hear this character of language and tone issuing from your mouth. You are a disgrace to the building. I'm ashamed to be living in the same building as you. If I run in to you anywhere, I'm calling the police.'

Her: 'I'm shivering. I've never been so scared in all my whole life.'

Me: 'Wait until I tell Mal about you.'

Her: 'Tell the White House if you want to. But I warn you, spread it around some more showing the world what a screwball you are and they'll come here and get you and then what? Your own children, your own grandchildren, they'd all disown you. And me, I'll laugh.'

Me: 'They're terrific tiles. In fact, if I say so myself, they're sensational. Plus which, you'd choke to death if you saw what great carpeting I had installed for next to nothing – and if I told you what I laid out for it – wholesale, wholesale! – plus with a friend high up in the company – your children and your grandchildren, God help them, the poor creatures, they'd all get cancer from just the news of what a deal I, your neighbor who hates you, had.'

Her: 'Do you hear yourself? Did you ever stop to think what a lunatic you are? Would you like to know what every single psychiatrist in the building has come to me and said to me about you? It would make you sick to hear it. Sick!'

Me: 'Lizzie baby, kiss my ass. And if my tiles and carpet, if they had an ass, you could come in here and kiss that too. Goodbye!'

Her: 'Oh, you'll pay, you bum! You have not heard the last of me. Nobody talks to Elizabeth Dalsimer like this and gets away with it. You realize I have sons?'

Me: 'So? I also have sons.'

Her: 'See you on the sidewalk with your furniture, shmuck!'

Me: 'You want to hear the last word? Here is what the last word sounds like.'

Naturally, I hurried up like crazy and hung up before the no-goodnik had a chance to wreck my exit line. Look, I'm just trying to show you what I have to put up with. And that's *just from that side*. As far as the other side goes, *it's worse*. But do I have possession of the evidence yet? Not that I am saying the Dalsimer affair is conclusive, am I? Or is it? I mean, we have to take into account that, in legalized terms, what that no-goodnik said to me amounts to what the judge would terminate as hearsay. This is the problem with people. Your chief evidence against them, the truly damning stuff, when is it not hearsay? For the most part, I mean. Well, it does indeed stand to reason the bastardos could come in the door and shoot you. Or probably decide they'd be better off if they just got you on your way down to Food Universe, or, for that matter, as the saying goes, back on your way back up the hill. You think it's easy with the cart, pushing? This is why, when I mentioned the situation to you earlier, I was especially careful, okay, *mi* – even picky, you might say, to pick the word – wait a sec, hold it a minute, it was the word – it was a word which was quite intelligent – insofar as, inasmuch as, it was expressive of the sense, or of the essence, of effort, of exertion, of a certain expenditure – almost a foolish one, or like a clownish 'thing', like an empirical experience in, you know, in folly, or, may it please the court, cartoonishly, à la cartoonish, lampoonish, goofy. Hey, come on, let's refocus here for a second, the word I used, it was hardly one of those words which exhibited me at the top of my game, was it? Wasn't it, more or less anyway, a pretty run-of-the-mill word? Slog, was it? Was it *slog*? Or SLOG? Give me a minute – we could work our way through the alphabet, you with me? You know, A B C and so forth and so on. Like is it, one asks oneself, an A-word? One proceeds. One interrogates oneself. One does not resort, nor advert to the course of the dictionary, does one? Doth one? Because there's no going through the 'thing' page by page. Unless it's page-by-page. Or ask yourself this, which is what I have spent many a sleepless night doing myself – which is WHY WOULD A PRACTITIONER BE SUCH A STICKLER FOR SOMETHING AS COMMON AND ORDINARY AND POINTLESS AS RECYCLING? Now *there's* an interesting word. Stickler. It's a beaut. To my mind (fuck it, fuck it!), a chap could pass a lot of very useful time (fuck that one too, you heard me, piss on it!) right up to the cusp of the grave considering the beauty of that word, not to mention the invention of it. Stickler. S T I C K L E R. Nice. Very nice. Rather wonderfully beautiful, the word as word and then the topic, the subject, the mystery of how it came to pass!

Who, one wants to know, devised it? What was going on at the time? WHAT WERE THE AMBIENT CONDI-TIONS? Was there money involved? Commerce? A payoff, a bribe, a little scratch, perhaps, *under the table*. As per, one guesses, surmises, virtually is positive of, had to have been the case, or the situation, or the BACK-STORY with the definitive woman. You remember, she who made it big with a whopper like that on her back! Don't tell me something wasn't going on there. One thing, or 'thing', you can depend upon about me, I WAS NOT BORN YESTERDAY. I know the score. I am fully fledged in the nepotisms of PEOPLE. You have heard of the entrepot? I said THE ENTREPOT? Few have. Believe you me, a word to the wise is sufficient. Or 'should' be sufficient. Ah, there's nothing like a sufficiency. I must tell you, I must fill you in, I must *put you in the picture*, there are times, there are instances, there are occasions, when I feel perfectly, superbly, sublimely – even insuperably – sufficient. A sufficiency. A proper sufficiency. In and of myself. In a manner, to a degree, by dint of a process that Dr Mal, that Dr Malcolm, that Drs Harry and Wayne, to put the finest point on it, would have no idea how to define or how to attain or what to make of it. And, mark you, persons of this sort, type, ilk are running the show around here and purveying their services as consultants to the general run of humanity. For all we know, for all we *can* know, there is no reason to disbelieve that the man Latimer and the woman Dalismer are not in it together! IN IT, if you will. Consider the names. How many syllables may be attributed to each? Plus which, do they both, these names, not conclude themselves in the selfsame MANNER? Have you not noticed? I have. And I shall continue to. Make no mistake of it. SIRS and MESDAMES, I AM NOT WET BEHIND THE EARS! A fellow does well when he is a STICKLER for such 'things'. As Mal himself has himself indicated. By setting the example, by taking the lead, by playing the docent, by showing the way, by enfolding one, cozzening one, cosseting one, utzing one under his wing! Jesus! It was there for me to see. As in A-word, B-word, C-word, see for yourself! Could it have been simpler? What could have been simpler? Why all this fuss? Are we not brothers and sisters, all God's children, Americans, or would-be, wannabe, let me be?

Whoa, time-out for a jiffy. It's necessary for me, it's become necessary for me, to make use of the facility. Be right back. It's only going to be a matter of a couple of drops, but if I do not act with all promptitude, with all celerity, with every inch of alacrity, the best practitioners in the building, not even they could tell you what the outcome would be. Yes, yes, I am mightily aware we've not discussed this situation before, but even you yourself cannot expect to be privy to everything anent me. Unless it's privvy. Oh, just joking. Mustn't take me too seriously. Nor seriously at all. It's the way I have. See you in an instant.

No, no, no false alarm. I'm above such horseplay. One 'thing' I do not kid around with is the kishkes. My son Atticus, he was quite young when he counseled me on this point, saying to me, 'Dad, keep it up and you'll come to lament the consequences flowing from a boggy bladder.' I of course took him to be playing with language or logic or the heinous business of ambiguity or amphiboly or an A-word, and look, he grows up, matures, ages into a top-flight, to my mind the toppest-flight novelist, commas back there, the presence or absence of them, probably misarranged or disarranged now that I've a mind liberated from urine to consider it. Whereas my other son, he too weighed in, or waded in, on the matter too, cautioning me to go take a leak when I felt the urge, the pressure, the viability to. That's Ethan. That's my other son. Or say I said he, or say his name, utter the man's name, the person's, the personage, eschewing the pronoun. Anyhow, he's in finance and was an Eagle Scout and is a patriot to the luppers or guppers or a word like that. A time-honored expression which I just can't manage to remember every minute of my life. Ethan is, predicate, egested.

That's the way.

It's the way, or ought to be the way, among, or amongst, the loving and the beloved.

There. That's better. That's ever so much better. Get rid of a couple of drops and you're as good as new. Sure, the dirty rats, there's no denying that they're out there right on this very floor, conniving, conspiring, all those C-words reeking with meanness in them. Check, I could stick to using the freight elevator or walk around to the front and use the passenger elevator, but do not delude yourself, if it's not on one elevator, then it's the other elevator, you're going to run into them. The building is awash with them. It'd be an infestation. Did you hear that? An infestation! Call themselves neighbors, but you know what? Neighbors, it's just another word for dirty rats, traitors, individuals in espionage, spies, spies, vipers, vipers, snakes of the worst variety.

Apologies.

Had to skip off again.

Look, it looks like it's going to start to come up a lot from now on. Once it makes itself known, so to speak, a man doesn't have a chance. On the other hand, it's nature, is it not? Some friend – nature! Who needs an enemy with nature living with you right in your own house? Myself, I don't capitalize it. You want to know why? The answer is it capitalizes itself! Big deal – just like that other word which if Latimer has capitalized, blame him and leave me and my family out of it. Absolutely, positively – sure, I've got daughters, two of them! – but in my condition, at this stage of the game, a man could go mental trying to remember everybody's name. Tonight maybe, when I am trying to fall asleep, I'll go through the alphabet the way I taught you to do. It works. Or, you know, so far, which is what you can say about everything, now that I am taking this pause for myself and really putting my mind to it, death and all the rest of that fiddle-faddle, children, grandchildren, the outrages in this building, what people all over the place are getting away with, words like definitively when definitely is the word!

You treat me fair and I'll treat you fair.

This is my advice to you.

It's wisdom.

Keep an open mind.

As for time, time will take care of itself.

Listen, what doesn't?

Like when Mrs Dalsimer was taken off to rehab on account of a fall, what did I do but right away go to the little chest of drawers in the front hall and take out a little card with my name on it and a little envelope to fit the card into, or in to, and write on the card 'Get well, Mrs D. Hurry home. I already miss you,' signed, 'Your sincere and affectionate neighbor for god knows how many years,' and then, making sure it was all ship-shape, I go and slip it under this lady's doormat so that it will be seen by somebody when they bring her back home and it wouldn't be hidden from sight for good and underneath the lady's doormat and no one would ever know that the lady's neighbor for almost forever did not put into practice the consultantship he'd been the beneficiary of at the behest of various and sundry human beings who are not going out of their mind sitting in the wings waiting to be named.

Entrepot, I saw it somewhere, with a little tilt like a roof up on top of it. There's nothing to these 'things'. What else do people have to do with themselves after they make children and make grandchildren and make trouble for the government and forget to package their shit and stick it in this bin and that bin and then in the last bin and forget to call it a can?

Flexure, on top – is that the 'thing'?

Becky and Jenny, I got it, I got them! – and didn't even have to lie down.

An instant, please.

There.

Oh boy.

All I can say is whew.

Okay, all clear.

You understand. I believe I was saying, or was going to say, well, that's it – it's, you know, you understand. Whereas with Mrs Dalsimer, who fell, matters are of a totally dissimilar character as of now. She and I, neighbors for the duration, as the old expression used to go, not to give a second thought to it, it'll be okay. Now that the woman can walk again even with a limp as of now, I'm positive it'll be milk and honey from here on out.

Milk carton, it goes in this can, napkin with honey on it, that goes in that can, what's the hassle, right? I mean, you do what you are able to as far as getting along with the other kids, it's good news for the kishkes and – wait another sec.

Just don't go away.

Now, then. Better, better – thanks for you being such a champ of a stickler, okay?

Come on, I know these 'things'. It's not magic. Yes, I'm special, of course, but I credit Mother. I credit Dad. I was just one of those crazy cases where a good upbringing did, I like to think, the trick. They're gone now, you know – Mother and Dad – but them being dead, it doesn't do a fig to detract from, or to distract from, nor to diminish my debt to them. Here's to you, Mother! The same goes out to you, Dad! You invested the time, the mind, the spirit, the attention, the patience, the stickleriness in me to cultivate, to adumbrate, to extenuate a pretty darn great outcome, allegiance to adumbrate a pretty terrific outcome. Be proud up there in the sky for me, as I myself am proud – despite the spate of difficulties I have been the unfortunate target of à la the particular insufficiencies à la my residential issues. If I go out there at say one or two in the ayem, or even three or four, so what if Mal is either out there inspecting – or I spot Mrs D. all set to reach out and check the doorknob to see if the lock wasn't fixed after she went away for –

A minute, please.

All right. Back again.

All's one hundred per cent again.

Is it such a tummel, such a ghastliness, such a big deal if there is somebody whose avocation in life is *to find fault with you*?

Of course not!

Doesn't everyone have to keep busy?

I mean, idle hands and so on, n'est-ce pas?

You think it's so easy sitting around waiting to pedal off without you meanwhilst having something to do? Pay attention to me when I tell you, the worst person could do very nicely with a little distraction, even if it's just like a hand is pushing you a little bit in the kishkes every two seconds because the last time you stood there and did your best to subdue it, as the old saying in another language happens to go, if you stood on your left ear for the rest of your life, you still could not get all of it out! So the man exists to find fault with people, is this a crime? You know what? It is an occupation. There is income involved. People, they couldn't live without it! Am I not myself a gold-medal example? Believe me, it wasn't so awful. In certain respects which I am not making mention of in mixed company, it was a pleasure, enough said? But you must – ein moment, momentito, eh?

There.

The salt of the earth.

The woman is, I say this with no fear of contradiction, the salt of the earth! A hip, a pelvis – don't kid yourself, it's no fun. Listen, if you know anything about the human body, you know there is no reason in the world why it couldn't be murder for all concerned. Even worse. Torture. A knee maybe. I knew a person, it was an elbow. You wouldn't wish some 'things' on your worst enemy. A bladder always on the point of knocking you down whereby even holding on to your shopping cart and squeezing and squeezing, it would not bring you relief.

The bones.

The nerves.

Jesus, do me a favor and don't make me laugh.

A human being wants a look at your new bathroom tiles, is this a felony? She should be turned away?

Denied? With life what it is? She fell. That's what I was told. Did she ask to fall? Should an individual such as this be treated with resistence? Or is that an A which belongs in there instead of an E? You see? Not everybody, nor everyone, is an expert. Chances are, there is a chance, my ire is misplaced. People, you have to realize, they're human beings. I was shocked when I heard it going around the building that someone right on the side of me should fall victim to such bad luck. It was shocking to me. I didn't know what to do. How to make amends? How to reach out? How to wipe the slate clean? Nobody left to discuss the situation with – no Harry or Harold.

No Wayne.

You say Mal?

I say forget it – I say *please*!

I say some 'things' are serious, are you still sticking it out with me?

Forgive me, I do not intend to keep sitting here and make an issue of it, but forgiveness is not always the issue!

Life must go on.

These paragraphs, what's with that?

Which reminds me to inform you of the fact that it hurts more and more. Fine, fine, but what would 'you' know about it, okay? Okay, okay, okay – right as rain again. Wish I could say good as new, or risk saying it in italics, but what human being in charge of their senses can legitimately impugn to you or impute to you or bruit, bruit the statement to you that they, your brethren, that they are as good as new when who wants to go down giving time, of all 'things', a hard time?

I promise you, Mrs D., Mal, me, what with viduity and so forth, there's no new anymore, or let us say any more, plus which good is not a question anywhere in the offing, not even for the newborn. Anyway, as I was preparing myself to say, in quotation of who remembers? – 'What in life is not life-threatening?' Which if I said, be a mensch and give me credit. A thousand misgivings. Have no idea what that means, or what I think I might mean by that, but when there's pressure, there's pressure. Forget it. Just kibbitzing. Which is spelt that way or another way, whereas, whatever, is there a difference? This is what living in this building has taught me. I'll tell you, it's been an education. Did anyone tell you yet there's a penthouse here? Or so it says if you get your information from the buttons in the elevator. Have I been there? Did an occupant invite me? Listen, I bear no grievance. To no one, least of all to the members of the practitional class, do I harbor the least accumulation of a sentiment imbued with what is nowadays referenced as resentment – i.e., a copia thereof? I say *fons et origo* is my witness. Huzzah, huzzah, the F8 key appears to have recovered its fortitude. Nice. Plus undiscontinuous sentences again, paragraphs, or a paragraph, fit for putting an end to this. Oh, shit, there can be no word such as undiscontinuance. Nah, here it goes with the F8 key back in unnecessary action – get this! – *undiscontinuance.* Dumb but soothing. Dumb but relaxing. Meaningless, madness, maniacal, but a friend to the heart in me no different from the dogs I loved, whose names will never take their leave of me even when sense has. Nice. I'll say this and then drop the whole topic. All I said to the guy is as to buttocks, do you, in the course of 'things', shift from side to side? And thence, whence doing it, be in any wise attentive to it, leaving the client, the customer, the cash-and-carry analysand unattended? For just that one fucking instant? The infant entreating for feeding and the tit withheld whilst somebody's thinking in a minute, in a minute! Which minute's eternity. Which minute's the closest you'll ever know of eternity. Or infinity? Emes, baby, emes! Like *fons* and so forth. Like what's the mystery? Frantic, desperate, lost, lost, suicidal, or at least homicidal, yon patient, yon client, yon paying customer, mook, muck, sucker, *gull* – a moment, please. With your permission, please.

Ah, fine, fine, fine, fine, fine. We're … good. Now back to the vernacular, hooray!

Is it anyway or anyways?

Yes, yes, yes, yes – I am human, I tire.

I am terrifically, you know, tired.

Oh, the rustlings out there! They are known to me. I hear them. At all hours. Listen to me, where am I? I am *in my kitchen*. I am sitting at the *kitchen table*, nursing, as is said, a cup of tea. No, never! Frito chips. Fritos. And it is *when*? Yes, yes, yes, yes! It is *at all hours*. Are you following this? Stick with this because, as you are my judge, it's probably going to be worth it. Believe you me, I am not the species of individual to waste somebody's time. What do we have? You know what we have? We have what? We have all that a human being can call his own.

The whole kit-and-kaboodle of it. The totality, the 'thing' of it, *the one and only thing* – F8 key, the F8 key, shit, *mesdames and monsieurs*, it did, it's doing, its stuff. It's time, baby, time! As if you didn't know! As if you in your kishkes were for one instant – what? – not noticing?

Okay, that's better. That's, I don't mind telling you, *hugely better*.

Just hoping I didn't lose any of these Fritos back there on the floor.

Oh, yeah, she's out there, all right.

Hard of hearing, hard-of-hearing, deaf as I am, I hear her in her careful, care-ridden, care-mad reaching for –

You hear me?

Are you listening to me?

Am I, mayhaps, cutting too close to the bone for you?

No, let me, with your permission, rephrase that.

Your feet are NYedding *nyoo* CLOSE TO *the fire?*

Yes Sir, nyes Ma'am, Nynohone niz safe, none NYexemp, *etter Nyed on* MY *snippers nyon and russ to the Nyedroom –* in MY BEDROO AND I HEAR HER IN *nya nyi*KITCHEN *shes the wiman my neig she has actuallkhy* HAD *nya nyerv* TO *engter without permiussion mu mitcen ad is call g out to me yoo* YOOHOLO HYLOOHOO YOOHOO *nyi*I'M COINU G TIK SEE THE TGK,ES *tkl,es tiles and don;t worry, not tro* ... *worry-p-pthere is no need forf yolu to worry I have I* HAV E O N SOCKS! IN H7*ny*EL,L. i mean 7 *does gthius thig this noyt* BEG THE QUESTun am I AM I NYgorn GORN *mysekf* goRnyn *not* in *nyedl* NYEDL INit HEL?

MANIFESTO

Because they are taking from me, because they are grabbing from me, because they crouch there ready and waiting to perpetrate theft after theft from me, heists from me, larcenies from me, because they are perched in the shadows for them to steal from me, for them to liberate outright from me, for them to poach the ranks and ranks of my best new neonate vocabularial zingers from me, because they can't bear it when there's no template for them to copy the crap out of me, because they plunder my top devices, because they stand around from morning till night for them to, you know, for them to crab the best cuts from me, because the whole filthy rotten stinking gang of them have got nothing better for them to do but to prepare themselves for their next fat chance to lift my terrific shit from me, because they have failed to exhibit the first fig of shame, the first plum, the first rutabaga, the first nectarine of restraint to keep their bloody hands the hell off of my prosopoeia, because they have shown not embarrassment to curb their appetite for the purloining of my genius, because they're copping my heart and soul from me, because of all of the foregoing criminality and then some, what choice do I, Gordon (Gordon!) have but to run from room to room in a state, goddammit, of fucking distraughtness, which, by the way, which word – distraughtness, distraughtness! – the bastardos didn't even have even the slightest shred of decency for them to take it easy on me a little and to maybe think twice a little before plunging right in and snatching my inspirations from me right the fuck out from under my nose from me the fucking minute I mint this shit – distraughtitude, distraughtitude! – not to mention them sneaking stuff from me precursively, even before there's a superhuman opportunity for me to get it into print somewhere.

Oh, but pardon me for stooping to make mentioning of it. Oh, please do pardon me and a half for me even bringing the matter up. Hey, kill me for risking the appearance of me sounding just a titter too, you know, too *proprietary* – and maybe like, you know, like maybe a trace *ungenerous* possibly or *unmagnanimous possibly* or like I'm possibly a bissel a little too much for you on the *look-at-me-aren't-I-something* side, which is fucking vile of me, okay? Which is totally fucking like putrid of me. Which is the most atrocious thing which I have ever done except for me going along with the whole affair in the first place and consenting to let myself be born.

Robbery!

Robbery!

The sons-of-bitches picked 'fraughtitude' right out of my back pocket!

Which is lousy of them.

Which is disgusting of them.

Which is pretty shitty of them.

For the fraud of them appearing to be the *fons et origo* of which neologism they will probably get themselves inducted into the National Academy of Authors and Koobs.

Hey, it was god-given, it was heaven-sent, it was an honest-to-pete breakthrough for me and for my sovereign enterprise in the installation of lexical allure.

They copped it.

The bums just came fucking sauntering along and copped it.

Not one single fucking by-your-leave to be heard!

Not a solitary may-I!

Not the courtesy of an audible thank-you perhaps, a whisper of recognition maybe, a nod of feigned indebtedness, mayhaps, not even a demi-nod of it, undertaken in my direction on the pages upon pages chuggyjam with acknowledging all of the tushies kissed, funds suctioned for woodsy retreats for the furtherance of troilisms with great shaggy canines thrust demotically into the healing meditative mix.

I'm sick of it!

You, you mooch, you goniff, you shnorrer, are you not sick to death of it, your craven cribbing from the created coffers of the *fons et origo* groomed and curried for keeps in the prized stall upholstered with velvet in yon Latimer's stable of jittery litterateurs?

My repertoire, my repertory, my store of novelty and panache, it's been kicked in the kishkes, been booted in la bonza, been rifled, been burgled, been overrun and sacked, been looted and emptied of it signature bits.

Jesus!

What the shit!

Does nobody care to know that my personal quarry of grandiosity – devised for my owm private bhgt and cfrsubhtion and goddamn crzubhgdt – has ben breaded, bfeeched, bredchded?

Holy Christ, I'm os, mde, med – fucking crazy ot of me med about it.

And will presenly ig, drat it, nyi will!

Ou hrd nyee – I, Grdnpo (Gosdfin!), yam gong ta Jeedus sjue!

Bastards.

Bastardos.

Momsers.

Muddernyuckers, nyull nyayy, nyodnyamit, nyu will!

DIDN'T WE JUST HEAR SOMETHING HUMANISH FALL?

That wasn't entirely on the level. The title, it wasn't, isn't, no, not to be relied upon. On account of the fact (hah!) that it was a man, or that, in fine, we think it was a man, with respect to whom might have fallen, not necessarily some yon gender-free unit in a collectivity of human beings, anywhere from female to male. We mean, since it's men who are principally falling at what often seems greater than the tolerable rate, odds are it's likelier it was the fall of a man we heard, that it's likelier the fall of a man was heard, not that of a woman, with respect to the sex of the human being heard to fall first and foremost in our tale.

Hey, look at that! – emphatically unintended – the rhyme which came to pass up there, or which, up yonder, occurred. Well, no one here meant for it to happen. Or no one's admitting to having underwritten a scheme. But, we ask you, is rhyme a crime? Rhyme's no crime – unless rhyme – the epiphenomenon of it – causes one outcrop to cause another outcrop, engenders it, precipitates it, in which case one could posit rhyme's criminal insofar as it encourages mimesis, concatenation, the narrowing of the diverse. Yet is there not, on the other hand, a sense in which rhyme can sponsor opposition, contradiction, the reversal of, or virage from, what was previous?

Or, if you wish to take our point, what was first?

Ah, what's to be said when firstness is all?

Anything worth the hearing of it?

In any event, we are more or less, or largely, given to postulate it was a man. Heard. Fall.

Which is interesting. Intriguing. Suppositive of investigation, deconstruction, unpackment – said rather than saying, for the refreshment in it, investigating, deconstructing, unpacking.

How about this?

Probing, delving, looking-into.

Not that there is any insufficiency of women falling. There isn't. Women fall. *People* fall. Which sex the fallen may be attributed to have fallen from the ranks of and, by reason of this epiphenomenon, to have therefore brought about one fewer – or, in the instance of the catastrophic, boundlessly less – of: this is a matter of little fecundity – statistically (if countable), socially (if reckonable), biologically (if these epiphenomena call for the chordal and a third adverb, accordingly, is wanted).

So where are we?

Epiphenomenally speaking, we are where?

The falling, alas, of people.

What a topic!

Talk about rich.

Answer this: How come the falling of people has come to occupy such a epiphenomenal emphasis in scribblings cropping up at home and abroad? Domestically and in the literating issuing from the scriblant class based, or operant, in alien lands?

Something – there's neither hide nor hair of a chance of our ever knowing what – is going on. Or clearer to say that something, epiphenomenally, is definitely going on, and there's neither a hide nor hair of a tip-off as to our ever knowing what.

What's indisputable, however, is this:

(a) People are falling, as when haven't they been?

(b) We believe we heard reported evidence of this epiphenomenon right before reporting on this.

(c) Yes, here we have to do with the triadic chordal again – so, sure, this C is just for that – to fulfill the tri-adism of the chordal requirement, in case, like me, or as with me, in two seconds you already forgot.

No one's saying it's easy. Being what we are – human, if you will, it's a pisser of an enterprise. No question, for plenty it's more of a pisser than it is for others, but for nobody is it – what is it the poet says?

A cakewalk?

Just getting born is murder – and getting dead?

Boys and girls, I just gave you the insuperable word, I'm too busy with this shit for me to listen to you nuddering me for another.

All right, the topic is the fallage of people, perti-nent to which it is our intent to spread before you, and, pursuant to law, attorneys appearing for the defendant, argument in support of fallage's inroads respecting the 9th District's ruling reached in July of last year – i.e. 'Let the parties settle, come to their senses, act in accordance with ...'

Wrong reference.

All wrong.

Eyesight's failing fast.

Heyoh, heyoh, let it be a Yukon Gold when it comes to a potato.

That was a tip for you.

Make a note.

Here's another one for you for when you're writing the word 'impasse'. See how it comes to an end? Attend the tip. Or tip-off. Don't just hurry along in the belief you're finished with it once it has come to *sound* to you as if you've completed your – wait a minute. The two 'it's back there in the sentence we failed to make our way all of the way through to the completion of. They are subjects, you do realize, those two 'it's of ours, so entirely discrete … skip it, just go ahead and skip it, insofar as *we cannot be held responsible for* – look, you're on your own. You fall? Fine, you fall. Only so much can be done. Linus Pauling, you know what he said? Or what it's said he said? 'Hold onto the bannister. When making your way up the stairs or down the stairs, hold on to, or onto, the bannister – if you want to get to live as long as I have.' Well, pride, it goeth before, you know. Not clear to us how it happened the man crapped out, but crap out the man did, didn't he? Which is, practically speaking, fallage.

Practically speaking, what isn't?

I–M–P–A–S–S–E.

No shortage of same.

By the way, here's another tip for you. You want to ease your way? (Two sentences, word 'way' in each, but are we to construe either to impart the meaning the other 'way' does?) Enough. Not going to hold your hand any more *in re* any of this. Anyway, eat Yukon Gold. When it comes to a potato, it's unbeatable. Yukon Gold. Boil – slice – or mash – add salt and pepper – a tit of oil perhaps – Jesus, that is some potato! Emes.

Or hang on to, or onto, it.

Altogether likely, or not entirely unlikely, the man said it that way and not the other way.

At any rate, he nevertheless fell.

Or he, nevertheless, at any rate, fell.

We know, we know, we know – the comma thing, the interjective thing – talk about what's murder. Imagine it, you fall for good, having deposited behind yourself, or your having failed to, too many of them or too few of them, never for a minute taking it into, or in to, account that your fallage might in some undisclosed – nay, even undisclosable – fashion be the result of, or on account of, insouciant or persnickety, handling of the comma!

Oh, you think not, eh?

Fool!

Nothing, not anything, when it comes to the final fall, doesn't count. Only a quitter thinks otherwise. Yeah, but go ahead and get a Golden Yukon on your plate and, yeah, live a little before you're not, you know, doing any of it any more at all. Or get a Nobel Prize. Didn't Mr Zimmerman do it? Listen, we've figured it out – if we can just keep the Swedes in business and leave it to them to get us some world peace, what'shisname – King, Stephen King – is even he fucking up the price of life too much for the poeticule

227

in him to fuck up? Ah, come on, be a sport – the man and his posse, haven't they been turning out their share of the real thing? Take the Oates lady, the Rushdie guy – you honestly think they can't recognize an opportunity when they see one? Where's your humanity? These people are not just potato-eaters, for Christ's sake, they'd be into, or in to, potato-growing if the fucking money were right and a medal came with it and the uppity Golden Yukon could be shoved aside in favor of giving some decent fries a fair chance for once in a tuber's life!

Shit.

Did we spell forsee right? It's not foresee, is it? Or maybe we didn't even use the word so far, not that any of this unforseeable shit couldn't have been foreseen.

True story, we're having more and more uncertainty as to how we're going to cope with this geriatric thing – unless it's for us to all fall down before there's just too much spelling of any rank ahead.

Will you look at this one?

Please.

It's kakistocracy.

Wait a sec – better we give it its due.

KAKISTOCRACY.

Please God the typesetter can render it in all small cap and make them letterspaced, unless it's letter-spaced. Who knows these things except, or apart from, the specialists? Anyway, it's our earnest recommendation you do what you might to master the composition of it.

It bears, in its fashion, on fallage.

Betokening, as it does, whether parochially or cosmo-logically, not to mention epiphenomenonally, signs and wonders.

Tell you what this morning's meeting with the staffers concluded. That we just had one. Or 'we've'. That we did, we did. A sign and a wonder. Mark it. It's 10 October 2016, or maybe 10/13, and word, or at least when it had left Sweden and made its way to us, or, you know, come to us, we right away all assembled ourselves in The Situation Room, as the auld enclave is referred to around here – and the staffers, they all let it be known we'd just had one of them for ourselves – a sign and, by gum, a wonder – no exegesis of either alert required.

Jesus Christ.

Talk about your climate change.

Unless it's climate-change.

Yeah, that's what it is, a change in the climate.

Whichever it is, hey, the righteous have had it again – a kakistocracy, it's overnight taken over its inexorable charge – we are, holy fuck, a fallen people, falling fast, whose deserts are the worst – while the better, some of the best of it, it's just been blown, like the man, all the way down.

Oh, in one stinking rotten lousy exhalation of the perilously polluted mind.

Yes, yes, yes.

No, of course not. It's not anything like the end of the world or anything – like where homo-sapiens lives. Honest, it's no more than another day where life, for the sake of the ersatz, is wronged.

Everything resumes its teeter-tottering equilibrium.

See?

You hear it?

The rate of fallage remains steadied before the morrow dares to show its blushing face anew, metaphors mixed in the manner only a laureate could fiddle out the kinks in doing it.

The works of mankind remain intact.

The oceans churn – but tire after a while and go ahead and fucking subside.

We're all okay – save for those who aren't.

But falling's going on, all right.

Big falling.

Hear it?

You can hear it.

It's plenty noticeable.

Especially if you're cashing in on it.

Shake it.

Celebrate it.

Sing yon songs.

Tap your tambourine, oh.

All it is is all it was – and that's just fine with us – for turbulently, then ever so quietly, flows the – fuck it, isn't the decrescendo always all in the rhyme?

A KEVIN BARRY HOSSANAH

Q: Mr Daedalus, are we disturbing you?

A: No, not in the slightest – just having me a wee bit of a time off my feet.

Q: May we speak with you, then?

A: By all means – yes, of course.

Q: You agree that you are the creation of Mr James Joyce?

A: I do.

Q: Tell us how it feels for you to be the instrument of someone's imagination.

A: It's probably all right, I suppose.

Q: Does this apparent nonchalance of yours extend to the name Mr Joyce saddled you with?

A: Saddled?

Q: Yes, dubbed you with, sir. Decided to designate you by.

A: Judge it odd, do you?

Q: Well, it's not your everyday sort of a name for refer-ring to a feller, now is it?

A: Says who?

Q: No offense, Mr D. Just trying to break the ice.

A: Well, you broke it, didn't you?

Q: Got a sort of Hellenic effect to it, don't it?

A: Now that you say so, I suppose I suppose so.

Q: That was neatly put, Mr D. You go for the fancy, do you?

A: And why not?

Q: But the name the man gave you, it's damned peculiar, wouldn't you say?

A: Yes, I would say. Sort of a strange one, wasn't he? And who's not? Nor is any name any queerer than another.

Q: You say you don't think it's got airs of a particular sort of la-di-dah variety or anything?

A: Jaysus, you might be onto something, for all I know. You reckon the scholars are having themselves a bit of a smirk at my expense?

Q: Logan's a fine name, Mr D. Nothing wrong with O'Grady, neither. Ah, put it out of your mind, old boy. Deed's been done, am I not right? Yet may we ask if you've any idea, might it be asked, why it was your yon Master Joyce picked out such a name for you, then?

A: Well, seeing as how it was to be the family name of me kid, what choice did the feller have?

Q: That's no way to reason, Mr D.

A: It's the kid which is the reasoner, isn't it? Something of a snot, I've heard them say.

Q: And who would that be, Mr D.?

A: Them. The readers of it.

Q: Commentators, then.

A: That would be they.

Q: Well, one can't quite escape one's being aware of there being differing views in the matter, can one?

A: One can.

Q: And what would some of those be, could you be so grand as to tell us?

A: I can say this – it's often suggested he hoped to make a point. Ah, but didn't the man have himself a brother christened curiously? And then there's his own son, and the daughter too, the lot of them laboring their whole lives under insignia that set them apart.

Q: Affiliates of the same Mr Joyce, you mean?

A: I do. Any fool can tell you it wasn't any of Miss Barnacle's doing, names as froufrou and unIrish as all that. You name a person, you set the course. It would be true of a dog too.

Q: You think so?

A: I do.

Q: You know the name Kevin?

A: I do.

Q: Would you say it bespeaks a vector in it?

A: Hector? Ain't that more of your Grecian formula?

Q: No, vector, sir. I said vector. Direction and all that. A destiny like.

A: It's an ordinary name, now ain't it?

Q: But he's no ordinary variety of man.

A: And how would you be knowing that?

Q: The feller's writings, I've read them all.

A: Ain't you the one, though! And what of it?

Q: Not a thing, sir. Just making conversation. Do you read yourself?

A: Think what you're saying, lad.

Q: Do you make time for books, then?

A: I make time for what amuses me.

Q: Would it ever be a book?

A: I'll be turning the pages of this one, won't I?

Q: In search of your name, Mr D.?

A: Is there a better excuse?

Q: So you'd say vanity's the thing?

A: I would.

Q: Is it the only thing?

A: It is. And thank Heaven for it.

Q: You don't think the world would be better off free of it?

A: I think there wouldn't be any.

Q: So it's not love that makes the world go 'round? Or money?

A: It'd be seeing one's name on a signpost.

Q: You don't say.

A: I do say.

Q: Who would you peg as the vainer – Hephaestus or yourself?

A: Who's he?

Q: Let's just say another artificer, okay?

A: Are we talking about Mr Barry again?

Q: Then you were misleading me when you said you were no reader.

A: Ain't misleadin' the first tactic of the artificer?

Q: Well, I wouldn't say no, would I?

A: Now you've got it, boyo. How else is the ice to be broken?

Q: It being, beforehand, all ice – right?

A: You notice I get Irish and unIrish betimes?

Q: Is it a trick, then?

A: What's not?

Q: D'ya have an opinion of the Kelman feller?

A: Fucksake, who's he?

Q: Have you anything to say about translation?

A: I might.

Q: We're listening.

A: Isn't there the odd bob in it?

Q: There is.

A: And the general idea gets conveyed?

Q: So they say.

A: Your name goes on it?

Q: It does.

A: Babel sort of a thing, in't?

Q: Babble, babble – thank you, sir, I see, we see.

A: Yr s'yin' y'folw'n' m'?

Q: This is pretty exciting, Mr D. I think I'm getting what you're getting at.

A: Ep'ph'n'm'n'lly spakin', wud'ya n'say?

Q: I would, sir, yes.

A: M'n'me's yit onit, in't?

Q: Yes, yes!

A: S'y'll b' wr't'ng a cheque, y's? Sah b'quik, th'n, b'quik!

Q: Sah wud ya b' sayin' ya dinna myind th' rangf'l aitch in d' toitle?

A: Dere's 'n aitch dit's rangf'l sumairs?

Q: Dere is.

A: Fugsake nay! Y' dinna say!

Q: Oy di.

A: Yin ohana, y'say?

Q: Oy do.

A: Fugsake nay?

Q: Aye.

A: 'y'?

Q: Rott'n 'gg fooks y' uml't, 'h?
A: 'm''n.
Q: ''?
A: '!

WHAT'S WRONG WITH THIS BOOK?

Well, yes, an exasperating read-through betrayed it (the
book) to look as if it's got a lot wrong with it, or,
anyhow, not enough right with it, and that it is defeated
by the presence of an under-supply of muchness in it,
which is (hardly at least) one of the outstanding weak-
nesses in it, the lackingness, the lackadaisicalness, the
slapdashery of the effort brought all too feebly to bear
on the paltriness of it. There's no nipping any of it
beneath the table (bigger type, deeper margins, looser
letting, a shift to nought but sesquepedalian diction) to
keep the savvy librarian from sniffing in the face of the
cagiest wholesaler. I know. My father was in business.
My father was a business person. You think I want
Latimer's press smirked at, sniffed at, sent thither? Or
some perfectly respectable representative of Latimer's
told to beat it, take a hike, go away, piss off, please leave
this shop unLished please? No! All on account of me and
my bad back and my not being up to my sitting for
longer spells in this unergonomically intelligent chair? I
am sitting in an ergonomically unintelligent chair. I am
sitting in an office chair from the twenties. Maybe from
the teens. It's a smart-looking affair but it's not smart in
other respects, which respects have everything to do
with function. It's a dumb chair, I'm sorry for it to hear
me declare. Latimer deserves better than this, and,
book-travelers hustling around on Little Island's behalf,
their having been sent off in decryment, they deserved
better than that too. I myself, I deserve better, but in my

book (hah!), yeah, it's appearance which is first and that's the truth of it. Even my grandchildren, every guiltless one of them, shall never fully recover from mopery were it known among them the old boy didn't have the mustard to evince the good sense (nice, that – not bad at all, the ince and the ense linked propinqui-tously) to go out and get himself an up-to-date replace-ment. The chair you sit in, it's got to count. When it comes to the facts, what doesn't? God yes, the chair that's sat in, it must matter colossally. For better or worse, it plays its part, whether throne or an up-ended cinder block. This one's not the worst, but even limping all the way, it wouldn't break a sweat giving the worst a run for the money. Not that one ought to be forgiven for indicating its talent for its going pretty darn swell with the other furnishings in the room. Oh, it does a bang-up job at that. Appearances, appearances – the felonious chair, it goes just grand, or grandly, with where it's been sentenced to spend its impracticality as a showpiece in this setting. Right behind it, facing oppo-site, there's another chair very like it – same vintage, bewheeled, all old-time office-y-effect design-wise – and no less obtuse as a device to park your backside on for longer than minutes. Did I say it faces the other way? It's drawn up to, like this one is, a long oak table. The wife used to sit at that table and in that, or upon that, back-hating chair. It was the selfsame setup for both laborers, long thick tabletops resting on baroque iron-work bases, a jacked-up drawing board on that one, a machine to type with on this one. We used to, through

238

till dawn, go at whatever was driving us, Barbara at her layouts for magazines and rocketship shapes for Raymond Loewy. Going to have to go back and check the spelling of that name. Maybe it's Lowey. Swiss fella. Did the Studebaker. Looked like you couldn't right away tell which way was the front of what many nowadays wouldn't know was a vehicular wonder. Also did the Coke bottle back when it was glass and famous for its seductive graspability, the claim being, by forces on either side of what was to become a topic of disputation, the consumer was enticed into taking hold of the thing owing to its mimesis of the body of a woman. Gone now – Loewy or Lowey and his modernism and his injections of 'monkey glands' to preserve youthfulness and entify a long life. So is Barbara – gone, too, long, as they say, before her time, diagnosed at forty-eight, dead at fifty-six, her shoulder to the wheel for seven years more than the year four neurologists had foretold for her. You don't want to know why. You just don't want to get what she got. Since celebrity's never not been a convenience for shorthand and since these celebrities were celebrated in the era most familiar to me, I'll just append that if you pay taxes in Latimer's land, these notables were landsmen of yours – Terry Thomas and David Niven, they went down to the same lousy luck Barbara did. Every day somebody, even people who were never even forgettably famous, do. It was quite a shock when the news showed up here. Barbara was dropping house keys more often than seemed unsuspicious. Lipsticks too. Tripping on curbs, wearing down the tips of her shoes. It was when she couldn't trim her fingernails that she went in to see the family doctor. He sent her right over to a specialist across the street. He told her he had a notion regarding what was going on, and she asked him is it treatable, and he told her no. She phoned me from a telephone booth on First Avenue. Called me at my office. There was a terrific downpour at the time. All I heard was screaming and my saying to the woman screaming where are you where are you where are you and running all of the way there since there were no cabs to be had and the rain was such a rain that I'd never been in a rain like that, running from 50th Street and Third Avenue to Thirty-sixth Street and First Avenue, my having screamed back at the woman screaming stay there stay there stay there, and all the way praying she would she would. She did. In a phone-booth in a deluge that had emptied the streets and which phonebooth stood there in the tempest as the last shelter she was ever again to have. They still had them back in those days, phonebooths. We still had each other back in those days, but never thereafter without the stipulation widening the divide between the dying informed of their dying and the dying yet to be told. Jim Watson got me through to Stephen Hawking for advice. You want to hear what the advice was? Take cod liver oil and vitamin C. Or maybe it was Linus Pauling who told me to load Barbara up with vitamin C. Don't remember. I can't remember. Stopped remembering a lot from that time to this. Now I sit in this chair even though I know it's bad for me. Back all aching and (what is the Kern word if Kern's it was?) racked, or wracked, with pain when I gather myself to get up to call it a day or, walking bent, walking crooked, make it to the kitchen to whip up some instant espresso and sugar substitute and fat-free milk with a battery-powered tszuj'r to froth up the glass. Friend of mine, Patty Marx, she uses so much Sweet 'n Low, her pal Phoebe made Patty a birthday cake in imitation of a packet thereof when Patty turned fifty. Patty would every day come over here not long after dawn back then in those worsening and worsening and unbearable days when, of course, of course, the unbearable is borne – her idea for her to be on hand when the night nurses were going off-shift and the day nurses had yet to show up. Her pal Doug McGrath, he'd often come by later in the day. They both put in time here when time was as sadistically inseparable from life as it always is, but the equivalence never quits making an impression on you. Bill Murray, who lived up above us, he'd show up off and on – to stand there flush in front of Barbara so that she could see him capering to make her laugh. Then she stopped being able to laugh – or to phonate communicatively at all – although she could groan in displeasure, refusal, despair – and weep sound-lessly, soundlessly weep. Or that's how I remember it. I don't remember much. Or I make embellishments up, the actualities all being well beyond my faculty for looking and saying. What am I willing to retrieve from back before the rainstorm? Plenty. Lives entwined from the first look I took at Barbara when we were assigned to places across from one another at Behavioral

241

Research Laboratories. That was in Palo Alto. Then we came to New York, and then we came to inhabit this apartment, and then it came to our setting ourselves up in this room when, after hours, when after the day's office hours, with our child in his bedroom, his having, as my father would say, made night for himself, Barbara and I would take up our back-to-back positions in this room and somehow manage to work night after night, the bulk of the night through, getting by – but not really, but not, time taught, without penalty – on snatches of sleep. Oh, the smuggery in my remembering how mad with happiness we were with every effect we created in this place. Did I tell you that Barbara was forever searching the five boroughs for vendors likely to be found vending the unlikely? That's how these honor-worn chairs got here. That's how everything did. I can't tell you if the one I'm sitting in right now, and which I sit in every time I sit at this table, is the one Barbara sat in or if the one she sat in is the one facing the other way behind me where it's every day stationed mid-table at the long table back behind me. When my back began to go, I tried my luck with that other chair for a time. They're different, but in sympathy as to period, the wood they're made of, the intricate iron fittings, unless they're steel, the rollers on the feet, or is it an ostentation not to call them wheels? Oh, another word just came to me that I used to hear my mother favor. Casters, wasn't it? Or maybe I've got that wrong too – as I bet I've done with so much in this book. I've reached the age of guessing, and of then abandoning the excruciation of guesswork and settling for what seems, in the exertion, a hint more reminiscent than that does. The mind, the tumult in it, the ceaseless concessions to shame and to dread and to unignorable ignorance and self-congratulation – delusional at best, all inexcusably, so humanly, an irrevocable lunacy, yet a friend to you in the grief of your ultimate friendlessness. That chair back there, the one drawn up to the other table still paired with this table rearwards behind me now, it stands higher than this one does – and when I first tried it for the sake of my back, I thought the height would do the trick. It didn't. Neither did cushions I took from the breakfast room chairs, arranging two or three of them in what I'd hoped would prove an improvement. Nothing came of any of any of these desperations, either. Put them back in the arrangement they cunningly belonged in where Barbara had laid them about where I took them from. The whole place, the decor and ever so much more, it's all Barbara's doing – just the way she deigned it all to look like in the mid-seventies and saw, in the mid-nineties, the last of the joy it entified for her. When I'm down in the street in front of our place, I think Barbara never saw this, the way they've redone the sidewalk extensions at the intersection. Go down into the subway station where you catch the train up here and think Barbara never saw any of this renewal, either – the way the trains are so different now, modern-looking, quieter-sounding, cleaner, sleeker, still an eye-opener for an old-timer like me. Wherever I go in the city I see what Barbara never saw and what I know she'd think was terrific. Most of all, most unimaginable of all, unimaginably, unimaginably, unimaginably, the power of our son's art. His novel, *Preparation for the Next Life*, I cannot tell you, I cannot tell you, I cannot tell you what its power has done to make of its title a pardon for me, a directive, a man's lullaby to another man. What would this flowering of genius and the acts of genius to follow it have meant to Barbara? Is it thus with everyone who's gone on to live when his reason for living has died – that the one living is seeing what the one not living cannot and the one living ceaselessly hears himself sighing oh oh oh, the wonder of the wonderment of being and of not being, the want of wanting time to be ceded back to the one person most cheated of the delectation of the prized. It wouldn't be anything like that if Barbara were sitting back behind me now – in one of the chairs we always sat in when we sat in this room. They're mated, all right, though with differences that do nothing to impair the harmony of their kinship. I am sitting in the one that's lower to the floor as I type the words you're looking at now. If Barbara were to get up from that higher chair to get up and go along the hallway and through the foyer and into the kitchen for coffee to bring back with her to her drawing board and to turn herself back to her work again in order that she might make the deadline she'd set for herself, she'd see everything's the same as it's always been in all the rooms she'd catch sight of on her way going and coming on along to where she started from in this room on that chair in her completion of her errand. Things are just the way she left them – on the 9th of September in 1994 – or, rather, was made to. It's really beautiful, as she herself surpassingly was – glowing, radiant, tidied to a faretheewell – every feature in defiance of what you'd expect to see bespeaking the dwelling of hard-working people and the person of a mother foretold she was to be taken from the indwelling her womb had wrought for her. There's the pair of chairs, handsome as all get-out, looked-at for their standard of the joiner's craft. No, they're not at all comfortable for anyone my age to sit in, but we sat in them, my beloved and I when we were young, and I, I'm still sitting here sitting in one now. It kills me to do it. Bet back in the day when they were made, word was they were the last word in office-ware seating. Now they're just good to show off if anyone ever gets in this far into the apartment. They curry attention, as do the photographs of their collector, which are everywhere on view here so that I am greeted by memory wherever I look. We'd sometimes go three, four nights in a row in these chairs – to meet deadlines and keep the wolf from the door. Pain was never the issue with us. Looking good and being punctual and seeing to the welfare of our child, these were pretty close to topmost among the aims I'd freely admit to. You know what? I don't have the grit to end this truest. I just realized that. That's the worst thing wrong with this book. Best I can do is refer your envisioning to these chairs of ours. You've probably seen their like in movies and in used-furniture stores. Maybe Atticus and Beth will want them when I can't get out of bed anymore or when some cowboy on the street has smashed me all to pieces with a scooter or a skateboard or a motorized bike on the way to meet a deadline unheard of back in the era when Barbara and I were racing to keep ourselves in the running and look presentable as we ran. I just moved my bottom a little, trying to inch it into a better fit. Heard the thing squeaking. Going to go back to a cabinet in the laundry room and come back here with a spray can of something to grease the works. There's plenty of moving parts invested damn cannily into the function of this chair. Might also get a bottle of lemon oil and a rag for to spruce up the wood – of this one and of that one, the oak of both chairs. That's as truly as I can manage to stop this maundering – leave you with a picture of the fiction or non-fiction of my stewarding, in my old age, the household where a pair of house-proud parents never eased off in their devotion to make of their digs a sort of museum in which to exhibit evidence of their creation. No, it wasn't the healthiest of habitations for a regular kid, but we took Atticus to be as fussy about the look of things as we were, so maybe, all in all, as I was instructed never to say, it wasn't the torment for Atticus you'd suggest it was, his having to get around the place on tip-toe not to dislodge or misalign anything Barbara and I were subjecting to the imperatives of display. Listen, my back hurts. Maybe it's the fault of this low-slung companion to Barbara's high-hipped cousin of it, but I don't think so. I think it's chiefly, truly, old age and its deserts. The long tables are still here, they're still here. I probably told you – but I forget, I forget – more and more I can't seem to retain all that much of what I said and how I've said it and what I've been taking care to keep to myself. One thing is – what the hell! – there's clutter here now. I'm ashamed of it. The bookshelves, they're in terrible disarray and the books in them, they haven't been dusted in years. Shit, can't see so well as to be able to spot what I might be sometimes on the lookout for, can I? Bending over to get up the droppage, it's not any more all that readily in the cards for me. But no, godamnit, as soon as I say what might remain in me to get to the last of this, it's absolutely sworn – emes, emes! – I'm going to get up to go get the spray can of silicone and the lemon oil and a rag or two and, godamnit, give these chairs their due. They've done their duty, lousy as their function is, and it's up to me for me to do mine. Just to say, Barbara, you made all this. You put every gleam where it went best. Thank you, thank you, thank you – for me you are there, there, *there*! – living, alive, my salvation, your preservation – my supernal comfort, your insuperable presence, here, here, *here*! – in every touch you took to bring into being the world I am trying to keep living in – that I feel safe in – that I can abide in nowhere else than – that Barbara and I sought to polish with all the endurance and pride we had. Now watch me – I'm getting up and heading to the other end of the place and then I'm coming back here to get down on my knees and do the bidding of my conscience and enact another crack at the fulfilling of my debt.

INVESTIGATIONS

'This Negger, Degger & Finn?'

'Yeah.'

'Private investigations?'

'Yeah, you got it, private investigators, yeah.'

'Private Dick Negger there?'

'Maybe yes, maybe no.'

'Might I speak to him?'

'Lady, it all depends.'

'Depends on?'

'Around here we say speak with, not to. Plus upon and not on.'

'Okay – may I speak with Mr Negger, please?'

'What name shall I give?'

'I'd rather not say just yet.'

'Lady, no name, no speak – to or with. But your reticence, it's no problemo. Just give me something for the log, okay?'

'Will Mrs Logger do?'

'Spell it.'

'L-o-g-g-e-r.'

'That double gee?'

'Yes – two gee's, please.'

'Hold on.'

'You said Negger, right?'

'Please.'

'Hold, please.'

'Negger here.'

'Private investigator Negger?'

'Speaking. You told the girl Looger?'

'Logger, thank you.'

'Got it. Two gee's. One oh, two gee's.'

'Yes, thank you. That's it.'

'And that would be Miss, Ms, Mrs – what?'

'Mrs, thank you.'

'So what can we do you for, Mrs Logger?'

'You handle private investigations?'

'We do.'

'Is what I'm saying to you now, is it private?'

'We don't have all day here, Mrs L. You got something you want to talk to me about, talk.'

'Your receptionist said your office prefers talk with, not to.'

'That's the policy here. She told you right.'

'But you just said otherwise.'

'I just said otherwise? When did I just say otherwise?'

'Just before now. Just a moment ago. I distinctly heard you say to, not with.'

'Listen to me, lady, we do investigations here. Private ones. We do not dabble in quibble. You got something you want us to look into, we're only too happy and glad.'

'Mr Negger, it's vital to me we get off on the right footing. You seem vexed with me. Have I touched a nerve?'

'Mrs Looger, we're running a business here. It's true – attitudes count, attitudinal variations, they matter. Believe me, no one here would argue the point with you, but if you're looking for the kind of work we do, then let's get on with it, to coin a phrase.'

'Mr Negger.'

'Yes, Ma'am – what's on your mind?'

'There's a book.'

'Yes, Ma'am, a book. What about this book?'

'Mr Negger, the book to which I refer, I believe it to be slanderous or libelous or what-have-you.'

'Mrs Looger, I'm listening. So how specifically can Negger, Degger & Finn help you?'

'Mr Negger, was that an ampersand you just said?'

'Look, Mrs Looger, if it was or it wasn't, what's it to paying the light bill around here?'

'That depends, Mr Negger. If you'll excuse me, Mr Negger, but my question, if you'll just give me a minute, it prospectively proliferates into a host of other questions, all of which I believe to be pertinent to whether we can do business or not.'

'Look, lady, I'm sure you're a nice lady and all that, but I'm, we're, in no position here for me to waste words with you. If this is a question of us dealing with speculation, you come in and we work out a work order and you render to ND&F the routine agreement papers and the standard fee for the initial consultation, etcetera and so on, and then we take it from there – doesn't that seem reasonable to you?'

'Could I speak to Mr Degger, then?'

'Hang on.'

'This is Degger.'

'Mr Degger, you sound far more cultivated than your Mr Negger.'

'Miss, this is an office. We do investigations. Is there something you want investigated?'

'Mr Negger's tone, to begin with.'

'Name, Miss?'

'Logger.'

'Okay, Miss Logger, what's on your mind, if I may ask?'

'There's a book, Mr Degger. I purchased this book in good faith.'

'And?'

'Well, Mr Degger, I'm confident you'll appreciate I don't want this known, but after having paid good money for this book and after having read it as much of it as I could stand to read, I believe it's not an exaggeration for me to say that it would appear the publisher is taking advantage, perhaps even deceiving, if I may use such strong language as that –'

'Begging your pardon, Miss, to cut you off, but this is beginning to sound to me like something our Mr Finn could handle more capably for you. Would you wait on the phone for a tick while I see if he's free?'

'Yes, of course, Mr Degger. Thank you. I'll wait.'

'Finn.'

'Mr Finn?'

'This is Finn. Who's this?'

'My name's not the issue, Mr Finn. Look, I realize I'm taking up far too much of your time there and I'm not even sure I'm in touch with the right investigative agency – it's just that, as a consumer, I feel it's my duty to put the right people on notice concerning what I take to be a possible instance of fraud. Do I make myself clear?'

'Yes, of course you make yourself clear – yet it's not at all clear what you want from ND&F. This fraud you speak of, would you be so good as to give me more of an idea of what you're talking about?'

'Consumer fraud, Mr Finn. I'd say it's a matter of out-and-out consumer fraud. The defrauding of a consumer.'

'And it's you who is the consumer?'

'Yes – regrettably, yes, of course. I am.'

'Would you narrow that down for me, zeroing in on, if you would, with what it is you expect ND&F to do with regard to this kind of case? Because, Miss, you do realize there are public agencies that deal with this sort of thing, consumer fraud and the like.'

'Mr Finn, there's a book.'

'Okay.'

'I bought this book from a licensed bookseller.'

'Okay.'

'Not a word of it corresponds to the publisher's claim for it on the flaps, if that's what you call them.'

'And you want ND&F to do what, Miss?'

'Take an action, of course.'

'Miss, tell me, did you approach the bookseller for a refund?'

'Heavens no. I read every word of the book. To ask for my money back when I have consumed the product, as it were, would that not be a form of fast-dealing in itself?'

'But you're dissatisfied.'

'Yes, but I made full use of my purchase, and there was no warranty given that I would find my purchase a satisfaction to me once I had had the chance to delve into it.'

'And you delved into it.'

'Every word, Mr Finn – no few of which are repeatedly repeated, I might add.'

'But your position is you paid for those words without knowing that, in a sense, you'd already paid for words you'd then be repaying for.'

'That's it exactly, Mr Finn – thank you. It's fraud.'

'I agree with you, Miss. You'll get no argument from me. But what do you expect ND&F to do about it? Our business is investigations.'

'Investigate them.'

'Investigate whom?'

'The author, the publisher, the bookseller. Could anything be plainer?'

'For which investigation you would foot the bill?'

'What?'

'Defray the cost of, Miss.'

'But I already paid.'

'Miss, pardon me if I go too far, but there's precedents in a matter like this – let the buyer beware and that sort of thing.'

'Yes, yes, of course, Mr Finn – but is not the publisher liable for perpetrating a deceptive practice?'

'Finn, this is Negger – we need you for a meeting. Might you bring this call to an end soonest, please?'

'Miss, you heard that, yes?'

'I did, Mr Finn. He's a terrible man – rude, rude, rude.'

'Three words when one would have done, Miss. If you don't mind me saying so, here we have it exemplified before us, the superfluousness of three for the price in time of one. It's what people do. It can't be thought fraud – unless one adopts the view, useless as to do so would be, that people, in their very nature, in the expression of their feelings, their interests, their traffic with others, are helpless but to commit a fraudulence, to, in a word, defraud. To expect otherwise is to expect people to conduct their commerce with others as bestselling authors do – by plan, at a safe distance, by script. But I must go. My colleagues are calling for my presence. I wish you success with your case, but I cannot be persuaded you have one. Try to extract a refund from the bookseller or from the publisher or send a letter to the author or to a newspaper or go online perhaps and do what you might to warn off other unsuspecting customers. Where there's a will there's a way, but there's little doubt this office is not your answer. I must, at any rate, run.'

'The book's called *White Plains*.'

'Haven't heard of it, Miss. Will there be anything else?'

'The person who wrote it, he admits to being crazy.'

'Really, Miss, I must ring off.'

'Would it interest you to know there's something in the book that's just like this? Isn't that plagiarism? Or self-cannibalism or something like that?'

'No doubt, Miss, no doubt. Now, I'm going to have to hang up.'

'Go ahead. Hang up on me, then. Where's decency in the world anymore?'

'I'm sure I don't know. Perhaps if you applied your concerns to the Swedish Academy, perhaps they'd have some illumination for you.'

'Them! Is that what they call themselves? Well, I never! What do they know about the furrows of English speech? Or, worse, American?'

'Ma'am, I'm sure I don't know. Mr Negger and Mr Degger, they both had bets on Mr DeLillo. Myself, I took tickets, as it were, on Cormac McCarthy, Joy Williams and Jason Schwartz. All of the foregoing, weren't they aced out by a harmonica player lacking the probity even to offer himself under the sign of other than a phony name? Could anything be more telling as to character and so on? Why would Swedes even – Swedes! – honor cowardice attendant to such a testament of fundamental perfidy? Now, if you ask me, there's a piece of fraud for you, par excellence, as the saying is said, but here at ND&F, we've aways made room for the cynic's observing as to where indeed would the wealth of nations be without a dollop of the day's duplicity? Now please, Miss, let me go.'

'Name's not really Logger, you know.'

'Yes, Negger passed me a note saying you'd declined to give your name as it would read in official records.'

'That's right. Want to know what it is?'

'It's of no note to me and my fellows, but if you'd care to leave it – since you've already robbed so much of our time from us in our workday.'

'Oates.'

'Oates?'

'Yes, Oates.'

'Not the famous writer Joyce Carol Oates?'

'The same.'

'Well, we here at Negger, Degger & Finn are honored by your interest in our firm, Ms Oates.'

'That's okay. Call all over the place all the time.'

'But you must be so busy with all of your involvements as a literary artist.'

'Artist, shmartist. Can't tell you all of the time I have on my hands. Just fucking with you people, anyhow. Had nothing better to do until the next PEN convention. Call it research for my next project. You guys have been great. Thanks. Hey, thank the other two private investigators for me too, okay? Think I'll just knock off another top-seller and then hit the sack for a little shut-eye before I sit down to work out my next tweet. See you guys. Been nice chatting with you. You people there with your ampersand and all that, you've all been pretty darn swell. Good luck to you.'

'And to you, Ms Oates. Do phone again.'

'No problemo, Finn. Words. It's no skin off my nose, is it?'

'Pleasure to pass the time with you, Ms Oates. An honor. Really.'

'Quite all right, Finn. Think nothing of it. I know.'

'You're some good egg, Miss Oates, I'll tell you. May I call you Joyce?'

'Yeah, sure – Joyce Carol.'

'I'll so inform Negger and Degger. They'll be glad to hear.'

'Sure, Finn – pass it around. I might be up for something tasty if Hillary gets in.'

'Why not? Hey, if Dylan, why not Hillary? Even Trump, okay?'

'Way to kudize, Finn! Could use a wordsmith with rapido comebacks like that. Might have a place for you in '20, you know?'

'Always here, Joyce Carol, darlin'. Always here.'

'Attaboy, Finn! Who the fuck isn't?'

'Was that the finish of this, then?'

'Finn, you got a better way out?'

'Can't think of a thing, Joyce Carol. Nervous and all.'

'Me too, my man – writer's jitters. Honest, it's the shits.'

'But that's so modest of you, Ma'am.'

'Joyce Carol, Finn – and don't you forget it. Now, up, big fella, up! Hiyo, Silver! – and away!'

THE DEED

Before I die, which, you know, could happen who can say when? – which could, for that matter, happen, for instance, right in the midst of my sitting here writing this, I would like (before that happens, before I die, that is) to get credit for, to receive credit for, to be in receipt of illimitable credit for, the achievement of an accomplishment thought unique, which is why I am bringing to your attention a man named Ariel, or so I am told his name is, this by the woman to be spoken of below, told, am told, that this is what the doorman's name is, for I certainly would be loath to risk my asking him himself, as they say when they say, or is the 'himself' of it too much of an irksome excrescence? An extimacy thing? No, it's 'loath' which is the obstructive word. Loath is not the word we should want here. I suppose replacing *loath* with 'uneasy with' or with 'disinclined to' or perhaps with 'afraid' or 'scared' or, this to be found to be wrenching matters around and, ah, switching field, or fields, as another of our sayings has been storied to go, adopting, as I do it, or am doing this, the vocabulary of an opposing quadrant of sentiment. So how about my instead of saying what I've said, I say 'too sensitive to' or 'so much in awe of' or 'thoroughly awed by'? (Question mark inside or outside the closing quotation mark? – back there, back there! – I don't know, I don't know, who knows how to do it, before we made it, anyway or at any rate or at all events, to here.)

You know what I mean.

Look, if you want to know what I am trying to mean, you'll know so and then, or therefore, will there exist ground for debate?

Check that.

Cheque that.

There is always ground for debate.

Well, to get right down to it (or, if it's cases you have in mind, then *them*) and therefore to appear to be abandoning, forsaking, quitting all this shilly-shallying around (unless that last bit is instead corrigibly said, or correctly instead said, thus: shilly-shallowing), this Ariel fellow (the name is known to me, or is, anyhow, proposed to me as known to her, as has already been amended, via the medium of the woman I visit in the building where the man (the *door*man) Ariel works, and where – mark this, mark this, you had better be marking all you are able to mark if you are nursing any expectation of your getting to get a grip on any of this, to grasp it even ever so wispily (looks all wrong, wispily, wispily), have license to it, access to it, make your, you know, your way with it, or headway with it – his colleagues in doormanship, Ariel's, Ariel's, though like him as regards occupational titling, or titlement, are colleagues in that regard only, for, though officially doormen, none, of the number, mans a door as the man Ariel does, which is utterly, totally, deed-wise, in the extreme, they (Ariel's collegians in doormanship) don't. Man a door, that is, although receive, whatever number of them there is, or are, remuneration, or are in receipt of it, compensation, one quite not irregularly assumes, take pay for it,

manning a door in the manner that they man it, whereas not so as with the man Ariel, remunerated no more
greatly but great in the extreme in his manning the door
he mans six days a week, the shift for which, the hours of
which, happen to coincide with my comings and goings,
or rather, in fine, with my going there, to the woman's
building, and coming back here to mine (my building), so that one might more corrigibly say, inverting,
or reversing, or transposing the terms of the conjunct,
goings and comings, rather than succumbing to, rather than giving way in an act succumbent to, the storied
phrase, or, if corrigibly sayable, say conjunct — namely,
comings and goings, which phrase or conjunct or con-
junction of nouns, to wit, the conjoining of the deno-
tations of the actions denoted, ought better be either
rearranged as proposed or set off from ambient prose
with the disquietude querying rectitude recommended
by imposition of quotation marks, as per the practice
still in fashion (vogue) in the place where these obser-
vations did enjoy, or have enjoyed, their origination.
What one is saying is this — the man Ariel, though denoted as a doorman, connotes himself as to inhabit an ideal
of the occupation so utterly realized, or reified, or (here
it comes again!) entified, as to differentiate himself from
all other doormen employed in the referent classification
by the owner, or owners, of the building (the woman's)
in question, or to hand, or under relatable consideration,
or made subject to same. Oh, God, how the man Ariel
fulfills the duties incumbent upon him, despite (in spite
of, preferable, preferable, this in ineluctable anticipation

of the phrase's resonating with the thinner vowelic concatenation, provoking, as it does, a not valueless, nor
irrelevant, Eliotic concitation) the indifference to these
expectations exhibited by the man Ariel's, well, to concede to the times, co-workers, ugly as the compound is.
Yet, one must attend, must one not, the temper of the
times and cede the present to one's coevals, or, rather,
the vernacular of same, if not to, any the less, the col-
lo – no, sorry, gone too far, taken it well more than a
mite farther than my pseudo-mastery may be any further held to merit the holding of merit – oh, but I have
seen them, all right, the lot of them *out of uniform* – rare-
ly in uniform, chiefly in shirtsleeves, if sweatered, then
swathed in cheap sweaters, or besweatered, in the utmost
ragged and tattered and holely variety of the kind, doormen to be evaluated as veritable unravelments in whatever costumes they man their given doors at, hair askew,
hair awry, if that, then of course hatless, for providence's
sake, *hatless* – or is it 'their having dared to turn up for
pay hatlessly'? – whereas Ariel, the man Ariel, the *doorman* Ariel, our demi-object, disquisitively speaking, this
Ariel, contrastively speaking, is he not the very word of
couth, the very word of kempt, doorman to a T, ever
seen (by me, by me!), or ever to be seen by me, ever not
gleaming with, not agleam with, impeccability in the
veriest extreme of it? I'm not, I swear it to you, shitting
you for an instant – I swear it, I swear it!

In any event, in *this* event, I could, of course, go on
(and on), you do indeed realize this, or will give me,
towards said end, the benefit of the doubt suing against

substantive belief *in* this, or *of* this – *in* the *in*terest of one's dissolving the tensions between language, calculated from the standpoint of one domain, and actuality, calculated from the standpoint of another, not to mention the mismention of the contingency of an additional realm wherein the stresses and the reciprocal mutuality of reactive subsidings aroused by the aggressivity of the narrativized object (demi-objects not excluded) are taken (doubly appreciatively, and not individuatingly), into appreciable account.

But we stray from the man.

From the doorman.

From Ariel.

We veer from him and therefore from our (unspoken, or not spoken) agreement with one another – to, in fine, or, as your German might put it, in fein – to produce a one-of-a-kind deed, a one-of-a-kind thing, a *made* thing, a, namely, an artifactual thing, or, fein, fein, a thing not all that counterfactually in contention with an artifactual one.

Or one such.

Or such a one.

No, sticking to the man Ariel (and to the woman, don't you dare sit there and submit yourself to the suspicion there exists, or obtains, or is, *is*, no reason for you not to forget her, or about her), he's, let's face it, our (the) safest course.

The man stands sovereign!

Visored hat!

Garment!

Posture!

Doorman!

The very thingness of the exception!

No slouch, no readiness to be routed from his station, become derelict, grab a snack-break, sneak a smoke, gather wool, doze, slump, fall, give for an instant in.

This man is like no man.

An eidolon.

Is an eidolon.

I can tell.

I know all this.

I can see all this.

I am kindred, do indeed sense the unswervable disposition of the man Ariel – a doorman on duty whenever on-duty, unless it's vice versa.

That's it.

There! I've done it!

Said 'eidolon'.

Rescued the word from the fate of the unsaid.

Really done something – for once.

Did a deed.

With no help from her – and none from him.

And you? All right – what of you?

The nerve!

Yeah, sure, some accomplices people'll ever be.

Oh, the aerialismo of it, the ensorcellment of self – an end to a book, or, for crying out loud – almost – of it.

UNSTORY

What follows is not a story. It is a listicle of statements uttered consecutively by two persons. That statement – the one just made – is not without the liability of its being read as an ambiguity. Hence, listen: two persons speak, each to the other or each to himself or to herself. They do this consecutively – the occasions of their speech alternating one with the other. That is, one speaks, then the other speaks – and so on – this until no speech is further to be heard.

We begin.

'May I say something?'

'Of course.'

'I was in the bedroom.'

'Yes?'

'I wasn't in it, I should say – I was passing it. No, I mean to say that I was coming out of the lavatory and looked toward the bedroom.'

'Did you say toward or towards?'

'I don't know. I don't remember. I wasn't listening to myself.'

'You should.'

'So is it toward or towards I should have said?'

'Not ought to have said?'

'I don't know. Was should wrong? Ought I to have said ought?'

'Perhaps you should have said ought.'

'There was a point I wanted to make.'

'What point?'

'I'm not sure any more. Let me think.'

'It couldn't have been very important.'

'That's what people always say.'

'You know what? It's no comfort.'

'What's no comfort?'

'Someone saying when you've told them you'd forgotten what it was you wanted to say that what you've forgotten could not have been important.'

'What do you mean 'them'?'

'I should have said what?'

'He, him, the person you're talking to.'

'Talking with.'

'What?'

'To is rude. With would be the seemly word to use.'

'Sorry. I didn't know that.'

'It's the preferred way.'

'Who told you that?'

'I don't remember. It's just something one knows, is all.'

'I'm somebody. I didn't.'

'You're not offended, are you?'

'These corrections, it makes making headway difficult.'

'Then don't do it.'

'I thought it was you that was doing it.'

'Who, not that.'

'What?'

'Say who, not that.'

'I'm not getting this.'

'You said, I quote, "you that".'

'So?'

'Better to say you who.'

'All right. You who. I'll do it.'

'Not a big thing. Just trying to help.'

'Thanks. I'm sure you are. But meanwhile all these comments on what we're saying, they're retarding speech.'

'But we're speaking, aren't we?'

'We're supposed to be talking with one another. Making progress.'

'Look at all we've learned. You saying that's not progress? What could be more progressive than learning, changing one's ways?'

'How about getting something said?'

'Point. Good point.'

'I'm confused.'

'Me too. I am too.'

'This is rather confusing, don't you think?'

'Which of us said something about coming out of the bathroom?'

'Lavatory. Whichever of us it was, bathroom would have made for a better word.'

'Better intrinsically, or better in context?'

'Which context?'

'That one – the one when one said lavatory.'

'Restroom, washroom, can, crapper, loo – what is your point?'

'Never mind. It's been forgotten.'

'Nothing is ever forgotten. Not really. You're just saying forgotten just to rid us of this contention?'

'Contention?'

'Contending.'

'Didn't one of us just say just twice in the same context?'

'One did. One had. Was it I?'

'I don't remember.'

'You're kidding. How can you not remember?'

'I suppose I wasn't listening all that carefully.'

'Not listening?'

'Mind drifted.'

'You're telling me. Mind's forever drifting.'

'Ain't it the truth.'

'Besides, what's so wrong about using the same word twice in a given context? Use the word three, four, as many times, so long as it makes for clarity.'

'But it's cumbersome. Not very graceful. Suggests limited range. Imprecision, a muddied mind, inattention, a wandering into the weeds.'

'The first thing I want to say is cumbrous. The second is shame on you, a hackneyed sentence.'

'What?'

'Wandering into the weeds.'

'Phrase. It's a phrase. Where'd you get sentence?'

'Phrase, then. But was, not is. Pay attention to tence.'

'Here we go again.'

'Better to have said there we go again.'

'Better to say better to say, not to have said.'

'You know what?'

'Tell me what.'

'When I said tence, did you see it with a cee in it or an ess?'

'The word.'

'Yeah, which?'

'Say it again and I'll tell you which.'

'No.'

'Why no?'

'Because now you're paying attention and then what you say you saw in your head will be falsified by the intense attentiveness.'

'But I thought you wanted for me to pay attention.'

'What was that for me for?'

'I see what you're saying.'

'You hear what I'm saying.'

'The question is why did I choose to insert that for me in there?'

'Couldn't you have just said me and not for me?'

'I could have. But I didn't, did I? So what of it?'

'Nothing. Just making comment. Indicating attention's being paid.'

'Thank you.'

'You're entirely welcome.'

'Not easy keeping up with this.'

'I know, I know, I know.'

'But I can see the profit in it.'

'Hear, not see.'

'Okay, hear.'

'That's better.'

'It's great, don't you think?'

'I don't even have to think about it. Absolutely, there's a real payoff in it. We're getting somewhere.'

'That's right. We're making progress.'

'You bet we are. We're really talking now.'

'You took the words right out of my mouth.'

'That's an awful cliché.'

'How so?'

'It bespeaks an aggressivity.'

'I didn't mean for it to.'

'But still it does, it does.'

'So does repeating things.'

'Things?'

'Words, phrases, expressions.'

'But one's hoping to make one's speech expressive.'

'Nevertheless.'

'Nevertheless what?'

'May I say something?'

'Go right ahead. Say something. I'm listening. I couldn't be more attentive.'

'All clichés, you know. You do realize that, don't you? You are not unaware of that, are you?'

'Sorry.'

'It's all right.'

'No, I mean I'm sorry for my losing the thread.'

'But there you go again. Losing the thread – really!'

'Well, it's true. Haven't you?'

'Haven't I what?'

'Lost the thread.'

'Let me think.'

'You think and I'll wait.'

'The answer is yes – I'm utterly confused.'

'Lost.'

'All right – lost. Have it your way, I'm lost.'

'But that's good, don't you see.'

'Being lost is?'

'Yes, yes.'

'I thought the idea of speech was to get something said.'

'There's where you're wrong.'

'You're certainly not saying the proper aim is to get lost.'

'That's what I'm saying, yes.'

'That's crazy.'

'Wrong again. God gave man speech to give him the means to get himself lost. Whereas you stay on track, you run smack into death.'

'Never heard anything nuttier.'

'Want me to take it back?'

'I'm thinking.'

'Better not to think. Better just to talk.'

'Just talk?'

'Just keep talking, is all.'

'But what if there's nobody there?'

'There's never really anybody there.'

'Talk to who, then?'

'Whom.'

'Okay, talk to whom?'

'Yourself.'

'Isn't that what the deranged do?'

'Isn't that what everybody's always doing?'

'I see what you're saying.'

'You hear what I'm saying.'

'Right. I do. I really and truly do.'

'Just don't give it a second thought, is all.'

'That's exhausted speech again.'

'Of course it is. So what? All it is is just to talk, which is what you're already always doing anyway.'

'One's always talking to oneself.'

'Isn't one?'

'I guess so.'

'That's right. Just don't fret about it. Take joy in it. God's gift.'

'Keeps you distracted like.'

'That's it, that's it – now you got it.'

'And don't think.'

'Not if you can help it – you bet!'

'Then how do we take care of the world?'

'Please, pay attention – are you taking care of it now? Listen, the world takes care of itself. Your job is words and so on.'

'Death's a word.'

'What?'

'I said death, isn't death a word?'

'Regrettably, no. Regrettably, it's a lot more than that.'

'Death is?'

'Right you are! That's the thing with death – it is.'

'I see what you're saying.'

'You hear what I'm saying. Or don't.'

'Well, which of us was saying something about coming out of the water closet?'

'The WC?'

'Yes, that – catching a glance of the bedroom.'

'No idea. Was it me?'

'You mean was it I?'

'That's the spirit. Now you're getting it!'

'You're saying it doesn't matter one way or the other.'

'Does it? Does it really?'

'Pretty nifty. Damn. You've changed my whole perspective.'

'Not likely. You're just saying that. It's always the same old perspective. All that changes, if anything else does, is one's way of looking at it.'

'One's manner of perception.'

'That's terrific.'

'It is, isn't it?'

'I got it, I got it – but how do we get ourselves out of this thing?'

'What thing?'

'This?'

'Oh, that's easy.'

'Okay, tell me.'

'Tell you?'

'You're so smart – go ahead and tell me.'

'Be uncivil.'

'Uncivil?'

'Turn on your heel. Walk away.'

'But I live here. How about you be the one who walks away?'

'Even better.'

'You're leaving?'

'Already left. Wasn't even really here in the first place.'

'So you say.'

'QED.'

'QED?'

'It's another language.'

'Hey, got something for you to think about.'

'QV?'

'Which isn't?'

'To each his own, am I right or am I right?'

'Her own.'

'There you go! See what I mean?'

'Hear, not see.'

'Oh, shit – here we go again.'

'Lucky sticks. Aren't we lucky sticks?'

'Hunh? Lucky stick?'

'Ice-cream thing. Forget about it.'

'No, really. Explain, explain. I'm really interested.'

'No you're not. Just easier for you to keep me here than for you to be with yourself.'

'How's that again? Say that again.'

'Sorry. Got to go take a piss.'

'That's okay. Me too. Go make it here.'

'Is that going to involve looking into the bedroom again?'

'Don't know. Might, could.'

'So we'd be right back where we started from.'
'See what I'm saying?'
'Hear, hear.'
'Ain't life grand?'
'Life?'
'Life, yeah.'
'Words, words – now let's go make a wee.'

POSTCARDS

Can't tell which one's the last one. Eyes aren't up to making out the USPS markings on the address side. No, I take it back. See now that I was looking at the wrong part of the line.

I see double. Too, can't see where the edge is. Or edges are. But, yes, one of the two cards I got out of the drawer where I drop my mail says 2 FEB 2015. The other says 20 JAN 2015. So I guess we know which postcard was the last one. Here's something I just saw – on both of them. After the dates I just gave you, it says, on both of the cards – PM 31. Or PM 34. I can't tell which. No idea what it would mean anyhow and certainly am not going to try phoning the post office to ask. Nor try to go there. My legs won't carry me that far. Not all the way there to it and then back, they won't. Besides, I'd have to stand when I got there and wait at a window and ask a question that would make me look dopey or strange. I don't want to look dopey or strange. Who does? Oh, I bet there's bound to be some sort of type who feels better looking ridick. I don't even look in the mirror any more to shave. Not that I shave that often any more. Just when I'm going out with Jonnie and her family for something to eat, that's when I shave – or make a pass at it. Trouble is I shy away from buying new blades. I seem to have bought quite a lot of them just before Barbara died. Can't imagine why. Anyway, there's been a pretty good-sized stack of them in the medicine chest. Or is it cabinet? I don't know. I don't remember. It must have been quite a while before I came to understand I hadn't had a postcard from Campbell in probably three weeks or more. Campbell ordinarily has a postcard in the mail to me no more than every two weeks. Unless he's in Vermont with his kids and their kids. That's in the summer, of course. But even then and no matter what, I'd get postcards from Campbell Geeslin no more than three weeks apart – and that's for years and years now. Barbara died in 1994. I mention this so you will understand how I have come to date everything according to that date – before 1994 and after 1994. Geeslin and I were sending postcards back and forth before Barbara died. I'm positive of that. Here's why – I was suing some magazine and had it in mind to ask if he would be willing to appear in court as a character witness on my behalf. The lawyers asked me to look around for somebody who would be a likely party to do this for me. I thought of Campbell right away. He wasn't the first one I thought of, though. William Shawn was – and Russell Baker – and William F. Buckley, Jr. But all of them had reasons. I'm not saying their reasons were not perfectly decent reasons, but you know, it would be sticking your neck out – because the magazine I was suing was a very big-deal magazine, old and distinguished and nothing to screw around with. That's okay. I'm sure the reasons for my candidates electing to back away were the best of reasons, you can bet, but there was also the matter of one's showing up in court and swearing to the claim that I was a generally okay fellow when the newspapers and the like were all saying otherwise. It was their view that my going to court over this thing, whose details I don't see the point of my going into with you, was an attack on the First Amendment. Freedom of the press and all of that. Maybe we'll talk about it later, but I doubt it. The only bearing it has on Campbell Geeslin was my getting, on that account, just that one time, to see what he looked like. How would the man look up there on the witness stand? I wasn't even thinking that the other side would have a fellow like that. But they did – I mean, a character witness. It took me by surprise when it happened, I can tell you. It puzzled me at the time. After all, how is it that someone testifies to a magazine's having a good character? Well, the guy they had, he didn't actually do that. He just got up there in front of everybody and pronounced me a pretty disreputable person – his having considered the matter and come to the conclusion that there was nothing more to be said for it but that it looked to him I was suffering from a lousy character – and that, Your Honor, was that – whereas the guy who came there to testify for me – instead of Campbell, you do realize, all I can safely recall of him was his letting the judge know he didn't really know me all that well, or even very much at all – that and that he had done, and maybe said he was still doing, some teaching in the writing field, and the like, at, you know, at Harvard and so on. But, sure, it did take guts. I'm not saying it didn't. Even for a guy to go a little too carefully out on a limb for me like that, it absolutely took some mustard, all right, the guy being a more or less prominent fellow in, well, in journalism – a top gun at *Time* magazine and there on your PBS screen doing think pieces for the *Nightly News Hour*, didn't they used to call it? – and, for all I know, still do. Call it that. Come on, it was a long time ago – the early '90s, okay, or did I already tell you that? So there was plenty of risk in it for the man – for my character witness, that is. Hey, my hat's still way off to the man. That man did a lot more for me than I'll ever get to do for him – and that rates pretty large, you know? Or high. As opposed, as they say, to Harold Bloom, let us say, who was a buddy at the time and who was pretty emphatic about his not wanting any part of this affair, not as a character witness or even as an observer in court. Skip it. Everybody – except DeLillo and Hempel – and Campbell, of course – ran, or at least got suddenly pretty scarce. Skip all that. All I remember Bloom saying was, no different from how he had put it when I was giving a class at Yale and was getting hassled by a deeply disappointed, unappeasable co-ed. Bloom's counsel? Get the hell out of it – and fast. In both instances, Bloom's advice was that, if I defended myself, I'd live to rue the day, coaching I shamefully took that one time back at Yale but would be damned if I were going to be seen truckling under to my being scared off again. Yes, by then I had Barbara to take care of. She was dying – from a disease we don't need to talk about. Fine, everybody's always dying – from the worst of diseases – to wit, death. The whole point of my sitting here shooting my mouth off to you about all of this is that, okay, maybe it's happened and that Campbell, my pen-pal, is dead. But even if he's not, isn't my pen-pal and all the rest of us, aren't we soon enough all going to be as dead as we can get? What's to get so upset about? The answer is plenty. That time when my nose was all stopped up and nothing I was doing gave any hint it was going to get me breathing through my nose again, I was in a pretty big sweat, you can bet. Talk, the way the man says, is cheap. No, you can't talk yourself out of terror. What can you talk yourself out of? A livelong itch where you can't ever reach it? It's ditto with Campbell's silence. What is it? Do I just need to confect a reason to carry on? It's right now in the middle of March, isn't it? I tell you, I'm getting good and crazy from this, which makes it since February 2nd since I've had any word from the man. I suppose I could get Jonnie to look on her machine to see if she can turn up Campbell's telephone number. He lives up in White Plains, whereas me, I'm down here in the city. I'm typing this. It's the only machine I have – but it's not a typewriter. It's a word processor, I believe the jargon is. Campbell types on a typewriter all of his postcards to me – and probably to anybody else he sits himself down to write to. I can't do that. Gave my type-writer away when I got this machine. It was dumb of me to do it. I never thought about how it would mean I couldn't type a postcard to Campbell – you know, with the postcard rolled in sidewise. Instead, I have to hand-write – which is not so easy for me inasmuch as the bones in my writing hand, they're a wreck. Eyes are too. But I have never eased off on my keeping up my end of it with him. Campbell's the older. Don't know by how much, never asked. Just can tell from the experiences he refers to. Guess it's something like at least a decade. Tell you this – not once has Geeslin bitched about my postcards, about how he couldn't decipher them and how there was only in them the littlest cataract of scribblings running narrowly down the center of the space. Not that I ever thought Campbell was going to pick up the phone and say, 'What did you say?' He wouldn't. It wouldn't be his way. Besides, I don't think we'd ever given one another our phone numbers. It would be awful for us to have to switch from postcards to talk, even just a little bit. Beats me why. Just know it would. The silliness of men. The pudence, I suppose. It's dumb – but probably not so easy to dump. I think DeLillo has lately said he can't catch on to what I'm saying anymore – and then when he calls and leaves messages, I can't really make them out. That's right – my hearing, it's not so forthcoming anymore, either. Haven't invested in an aid. Man, even I can't read all of what I've written. Words here and there, sure. You get the drift, is the thing. Guess a lot. More and more. The enfeebling of the faculties, given the run of the years. The young, they have no idea – which is nature's ideation at almost its most merciful. Last postcard I wrote to Campbell, I'm pretty certain it went out about a week ago. Or did I say that already? I may have said a lot of this already – but if you're patient with me, chances are the picture – well, the essence of this – it will eventually come across. Besides, what's the hurry? Dawdling's exasperating, I agree, and the fumblings of senexes, it can drive everybody wild – but you never know when the geriatric will stumble into a shocker – if only by accident or the recklessness of those who take it that it's too late for them to have anything much to lose. Wasn't I saying I've got to write down the middle of the post-card for fear of my not being able to leave off before an edge comes up? Point of the pen drops off the edge and then I can't retrieve memory of what it was I was writing. We could, you know, we old people, drop off the line together and end up somewhere quaint – or unacquainted with. So which was it Campbell worked for – *Time* or *LIFE*? Or was it, after that, *People*? Anyway, it was somewhere like this where Campbell Geeslin had had a look at Barbara Lish. Barbara was designing pages where Geeslin was an editor, I think. That's the connection. She must have mentioned to me something about him, his Texas thing, so that, when I started *The Quarterly*, it occurred to me there was a way wherein Campbell would be terrific for an entry I wanted to add. Correspondence between Texans sepa-rated by lots of years. And, as it turned out, by what they now call gender. She was from oil country, daughter of a rigger, whereas Campbell's father was the mayor of the town of Brady. Over the years of post-cards, Campbell's reported on a lot of his father's accomplishments. Being mayor of Brady was just one in a major bunch of them. Anyway, me, I'd never had a look at him the way Barbara had. We'd only, to this day, met that once when my lawyers allowed as to how

I had better size the man up before deciding he should take to the witness stand to lend a bit of buttress to my case. It was terrible. I was so ashamed. Campbell said he'd do it, of course, testify for me, be a buddy in the breach for me, whatever it cost him, which was going to be plenty, considering Campbell was still making his living in the magazine business, and therefore making himself subject to retaliation. Harold Bloom, take note. Called, in the end, another prospect – who, for my money, once on the stand, made me look worse than I am. Some character witness, oh boy. The other side, however, they had the slickest fellow. Like somebody you'd see in a movie and like the hell out of right away. Can't remember his name. Only that he was an editor at *The New York Times*. The man looked like Walter Cronkite and the man sounded like Walter Cronkite too and everything he said against me and against the merits of the war I was waging, it convinced me I was a bounder, a degenerate, a no-goodnik with no hope of even any last-reel redemption in sight. But I won, anyway. Prevailed, as I've come to say. The judge decided in my favor, even though the sense I had was that he didn't have much use for me, either. The judge. His Honor. Campbell wasn't there. This time around, despite my having had all sorts of prior experience with an assortment of His and Her Honors, I was good and scared. The only people seated on my side of the courtroom were DeLillo and Hempel, which I'm next to positive I've already said. Barb wasn't there, of course. She was already mostly paralyzed by then. Funny thing was, Brodkey was there. In the capacity of a reporter for *The New York Observer*. Man wrote some pretty rotten stuff about me – not to mention about my attorneys as well. It took the wind out of me, a guy I'd done such a lot for, turning on me like that. He even, when he was dying from AIDS, contributed an article to *The New Yorker* saying, as for what it was like to be dying, that it wasn't so badawful for him insofar as it meant he wasn't going to have to see the likes of me anymore. I think that's pretty exactly how he put it, except he cited me by name. He was right. Brodkey, he never did see me again – or, anyway, I him. As for that one time I saw Campbell, it gave me quite a start. To begin with, the man wasn't going to win any beauty contest, was he, and, second, he'd have probably gotten me convicted of something really ghastly, solely by reason of his being even just a pen-pal of mine. Listen, you weren't going to give him a job on anybody's television reading the nightly news. After that woman from Texas asked to get out of answering Campbell's postcards, cards going either way printed in a section I had for it in *The Quarterly*, I took over. Then, when *The Quarterly* folded, or, how I'd prefer to put it, was folded, Campbell and I just kept going, popping postcards into the mail back and forth between White Plains and here right up until this silence which developed and which I told you about when we first started with this – this what? What's it to be? How come is it that I'm sitting here using the little I've got left of my eyes to talk with you about Campbell Geeslin and me and about how nervous I am right now, and strange-feeling, now that word has stopped coming to me from him. Or that there's been this hiatus to deal with. Please God it's that. Just an interval, an interruption, not anything worse. Twenty-five years of it at a minimum, trading postcards the way kids back in my day traded baseball cards and bubblegum cards. Is that it? Is my distress, is it like this puerile thing? Hey, isn't saying 'thing' back there, isn't *that* like a puerile thing? The prospect of his showing up in Superior Court in downtown Manhattan aligning himself against the prerogatives of the people in the line of work that had been supporting him and his wife Lyn and their kids for as long as he's done, nothing puerile in that for Campbell, is there? Or transpose it. Nothing puerile in Campbell for that, no! Or there wouldn't have been. But I picked another guy as my character witness guy. Campbell was willing. It was I who wasn't. Maybe that's why he's gone silent. Maybe, after all the years of our being postcard buddies, Geeslin's finally seen through me and taken me for the bounder they say I am. A traitor. No stand-up guy in a pinch.

Just another fake you can't depend on. Is that what Barbara took me for when sickness struck? Did she have it in her heart that I let her down? If she were still able to speak and didn't need me to take care of her, would she have said that? Well, she might have been thinking it, no matter how wild I was with nursing her. We needed a ton of them – nurses. None better than Jackie Brown. She was the one with steel in her. A person like Campbell Geeslin. No quitter. Give you all that she had. No

wearing her down. No wearing her out. Still phones
from time to time. Will I ever do anything to make it up
to her? The years and years of it. Jackie Brown. Jacque-
line. Was a whiz at jerry-rigging all of the machinery
we needed. It wasn't just people that couldn't take
it anymore. Those suction motors – and the oxygen
and feeding apparatus. Everything fell apart. And
then it did for Campbell too. His Lyn died. We were
widowers, fellows putting on an okay front most of
the time. Sometimes not, sometimes trading our sense
of our being taken by surprise, of nothing ever again
meaning enough to us to make much of a fuss about
our coming to a stop ourselves. Lamentations of lone-
liness, of weariness, of desolation, of ruin. Survivors
squeezed breathless with bewilderment, astonishment,
guilt – the amazingly abandoned attended endearingly
by children, by grandchildren, but so what? We were
outcast men, and sometimes said so out loud. Feeling
embittered, offended, betrayed, goofy with the notion
we'd been tricked by the women we'd been giving our
lives to, and now they'd moved on, leaving us behind
for us to act like boys again, ashamed for our no longer
being responsible for keeping up the act of our being
men. We – the aggrieved, the off-kilter, the disappointed, the spent. Nothing will ever again taste as
it had – but how, indeed, had it? There is no remembering anything, no getting anything anywhere near
to where it once was – nothing comes back but accusa-
tions – none of them unfounded, not a one of them not
cruel, all of the past a demon daring you to go to sleep,

your slumber all tauntings, all punishments, all implac-
able deserts, feverish, feverish, nightly renewed defeats.
Yet old as Campbell was – is, is! – has he not told me he
mows the grass, washes the car, bakes biscuits, turns the
soil wherein Lyn's plantings refuse release from their
faith with her husband's heart? Well, there's Barney,
Campbell's pervigilant physician, keeping the old man
to the mark. Me, nobody stops me – if I am not eating
actual food-like food over at Jonnie's, I'm eating – with
a vengeance – poison. Twizzlers all through the sleepless night. Fritos. Which, apart from age, is another
reason I'd had it in mind that, between us, I'd beat
Campbell in the drift to dust. Hey, wait a sec, I'm not
saying anything has really happened, you do realize. I
mean, I don't actually know anything for sure, do I? All
I know is that never before in all the years – didn't I say
it's been at least twenty-five years of postcards being
posted betwixt the municipality of White Plains and
the city of New York? – Campbell Geeslin's never, not
once, permitted, given leave to, let occur a lapse like
this to come upon us like this and disrupt the symmetry
of our mutual payment of courtesies like this. Look,
I'm right here waiting to goddamn it to hell hear from
the man! By God, didn't I just two seconds ago rotate
Barb's Rolodex to check if there's a telephone number
written on the card I years ago – years ago! – notched
into the wheel for him? A 914 telephone number,
goddamn it to hell! And there it is, there it is! So, no,
no, I don't have to ask Jonnie to fire up her machine to
look up the man's number for me. I've got the number,

got the Rolodex card, got what I need right here to the side of me and this keyboard. What a shock – that the info's been right here to hand all the time. But I don't want to phone. I don't want to call. I can't, I can't. No, not on your life, I could positively not. Wouldn't it be embarrassing for both of us? A kind of unforgivable agony of encounter and confronting, wouldn't it? Plus, I believe I know Campbell Geeslin well enough for me to be pretty absolutely convinced it would be terrible for him to have to suffer through a show of my hysterics like that, his having to talk on the phone with me as if it's some kind of psycho emergency. I'm going to send another postcard instead. That's what I am going to do. That's the sensible thing. I'm going to say, 'Hey, are you with me?' And add my phone number to any last-minute postcard. You never know. It could be Camp-bell's typewriter's finally given out on him – or there was no getting any of his beat-up old ribbons re-inked anywhere anymore. Fine, fine, I tend to worry. I tell you, I'm a worrier from way back. My mother always said I was going to worry myself into the grave. It's probably true. The other night I couldn't breathe so hot when my nose was all clogged up. I got tremen-dously scared. Thought of calling up one of my kids. Or Jonnie. Say it was worsening even with nosedrops, cry havoc, get an ambulance, get the fire department, alert the morgue. But instead of it coming pretty close to my doing something rash like that, I just kept walking and walking around the apartment. All night long. No joke. I'm not exaggerating. Breathing and breathing for all I was worth. Through my mouth, scared I was any minute going to gag. Or didn't I somewhere already tell you all this? It seems to me I might have. Anyway, I was terrified – afraid that in seconds I was going to choke on saliva – which is easy for you to do when you're an old guy and out of your mind with anxiety. Every so often I'd try more nosedrops, plus swallow antihistimine pills. Did I spell that right? I don't have the presence of mind for me to set this aside for a second and look it up – but you know what I mean, the stuff you take to clear your nasal passages. Hey, I was really pretty frightened. I didn't think I'd make it to the morning, and in the morning I just kept it right up – going from room to room, trying not to gasp, trying not to panic, trying not to do anything that would risk making me aspirate. That's how Barb died – choking, aspirating, right in the hospital with all kinds of people around her to keep an eye on her and make sure she didn't seize up. It didn't work, did it? Skip it. No, I'm not going to add my phone number to the postcard. I mean, it would slay me if my pal from Brady were to call me and say for me to just please quit it, not for me to be such a twit of a fellow, thinking the worst all of the time. I'll just send a regular, calm, horsing-around postcard. Just go ahead and scribble down the middle as always. Believe me, I do not want to do anything to disrupt matters between the pair of us, old as we are and fragile, fragile and, speaking for myself, so frail, so frail. Jesus, this seems to me terrifically like something I've already said. Did I? Have I? Is it true? That's right – after all of the years, it's crazily come to pass, the two of us, we're definitely a pair, aren't we? – Campbell Geeslin and I, stupendous in our need. I certainly, I have to tell you, am not going to start believing Campbell Geeslin's up there in White Plains having made up his mind he doesn't want to play 'friends' with me any more, that he's more or less totally fed-up with the whole jumped-up deal. Oh, crap – that's nuts, you know? Impossible. Honestly, I'm telling you, that's one hundred per cent out of the question. It's got to be something else. It's got to be. In fact, I'm sitting here looking over the last postcard to come here from him and the one before that. Believe me, the ink looks pretty darned faint to me on both of them. But, you know, my eyes are bad.

Hold it! Hang on for a bit. False alarm, false alarm! Guess who just phoned. Jesus Christ, my buddy Campbell Geeslin just did. It's incredible, isn't it? You're not going to believe it – it's the eighteenth and I swear it, I swear it, what happens but that Campbell Geeslin just calls me, the first time ever in all the years! – and he says to me, the man says to me, in this reedy, rumpled voice it turns out I hear he has – his saying something like hey, cut it out, Gordon, he's been snowed-in – snowbound! – and was all out of stamps. My God, I don't believe it – but thank God, thank God, it's all of it, Jesus, it's all of it okay again. Everything is absolutely perfectly swell again. What a winter, eh? The man said he'd gotten my card and could tell I was in a state and, lo and behold, did the merciful thing and phoned. Pretty terrific, dammit. Boy oh boy, am I relieved. Or didn't I tell you I sent

Campbell a pretty frantic postcard about a week ago, it seems to me it probably was? Didn't I tell you that? With my phone number on it, I think. Because I'm so excited. I'm not sure if I did or not. I think I actually might have done it. No matter. I can guess what it said, the words arranged right straight down the middle, grabbing onto a vertical axis to keep them from running out of room on the way to an edge. The edge. No, couldn't sit still for one more instant without my sitting myself down here for me to make a circus of myself. It's disgusting. I'm just disgusted with myself. What the dickens is wrong with me? Hey, I'm what? Authentically skittish, authentically jumpy – or just looking to hurry up and parlay somebody's bad luck – ah, God, my buddy's bad luck, anybody's first sign of a likely misfortune – eager to snatch at an opportunity for me to whip myself into center stage and make a spectacle of myself! I suppose I ought to be ashamed, and I am. Well, I wasn't not even a lick ashamed of myself there in the thereness of that courtroom, was I? I was just afraid – and bent on appearing to appear the good guy, the wronged party, a perennial victim of the world's broad back turned ever so dismissively against me. When, if the truth be known, if the truth all be told, all my life I have always been playing the angles. And worse, never for more than the puny gains in it. Mainly probably for me to wrest every blessed inch of favor for myself – attention, attention, hand it all over to me, whatever the theft exacts from others. Are you fucking fooling with me? I'm no sidekick of anybody's – I'm nothing like the man from Brady. Listen, you know what I'm going to do? I'm going to send a postcard to Campbell and tell him I'm sorry as all get-out for trying to score one off of him. Lord, Lord. I bet he's right now trying to dig himself out, an old man like that, some huge shovel in his Texas hands. And what am I doing? I'm up here on the tenth floor sitting on my tuffet tapping on the visually enhanced keys. Shit, I'm not going to get myself worried into any grave. You know what it is? The grave, the grave, reader, oh, reader, you'll see me not so worried into it as sickened into it, sick to death with the sickness of the theater in myself. The pleasure of the pose – who knows from real or feigned? A last deceit, the grave. Live another bit impersonating – no, *being* – the profiteer working the cheap seats for the hullabaloo in it in the submission of myself to death. Oh, you know, live yet another – one further, one further! – little bit. Performance, irreality, selfing the selfhood – right up to the very end.

Yes indeedy – that's the jazz.

Quick, Gordon, quick! – ready some sentences, any sentences. It's not double-dealing. It's honest. It's all Gordon, all. I mean, what other cards have there ever been for me to play?

DOES THIS MEAN ANYTHUGNG?

Do you think it means anything? Foretells anything?
Forbodes? That laat word, is it spelt right? Would it be
better spelt, rightly spelt, if it were spelt thus: forebodes?
Now that I see the spelling spelt thus, forebodes, it does
not look right to me. Oh, pity, just got a look back, saw
'laat'. Meant to say last. XDorry. You thin this means
anything? I mean fea,lly means it. Ohm God, now see
spelt one, two, gtheee words wrong. No, now two
more. Thagt's three plus two. Spelt five wirds wrong.
Now see wo more. No, three. Dol that's five plus three.
Gves eight. Uhp-oh, looking back. There's wo forf
two, Dol for so, Gves for Gives. Thfee more. That's
eleven. Plus Thfee for Three. Oh, skipped Uhp. Uhp
was supposed to be Uh. That's thirteen. Thazt's four-
teen. Thagt's fiftee. That's sixteen. Very foreboding.
Bodes badly. Bodes not well. Is it a A foretelling I am
beng told? It doesn;t look good. Oh, gthat's seventeen.
And ghat's for that, that's eighteen lor orobaakh nineteen. Plus shat's for that's agaub. No, nineteen, twenty. Do yoiu thuib this means anythung? D yurt thunk
it's the keeys or me? It may be it mneans the oewriter'w
keys are too close tigethet the way thewy're arranged
on te thypewiter'skeyboard. Not eniugh room fr mh
fingertips to touch te keys cledanly. Or des it means
mhy fingertips are undergiing a chaned. Growng
largwer. bgger Thckere. Becoming hideus. Asfinger-
tips go. If that's the ase, then it means my body is changing. It cannbot be that my vsy isa changng fr the better.

Can it? I just heard somethung below me hit the celig of the aoartment beneath mine. ZA bhammer? It woulkd alpoeafs a workman is hammering on the ceiling of the apartment beneath mine. O has it hapened that beneath is no longer te word in e is meant to choose to express such an ibsrvratiin. ??? Perahsos it'sd underneath o below. There it goes agaiun / Or went agaun. Yes, did I nkit receiv e a legtgefr fro m tnhr persl who new,hy bught that apartment that t woujlkd be undergling a renoi aton for the next en mk tbs? K djd I did. o this isd the edence of the dependabikitgy of tha lettefr. The ,legter said that if tere is any damage caused my apartment, the premises, tghe owner if the apartment below, the new owner ofd the apartment below, wulkd indeminify me agauanst all kosses suffered by myb walls floors and so on. Tha's right. Persons of authority czmse in. Sekeks s ago. Came wth camewrs. Persons repfresentingb the new owner and persons presumaby represednting me. That staff here. jperintendent, assistangt sulintendent, Tooik pictures lof everythung. EDne en of te insides f cosets To estabeisg the status of the pre/renvwtion state of things. In my apatt,ment. There t gies agaun, More hammmerfgn. Must be hammeringon fhe ceiling down tghere fr I xcan feel it on my feet uo here. The eloor is reasing reacting. Trembl,ing. Does tbis means anythunbg. Is a ytbung foretolkd by thius. I'mgoign yki go lok the word forfblde. up I a, going t ceck to see how it's selt. Lisen, hw I ba ve lokked it up and sen seen , I wn;t be ckming back. This is tg fre this. This is it fr thnbg. Can;t keep cubtng. Xloe,,n hg XS Se,k, Spe,,king. Canng

keep the ckut cujn count sarfiught. Gkos-bye. Sorrgreu
fr wastbg yojur tne. Xkrrg Zkrrgr. Am so ashamedcx.
Glold nrist.igt means smetghing, all rgnt! I know that
everytung nmeanns sinethung but tid fealy means ut!

'Be glad you got what to eat.'

That was one of his admonitions.

A, you know, a compressed, unless it's a condensed, one.

'You know what? You should get down on your knees and thank God you got what to eat.'

That's another one.

Which is one, this other one, like others you'll probably hear me recalling for your divertisement, that's got in it hard evidence of some importuning asking for the intervention of divinity itself.

Ears all set for the more calisthenic admonishment following?

'You should get down on your hands and knees and give thanks to God you are sitting there in your place at this wonderful table with what to eat staring you in the face in front of you like an invitation fit for a prince.'

You bet, I see it too – no insufficiency of room made for the deity, gotcha.

Plus, as exhibited, a kind of demi-prostration recommended.

Look, I'm mentioning some of the admonitory labors of Philip Acropolis Lish, my father, a person known to me and to my sister Natalie – Natalie Staircase Lish – as Dad. Or as Daddy or, shockingly, Phillie – if 'twere Natalie which 'twere the source of talk aimed at him or framed to be thought talk of him.

At the dinner table, you understand – because what

did I know of what intercourse or concourse involved them otherwise?

(Now, now – you better cut that out! – Gordon Cartilege Lish will brook none of that filthy fiddle-faddle in an embookment of his making.)

Okay, back we go to the sanctum sanctorum of the dinner table.

Which site was where Dad (my father) was not at all irresponsibly, nor in the least unlovingly, to be counted upon to vocalize around with the basic format of his apostrophic observances.

For example, you (i.e., I) might say, 'I can't stand stringbeans. I am not going to have anything to do with any of these stringbeans.' Or: 'I can't stand calve's liver. I am not letting this fork get anywhere near it.'

Whereupon Dad might say, 'You, my fine-feathered son, you should get down on your hands and knees and thank God in high Heaven that you got what to eat in plentiful supply when it comes to sitting down like a civilized person with your family who adores you for mealtimes.'

I'd say, 'Make me eat them – [or it] – and I promise you I'll throw up.'

Thus challenged, Dad'd, my father'd, not implausibly, say, 'Go ahead. Vomit. Who knows, who can tell, am I as your father a prophet? Maybe the odds are your family will be at liberty to lament in the context of their neighbors and associates that it was our terrible misfortune to have a child as a son who, believe it or not, was all by himself one of those one-in-a-million ghastly cases you read about in the papers where, lo and behold, the individual not even in long pants yet is sitting at the dinner table with his beloved family and they have to see him choke to death on his phony regurgitation.'

Mother, my mother, also my sister Natalie's mother, she'd say, or might – since, check, check, this is all just some last-minute hypotheticalizing or, for your personal sake, illumination, right? – the lady might say, 'Pay attention to me, Charlie Hollywood, the home-maker of the house laid out good money for that. Eat it. You eat it or you leave the table.'

(Despite that it was sometimes them.)

Anyway, I didn't tell you yet – her name was Reggie Electrolux Lish.

Plus which, she had for you no shortage of admon-itory assaults of her own design, either, as you could, I might mention, have heard for yourself if you'd been on your toes listening, but, yeah, yeah, it was Dad who took control of the leisure space in the room to confect threats that had in them the yeast to establish themselves in the compost of your mind and to root and mature there, to flourish like some jungley vicious foliage repli-cating itself like crazy there – in your brain, your brain! – achieving, planting season after planting season, the mythopoeia of utterability therein, an admission I am not ashamed to make in mixed company, which is, for your information, my eighties and your teens probably.

Well, eighties, not *my* eighties.

Natalie, my sister, in case you've let your literacy founder, yes, yes, she ate it – she ate it, whatever it was.

Or they – or them.

Natalie, so far as I, Gordon Cartilege Lish, can remember, ate, in addition to the two preparations I've already, for your edification, listed, nutritional standards routinely (a little redundancy, superfluity, what's a mere bissel of pleonastic grammatizing betwixt old bookmates such as we've – fingers crossed, darlings, rachitic fingers crossed the best I can – become?) to be availed to those members of the Lish Family seated in their seats at the Lish Family table.

You ready?

Okay, I'm going to go out of my way to stick a colon up there in, check, check, in a completely unnecessary but genially produced evidentiary show of there not having occurred any attenuation of the confidence you can keep drawing on without your diverting into the reserves you should by now have ready to relegate to me.

: tapioca, brussels sprouts, rutabaga, canned lima beans, canned asparagus, canned corned beef hash, chocolate pudding with that skin thing on the top of it, warmed-up milk (that's milk with the chill off) also absolutely with that grayish skin thing where else but right up there on the top of it where you had to figure out a totally subversive technique for dealing with it, for defying it, for seeing if you could break into an end-run around it – where are we? – oh, yeah : check, check – stewed rhubarb, stewed prunes, stewed tomatoes, plus canned sardines in that creepy oval-type can with tomato sauce filling in all over it in the inside of it with regard, I'm guessing here, I'm just spitballing here, to

take care of the need to accomplish the look of its pre-
senting you with the impression of your getting your
money's worth of plenty of former marine commotion
in there inside of it. Plus eggs, oh yes, oh yes, oh yes,
eggs which if they were soft-boiled – hey, I mean really
soft-boiled – like soft, right? – like you know what I'm
saying when I say like super-soft, soft like right-out-
of-the-chicken soft? – which excess of ickiness, in our
household, by reason of that very distinction, seemed
to be all the eggs needed for them to qualify for them
making the grade to be qualified for their making their
hideous way into the theory of any construct of mealtime anytime, not to mention the one we're chiefly taking the trouble to take under consideration here, which
we, the Lishes, speaking in our own personal vernacular, didn't call dinner, by the by, but never called it anything but supper.

Anyway, yeah, that's it.

That's heaps more than enough of it.

Any more enumerating and I am going to throw up.

Unless I should have said skim, not skin.

I guess there's no question but that skim's definitely
the more picturesque way of saying what I had in mind
to, expressively, be heard saying.

They all – you know who I mean – they would all of
them sit there and eat that icky shit with relish.

Them.

Dad, Mother, my sister, my wretch of a sister, my
long-dead sister Natalie Lorraine, or Lorraine Natalie,
herein resurrected as Natalie Staircase Lish, yes?

First.

First eat (lick?) the skim off before even venturing with the tip of a spoon into the pudding part.

Jesus.

And you do, I know, realize what I am saying when I say calve's liver, mmm?

Unless it's calf's liver.

Either way, it was brought by tumbril to the table with its entire repertoire of veins raging inhumanely in it.

Real thick pretty recently pulsing veinous ones.

Like just this side of fully fledged rubber.

Rubberoid – that's got to be screamy enough for you.

Ultra-organic before anybody had any idea of cooking up a scheme like that bigtime bullcrap like that all bullcrapped up for it to be cashed in on on (yes, that's right, that's right) a national-sized basis.

Vessels – just sit there and visualize it for me a little bit, check?

'Be glad you got what to eat,' Dad would warm up with, getting ready to delve down into the dark matter of his georgics and package it for the consumption of the non-conformist in all too vivid, helpless view.

Me, I had no way out except to complain of colic and keel over under the table in a faint.

Which I wasn't one hundred percent sure how to fake.

Not that, however medically bad-off I was pretending I was, I couldn't get the message of Natalie chewing her head off and – talk about believe-it-or-not again – actually gurgling suckishly when swallowing.

My father, Dad, you could tell from the floor the man'd meanwhile be keeping himself very well fed what with his addressing his delight to some green pickled tomato very likely, or instead, not impossibly, to some red pickled one, this dignitary slicing away for his delectation these nice big slices of variegated pickled goodness.

'Get up here and eat it,' Reggie Electrolux Lish would, imperative-wise (imperiously?), call down to the floor. 'Gordon Cartilege, I, your mother, am telling you for the last time that what you are doing is failing to exhibit the slightest respect for what I, your mother, paid for that,' she might refine the issue with, closing with the apodictic pronoun whose invocation was, in my opinion, thereupon (therewith?) conceived to make everything worse. (Sorry, but now that I'm getting more and more, tonally, confusitated, would really be particularly felicitated if I could just get us all to hang around for a sec while I see to it, at this late stage of the game, that I get the word *asseveration* incorporated somewhere in this book, unless it's into. All set again? Here we go): 'It's good for you,' was often how, in conclusive asseveration, Mother, my mother, would wrap up her endeavor to authorize the authority of her role, endowing it with what is nowadays, without concern for the damage done the general hope for a peaceable society, known to the young at heart as traction.

Whereupon Dad would get more and more, or increasingly, if this is your four-syllabical preference, rococo, as witness this: 'If God above was here in the flesh to see what a travesty you are lying there turning this festive occasion into, he would do everything in his power for him to wave a wand and work a miracle to explain to my own personal sonny boy that when you got what to eat laid out in front of you on a table which didn't come cheap from the furniture store, you sit like a gentleman and you eat it like a mensch and you spare your parents, which are your mother and father, from us having to confront what it looks like when we are forced to confess before God himself that we missed the boat and raised a spoiled, God help us, a good-for-nothing, not to mention an ungrateful child who's got the gall to go foodless in front of his family like he alone is better than the whole wide universe and should be dubbed a person with a superiority complex when he can't manage even to keep from collapsing off his chair like he's a thoroughly unbalanced individual.'

Natalie – Natalie Staircase Lish – testing with her horrible tongue whatever disgustingness was inside of the experienced interiority of her mouth, might, at any point, hurry to enrich matters, with, for perfect example, even though I am developing all of this positively solely from memory: 'What I pray God take into account is the question of whether or not my brother is absolutely aware of the tragic fact that he is making his mother and father sick?'

Or with: 'Gordon Cartilege Lish, I, your sister, am begging you will you please before we all plotz learn what it means for a member of this family to grow up for their mother and father's benefit and get up off of the floor and eat what's on your plate and which is going to waste when people you haven't even studied in school yet are starving and dying for lack of decent nourishment.'

Or, raising the stakes (as if there were anything other than this for human beings to do with stakes): 'Can't he comprehend that meal after meal my brother is making believe that there is something wrong with his intellectual development while what he's really actually in my opinion doing is killing the people of his family?'

Which did I hate more?

Them?

That tableful of them?

Or what they saw to it the groaning board was appointed with?

I liked crackers – and black olives – but only if they came out of a certain kind of jar.

I liked sticking the lambchop bone down into the ketchup bottle and savoring the result if somebody had already had the courage to bite off the lambchop proper away from the lambchop bone and even if there weren't any crispy stuff left on the lambchop bone for me to nibble from either side of it, one side of it – forever terrifically mysteriously – always somehow capable of its boasting of more crispiness to be scumbled from off of it than the side opposite of it was.

Yeah, yeah, I was mad for crackers.

Yeah, yeah, I still am.

And can, to this day, retrieve from death my father best – you heard me, best! – when I let my mind go loose in search of an impersonation of Dad's utterance of the trio of words he invariably invoked at mealtime when the fare before him – my father, my father, my dear dead sister and mother and father! – couldn't get to first base finding his favor.

Vile.

He would say.

Putrid.

He would say.

Atrocious.

He would say.

Philip Acropolis Lish.

But no reason, no reason at all the friendliest critic would be willing to grant it, that you need be intrigued to be made a party to any of this surrendering, succumbing, resuscitating. Me, however, I'm telling you it makes me happy as a clam in high water for me to sit here kvelling and fooling with these keys laid out in front of me, add-ons, store-bought added-on stickers of big red stuck-on letters of the alphabet, not to mention the ancillary back-ups of punctuational what-not and what-like stuck on the keys along with what's stuck on them as letters and hear – hear! – all by my lonesome – man oh man, just by these solitary devices – making up this last made-up word of them – retrieved, saved, kept forever in me for my loving of them.

The Lishes.

The essence of them all the more hidden for their being hinted at in these acts of revivification.

Or is the word I want shebang?

Can't say why but it's somehow in me for me to cry out shebang – hey, anybody still dawdling on the hook for this – shebang, you hear me? – that's the word! – shebang.

My people.

My people.

Mine, all mine.

Unless it's mine for me always to be theirs.

Oh, let me tell you something – no kidding, let me tell you – oh, when it was all of us who lived!

'Mary Rollins was born in Topeka, in a high white frame house shaded by elms. There was a verandah on the front of the house, and in the back there was a screened porch where the rough coats were hung up to dry.'

Thus begins the stately story 'A Kansas Girl', the only piece of writing, or so at this late age, I can, with certainty, say, that has made me – insistently dry-eyed I – cry. Well, no, not cry, no – but, time after time, reading to students what I've just recited to you, sense myself prepared for, preparing for, the onset of tears, which effect I could, of course, forever foretell, feel coming at me, fear were waiting to overtake me with an imperious irresistable welling-up in me, wrought by words that would inevitably get the better of me as I neared the close of the piece, the price to be paid for my having elected to read, surely mainly to the willfully deaf, to the precociously hardened, my all the while hoping to bypass tears, in the manner of an oldtimer of a teacher, to outstare the threat of a public breakdown, all the while praying to *this* time duck the wallop loaded into the closing remembrance.

The story was written by Edward Loomis, who *did* make me cry, wailingly, as I recall it, to an audience of one: Frances Fokes, the person I married when I was very young and was – this I recall exactly – attending college on a 'probationary basis' (did the administrator who devised the conjunct make himself alert to its embedded, and accordingly, choric, echoic, rhyme? Or, anyhow, assonantal sympathy?). Denise Riley, the finely wide-ranging commentator on matters of the kind, would, I want to imagine, think yes, that the coiner was never not wise to the voodoo of the coinage, and might, further, choose to adorn her assent with remarks concerning the rhymester's not unlikely indecision between the favoring of the allure of 'basis' against the pressure of the equally appealing status of 'status'.

I had been, at nineteen, a disk jockey in New York, and had fallen ill while *on the air* – this histrionic event occurring well before the definite article, in the American sprint to code in place of speech, was stricken from the phrase, an excision brought to the fore by (we can only agree, impotently, to accuse whatever tireless, iniquitous force forces such changes) – okay, I give up – in the end, what can be the agency but time's lieutenants, then? Yet I nevertheless blame the devil obtaining in the tongue of one's viciously complicit descendants – and thereafter (enough of that palaver, back to your so distractingly distracted host again), after the collapse and the months of bedrest, was delivered, I, by gum, still arranged on the flat of my back, to the American desert in the American South-West, in order that I might be coaxed toward recovery by reason of the ingeniously coincident copias of sunshine and aridity.

It worked, for an interval, at the unfolding of which remission I took up paying labor (it was advised that it be employment in the American out-of-doors) as a wrangler at a 'guest' or 'dude' ranch, where I played at cowboy until I was enrolled (on a probationary basis)

as a student at (in? of?) the University of Arizona, my
having failed to achieve a secondary-school diploma,
my not, theretofore, having been graduated from an
institution granting such certification, despite a wide
spate of inearnest tries.

It was at this citadel of elevated learning that I entered
Edward Loomis's class in, I don't know, was it captioned
'English'? – where Loomis, writer on cavalry horseback
seen slashing all about on campus with a satchel's-worth
of importantly praised MSS in his motorcycle's saddle-
bags, a former Army Ranger much 'shell-shocked' by
virtue of action in both 'theaters', as went the idiom
of the day (and which may still, for all I know, so go),
asked the youngsters in the class (I was somewhat older
than they, was, not unnotably, as I've already more
than hinted, a hubby without portfolio, and, as howl-
ingly exemplified by the unsubduable colic of the infant
Jennifer, a father in thralldom to the impersonation of
paternity, a fellow on the march towards any blurry
initiation into whichever careerist endeavor it would
happen, most easefully, be indued to surrender its
demands unto me, thereby vouchsafing me the shelter
of asylum from shame) – I repeat (all this distance from
the headwaters of this sentence), asked, Loomis did, the
man asked that the class perform a concise act of written
recollection of some sort, furnish him with a specimen,
give him to guess who (whom? gosh, I'm so confusitated
here at the long-sought last) each of us thought we were.

Promptly construing this performance to mean
a scriblance under the sign of 'fiction', I turned into

313

Loomis, as immediately as minutes after the task had been announced to be done, a passel of pages whose emblems he thereafter, the instant the class next met, was to be heard orating to my brand-new colleagues (and, worst of all, to *me*), this, all the while doing so, mockingly, laying especial stress on the piece's congestion of a lifetime supply of pretensions. Well, hell, you've by now suffered hearing more than a tolerable share of the kind I'm not averse to firing off in fits of indefensible liability. Does anyone, at the moment, know better than you how puffed-up a prig I (I?) can be? Not to let it vex you. Yeah, I'm as thin-skinned as they come, but also old, in virtue of which sorry condition I've weathered some conditioning and, presto, am quite used to my making a spectacle of myself and paying the violent price for it. So sneer all you want, if it is to sneer that you want. But don't expect me to sneer at myself in harmony with you, but neither will I promise not to see if you cannot be sued in a small-claims court. Besides, we're so near to the close of this, aren't we? Best if we might manage to bid one another adieu in, if in degrees of relief, not without some approximation of an august dissemblage of bonhomie, of even grudging cheer.

Oh, wait, that fillip back there – carelessly ambiguous, wasn't it? Well, as I've been again and again exhibiting – syntax and the rest, go ahead and approach it playfully all it tempts you to do, but never delude yourself into believing you're going to get to strut away from the slugfest without the cost of teasing a bully not in evidence on your mug. Or is it mugg?

Where were we?

Oh yeah – in Tucson, in the fifties – at, ugh, the U of A.

Husband, father, seasoned radio broadcaster (started farting around in the medium when I was in my medium teens), your host, plenty enough stunned and in no little of a huff, your student on probationary basis, he quit Loomis' classroom, took himself right up out of his seat and right out the door, hustling himself agog along one of the college's hateful corridors, did he, did I, somewhere before Loomis had quite finished with his demolishing my exertions (not *them*, by gum – who knew from *them*, by gum? – who even really *cared* about them, by gum? – to hell with my fiction-eering but what about me, me, *me*, by gum!), my barely managing to hold back hysterics (please treat this as the prospect of lunatic sobbings, berserkly distraught paroxysms of gulped-back condemnings prefatory to the school building's recoiling from the materiality of pre-homicidal bawlings) until I had restored myself to safe harbor.

Home.

To the one-room habitation we – Fran, Jen and I – huddled in, feeding on chicken backs (ten cents a pound) and kidney beans (fairly freely swipe-able in them thar markets in them thar high-tension days).

To wife Franny and to baby Jenny – all of us shrieking.

Fucking bully!

How dare he!

Didn't he know I'd been *sick*!

Years thereafter, when Loomis was chairing the English department at Santa Barbara's edition of the University of California, we became bounden friends, by means I, at this point in our fading relations (yours and mine), no longer retain the spritzo nor the patience to attempt qualifying. Listen, we became pals, so bindingly so that I was willing – once, just once, in a unique stand-off with terror – to ride along with him as his passenger as the man's ferocious motorcycle flamed southward on the American freeway leading from LAX to the Loomis family residence in Goleta, and, more convincingly still (of bindship, that is), to be told, in strictest confidence by him, this when he had shown up in New York for book business and the two of us were stoking ourselves on bourbon (J.T.S. Brown, hot damn, it was) in the ground-floor bar where Knopf, floors heavenward, then kept exalted offices, a confidence made the more vivid and forbidding, given my pal's then placing into evidence his hands, (*hands!*), oh the massive beefs of them jamming the claustrophobic hiatus between us, turning them for our growingly mesmerized mutuality of mere (not in the least, you bet, at all merely mere) sitting on our barstools gazing at the handness of them, the taking of an inventory, you understand, the man displaying the frightful bulk of his weaponry, taking stock of its then level of lethality, them, these hands, Gordon, the hands of an American warrior, now this side, Gordon, now that side, Gordon, commanding my alarmed witness of the ghastly experience to be descried in them, the terrible

capacity immanent in them, the potentiality in them, the unspeakable feats undiminished in their responsiveness to the hair-trigger obedience to them, from heavy use in *both* theaters, the power in them, by gum, never not all set to rage in them, now this side, Gordon, now that side, Gordon, that he, Loomis, was preparing himself to return to California to shoot a villain (some improbable boy of a suitor behaving unacceptably – nay, a pest conducting its besotted creatureness pestiferously – buzzing its flaunt of unwanted wooings in the face of one of Loomis's many daughters), a deathbound wretchedness, this unignorable fuckhead, for his refusal to leave off the buffoonery of pursuing one of the father's four, five, six? – what number had Loomis enumerated for my benefit? – how many daughters?

You heard me. I heard him. My old teacher, my sole teacher in the scribbler's scam, he was giving his old crybaby pupil (for that's, sound-wise, what I'd been!) to know he was going to plug this punk first thing on his arrival back in Goleta.

Listen, those of you not yet having had more than your fill of it – of listening, by Lucifer, to all of this, yeah, philandering – the man Loomis, the story writer Loomis, the novel writer Loomis, the scholar Loomis, the University of Arizona associate professor Loomis, the University of California department chair Loomis, he'd been a killer in bookended theaters of war, hadn't he? – he'd been the son of a Denver superintendent of schools, hadn't he? – been an American Ranger, been in abundant receipt of American medals, been, damn it all, at the age of twenty-one, an honorand of a doctorate ratified by Stanford when it was the redoubtable Yvor Winters himself who had to be not displeased with your lucubrations – been, had been, most chastening of all (or don't I mean bracingly?), the maker of the sentences you were supposed to have listened to along with me when we first made our way into this afterword – the man Loomis, this man Loomis, my friend, my cicerone, he said he was going to *do it* and, by gum, by gun, he *would do it*, there could not have intervened the slimmest entreaty he wasn't – if the guy so smitten with infatuation did not ... well, you know how it goes, it must be that, yeah, the guy *did*, indeed, leave off his tumescence, think better of the fervor made perfervid by the J.T.S. Brown, quit the fevers of book-busybodied New York for a nice placid flight back to family and professorship, and for which, thank goodness, a reunion with the post-war docility the man, this great man, had done some two years of time in a V.A. hospital to regain, under the proverbial lock-and-key, to (another word, why not?) resecure. No young punk got himself post-armisticely lit up, blown away, rubbed out, whacked, deducted from the populace, compelled to contribute to the inexorable campaign to tighten the obese ranks of those domin-ions entitled to be internationally overpopulated, nationally underrepresented, locally confounded, and generally pissed-off and all set to tip over the world about it. Or is it over it?

Well, sure, Loomis died. Ed Loomis died. His family, and mine, they, both installations, came, as the most ardent instauration can so often maddeningly manage to do – flutteringly, oh-so-fussingly – irreparably apart, bruises, uncompromisingly, succumbing to nature's commandment to mature themselves into cicatrices. But no matter – Loomis had had a run of rare satisfactions – surviving, in two unrehearsed theaters of war, the loss of not even one part of himself, save for, impermanently, a piece of his mind; surviving the indignity of a rubber room reserved for veterans to audition in silence the incomparable noise of combat they were not at all sophisticated enough to hear at its ghastly premiere; surviving a rancorous divorce; surviving the test of the faculty scrum, the ceaseless scrimmage of decency versus indecency, the constant bing-bang of seeking and ceding advantage, the whatnot, the crazy human whatnot, and, not at all impossibly, surviving the eating of himself up alive in consequence of the murderous feeding upon the heart of the artist reckoning with the foreshortening of his reach in the rivalries of art.

Yes, of course he died.

But – God, God! – was preliminarily sent into the humiliations of some sort of semi-public retreat.

Who knows why?

I knew only that the letters that had been covering the miles between us were no longer concerned to risk the ride from coast to coast.

I'm perfidy itself when it comes to researching details.

I let go ever so nimbly, ever so numbly, ever so fast. Relieved, I suppose, more than aggrieved.

Yet show up at my door and inquire of me what, darn it, in the world of indomitable wordways has not weakened in its charm to send gouts of feeling rushing to my eyes, and I'm going to go to my grave, by my heart, by my heart, still citing for your illumination Edward Loomis's 'A Kansas Girl', which story's falling exultation – retired schoolteacher Mary Rollins having taken herself to see the grandeurs of the Grand Canyon – is enacted thus: 'She stayed two days, and was happy, and her trip was a success – on her return to Kansas City, she was ready to die, and seven years later she accomplished this end: her mind was pure and once, in the hospital, she thought of her father, remembering as a child she had been able to call him to her, where she lay pale and cool in the narrow bed – a good father, who would be coming toward her out of the glistening throng.'